Praise for Lauren Oliver and PANIC

'Stark, fast-moving'
The Times on PANIC

'I can honestly say that I now know why everyone's
been raving on about Lauren Oliver!'
escapeinabook.blogspot.com

'Sharp, savage and unputdownable'
Star Magazine on PANIC

'If you thought *The Hunger Games* was frightening,
you've obvs never played PANIC'
Teen Now Magazine

'This book is brilliant'
Guardian on PANIC

'Lauren Oliver can do no wrong'
wondrousreads.com

'Oliver writes in such a beautiful way, it's hard to put
the book down'
Press Association

'Lauren Oliver masterfully creates new worlds and
characters that leave the reader little choice but to be
swept up and away'
New York Journal of Books

ABOUT THE AUTHOR

Lauren Oliver is the author of YA novels *Ringer*, *Replica*, *Before I Fall*, *Panic*, *Vanishing Girls* and the Delirium trilogy: *Delirium*, *Pandemonium* and *Requiem*, which have been translated into more than thirty languages and are *New York Times* and international bestsellers. She is also the author of two standalone novels for middle-grade readers, *The Spindlers* and *Liesl & Po*, which was an E. B. White Read Aloud Award nominee; the *Curiosity House* series; and a novel for adults, *Rooms*. A graduate of the University of Chicago and NYU's MFA program, Lauren Oliver is also the co-founder of the boutique literary development company Glasstown Entertainment. She lives in Brooklyn, New York.

Find more information at www.laurenoliverbooks.com, or connect with Lauren on Twitter (/OliverBooks) and on Facebook (/laurenoliverbooks).

panic

LAUREN OLIVER

HODDER

First published in America in 2014 by HarperCollins Childrens Books
A division of HarperCollins Publishers

First published in Great Britain in 2014 by Hodder & Stoughton
An Hachette UK company

This paperback edition published in 2021

1

A CIP catalogue record for this title is available from the British Library

B format Paperback 978 1 529 37768 2
A format Paperback 978 1 444 72306 9
eBook 978 1 444 72304 5

Printed and bound by Clays Ltd, Elcograf S.p.A.

Hodder & Stoughton policy is to use papers that are natural,
renewable and recyclable products and made from wood grown
in sustainable forests. The logging and manufacturing processes are
expected to conform to the environmental regulations of the
country of origin.

Hodder & Stoughton
Carmelite House
50 Victoria Embankment
London EC4Y 0DZ

www.hodder.co.uk

SATURDAY, JUNE 18

heather

THE WATER WAS SO COLD IT TOOK HEATHER'S BREATH AWAY
as she fought past the kids crowding the beach and standing
in the shallows, waving towels and homemade signs, cheering
and calling up to the remaining jumpers.

She took a deep breath and went under. The sound of voices,
of shouting and laughter, was immediately muted.

Only one voice stayed with her.

I didn't mean for it to happen.

Those eyes; the long lashes, the mole under his right eyebrow.

There's just something about her.

Something about her. Which meant: Nothing about you.

She'd been planning to tell him she loved him tonight.

The cold was thunderous, a buzzing rush through her body.
Her denim shorts felt as though they'd been weighted with
stones. Fortunately, years of braving the creek and racing the
quarry with Bishop had made Heather Nill a strong swimmer.

The water was threaded with bodies, twisting and kicking,
splashing, treading water – the jumpers, and the people who

had joined their celebratory swim, sloshing into the quarry still clothed, carrying beer cans and joints. She could hear a distant rhythm, a faint drumming, and she let it move her through the water – without thought, without fear.

That's what Panic was all about: no fear.

She broke the surface for air and saw that she'd already crossed the short stretch of water and reached the opposite shore: an ugly pile of misshapen rocks, slick with black and green moss, piled together like an ancient collection of Legos. Pitted with fissures and crevices, they shouldered up toward the sky, ballooning out over the water.

Thirty-one people had already jumped – all of them Heather's friends and former classmates. Only a small knot of people remained at the top of the ridge – the jagged, rocky lip of shoreline jutting forty feet into the air on the north side of the quarry, like a massive tooth biting its way out of the ground.

It was too dark to see them. The flashlights and the bonfire only illuminated the shoreline and a few feet of the inky dark water, and the faces of the people who had jumped, still bobbing in the water, triumphant, too happy to feel the cold, taunting the other competitors. The top of the ridge was a shaggy mass of black, where the trees were encroaching on the rock, or the rock was getting slowly pulled into the woods, one or the other.

But Heather knew who they were. All the competitors had to announce themselves once they reached the top of the ridge, and then Diggin Rodgers, this year's sportscaster, parroted back the names into the megaphone, which he had borrowed from his older brother, a cop.

Three people had yet to jump: Merl Tracey, Derek Klieg, and Natalie Velez. Nat.

Heather's best friend.

Heather wedged her fingers in a fissure in the rocks and pulled. Earlier, and in years past, she had watched all the other gamers scrabbling up the ridge like giant, waterlogged insects. Every year, people raced to be the first to jump, even though it didn't earn any extra points. It was a pride thing.

She banged her knee, hard, against a sharp elbow of rock. When she looked down, she could see a bit of dark blood streaking her kneecap. Weirdly, she didn't feel any pain. And though everyone was still cheering and shouting, it sounded distant.

Matt's words drowned out all the voices.

Look, it's just not working.

There's something about her.

We can still be friends.

The air was cool. The wind had picked up, singing through the old trees, sending deep groans up from the woods – but she wasn't cold anymore. Her heart was beating hard in her throat. She found another handhold in the rock, braced her legs on the slick moss, lifted and levered, as she had watched the gamers do, every summer since eighth grade.

Dimly, she was aware of Diggin's voice, distorted by the megaphone.

'Late in the game . . . a new competitor . . .'

But half his words got whipped away by the wind.

Up, up, up, ignoring the ache in her fingers and legs, trying to stick to the left side of the ridge, where the rocks, driven hard at angles into one another, formed a wide and jutting lip of stone, easy to navigate.

Suddenly a dark shape, a person, rocketed past her. She almost slipped. At the last second, she worked her feet more firmly onto the narrow ledge, dug hard with her fingers to steady herself. A huge cheer went up, and Heather's first thought was: *Natalie.*

But then Diggin boomed out, 'And he's *in*, ladies and gentlemen! Merl Tracey, our thirty-second gamer, is *in*!'

Almost at the top now. She risked a glance behind her and saw a steep slope of jagged rock, the dark water breaking at the base of the ridge. It suddenly seemed a million miles away.

For a second the fog cleared from her head, the anger and the hurt were blown away, and she wanted to crawl back down the rock, back to the safety of the beach, where Bishop was waiting. They could go to Dot's for late-night waffles, extra butter, extra whipped cream. They could drive around with all the windows open, listening to the rising hum of the crickets, or sit together on the hood of his car and talk about nothing.

But it was too late. Matt's voice came whispering back, and she kept climbing.

No one knows who invented Panic, or when it first began.

There are different theories. Some blame the shutting of the paper factory, which overnight placed 40 percent of the adult population of Carp, New York, on unemployment. Mike Dickinson, who infamously got arrested for dealing on the very same night he was named prom king, and now changes brake pads at the Jiffy Lube on Route 22, likes to take credit; that's why he still goes to Opening Jump, seven years after graduating.

None of these stories is correct, however. Panic began as so many things do in Carp, a poor town of twelve thousand people in the middle of nowhere: because it was summer, and there was nothing else to do.

The rules are simple. The day after graduation is Opening

Jump, and the game goes all through summer. After the final challenge, the winner takes the pot.

Everyone at Carp High pays into the pot, no exceptions. Fees are a dollar a day, for every day that school is in session, from September through June. People who refuse to pony up the cash receive reminders that go from gentle to persuasive: vandalized locker, shattered windows, shattered face.

It's only fair. Anyone who wants to play has a chance to win. That's another rule: all seniors, but *only* seniors, are eligible, and must announce their intention to compete by participating in the Jump, the first of the challenges. Sometimes as many as forty kids enter.

There is only ever one winner.

Two judges plan the game, name the challenges, deliver instructions, award and deduct points. They are selected by the judges of the previous year, in strict secrecy. No one, in the whole history of Panic, has ever confessed to being one.

There have been suspicions, of course – rumors and speculation. Carp is a small town, and judges get paid. How did Myra Campbell, who always stole lunch from the school cafeteria because there was no food at home, suddenly afford her used Honda? She said an uncle had died. But no one had ever heard of Myra's uncle – no one, really, had ever *thought* about Myra, until she came rolling in with the windows down, smoking a cigarette, with the sun so bright on the windshield, it almost completely obscured the smile on her face.

Two judges, picked in secret, sworn to secrecy, working together. It must be this way. Otherwise they'd be subject to bribes, and possibly to threats. That's why there are two – to make sure that things stay balanced, to reduce the possibility that one will cheat, and give out information, leak hints.

If the players know what to expect, then they can prepare. And that isn't fair at all.

It's partly the unexpectedness, the never-knowing, that starts to get to them, and weeds them out, one by one.

The pot usually amounts to just over $50,000, after fees are deducted and the judges – whoever they are – take their cut. Four years ago, Tommy O'Hare took his winnings, bought two items out of hock, one of them a lemon-yellow Ford, drove straight to Vegas, and bet it all on black.

The next year, Lauren Davis bought herself new teeth and a new pair of tits and moved to New York City. She returned to Carp two Christmases later, stayed just long enough to show off a new purse and an even newer nose, and then blew back to the city. Rumors floated back: she was dating the ex-producer of some reality TV weight-loss show; she was becoming a Victoria's Secret model, though no one has ever seen her in a catalog. (And many of the boys have looked.)

Conrad Spurlock went into the manufacture of methamphetamines – his father's line of business – and poured the money into a new shed on Mallory Road, after their last place burned straight to the ground. But Sean McManus used the money to go to college; he's thinking of becoming a doctor.

In seven years of playing, there have been three deaths – four including Tommy O'Hare, who shot himself with the second thing he'd bought at the pawn shop, after his number came up red.

You see? Even the winner of Panic is afraid of *something*.

So: back to the day after graduation, the opening day of Panic, the day of the Jump.

Rewind back to the beach, but pause a few hours before

Heather stood on the ridge, suddenly petrified, afraid to jump.

Turn the camera slightly. We're not quite there. Almost, though.

dodge

NO ONE ON THE BEACH WAS CHEERING FOR DODGE MASON – no one *would* cheer for him either, no matter how far he got.

It didn't matter. All that mattered was the win.

And Dodge had a secret – he knew something about Panic, knew more about it, probably, than any of the other people on the beach.

Actually, he had *two* secrets.

Dodge liked secrets. They fueled him, gave him a sense of power. When he was little, he'd even fantasized that he had his own secret world, a private place of shadows, where he could curl up and hide. Even now – on Dayna's bad days, when the pain came roaring back and she started to cry, when his mom hosed the place down with Febreze and invited over her newest Piece of Shit date, and late at night Dodge could hear the bed frame hitting the wall, like a punch in the stomach every time – he thought about sinking into that dark space, cool and private.

Everyone at school thought Dodge was a pussy. He knew

that. He *looked* like a pussy. He'd always been tall and skinny – angles and corners, his mom said, just like his father. As far as he knew, the angles – and the dark skin – were the *only* things he had in common with his dad, a Dominican roofer his mom had been with for one hot second back in Miami. Dodge could never even remember his name. Roberto. Or Rodrigo. Some shit like that.

Back when they'd first gotten stuck in Carp (that's how he always thought about it – getting *stuck* – he, Dayna, and his mom were just like empty plastic bags skipping across the country on fitful bits of wind, occasionally getting snagged around a telephone pole or under the tires of some semi, pinned in place for a bit), he'd been beat up three times: once by Greg O'Hare, then by Zev Keller, and then by Greg O'Hare *again*, just to make sure that Dodge knew the rules. And Dodge hadn't swung back, not once.

He'd had worse before.

And that was Dodge's second secret, and the source of his power.

He wasn't afraid. He just didn't care.

And that was very, very different.

The sky was streaked with red and purple and orange. It reminded Dodge of an enormous bruise, or a picture taken of the inside of a body. It was still an hour or so before sunset and before the pot, and then the Jump, would be announced.

Dodge cracked a beer. His first and only. He didn't want to be buzzed, and didn't need to be either. But it had been a hot day, and he'd come straight from Home Depot, and he was thirsty.

The crowd had only just started to assemble. Periodically,

Dodge heard the muffled slamming of a car door, a shout of greeting from the woods, the distant blare of music. Whippoorwill Road was a quarter mile away; kids were just starting to emerge from the path, fighting their way through the thick underbrush, swatting at hanging moss and creeper vines, carting coolers and blankets and bottles and iPod speakers, staking out patches of sand.

School was done – for good, forever. He took a deep breath. Of all the places he had lived – Chicago, DC, Dallas, Richmond, Ohio, Rhode Island, Oklahoma, New Orleans – New York smelled the best. Like growth and change, things turning over and becoming other things.

Ray Hanrahan and his friends had arrived first. That was unsurprising. Even though competitors weren't officially announced until the moment of the Jump, Ray had been bragging for months that he was going to take home the pot, just like his brother had two years earlier.

Luke had won, just barely, in the last round of Panic. Luke had walked away with fifty grand. The other driver hadn't walked away at all. If the doctors were right, she'd never walk again.

Dodge flipped a coin in his palm, made it disappear, then reappear easily between his fingers. In fourth grade, his mom's boyfriend – he couldn't remember which one – had bought him a book about magic tricks. They'd been living in Oklahoma that year, a shithole in a flat bowl in the middle of the country, where the sun singed the ground to dirt and the grass to gray, and he'd spent a whole summer teaching himself how to pull coins from someone's ear and slip a card into his pocket so quickly, it was unnoticeable.

It had started as a way to pass the time but had become a

kind of obsession. There was something elegant about it: how people saw without seeing, how the mind filled in what it expected, how the eyes betrayed you.

Panic, he knew, was one big magic trick. The judges were the magicians; the rest of them were just a dumb, gaping audience.

Mike Dickinson came next, along with two friends, all of them visibly drunk. The Dick's hair had started to thin, and patches of his scalp were visible when he bent down to deposit his cooler on the beach. His friends were carrying a half-rotted lifeguard chair between them: the throne, where Diggin, the announcer, would sit during the event.

Dodge heard a high whine. He smacked unthinkingly, catching the mosquito just as it started to feed, smearing a bit of black on his bare calf. He hated mosquitoes. Spiders, too, although he liked other insects, found them fascinating. Like humans, in a way – stupid and sometimes vicious, blinded by need.

The sky was deepening; the light was fading and so were the colors, swirling away behind the line of trees beyond the ridge, as though someone had pulled the plug.

Heather Nill was next on the beach, followed by Nat Velez, and lastly, Bishop Marks, trotting happily after them like an overgrown sheepdog. Even from a distance, Dodge could tell both girls were on edge. Heather had done something with her hair. He wasn't sure what, but it wasn't wrestled into its usual ponytail, and it even looked like she might have straightened it. And he wasn't sure, but he thought she might be wearing makeup.

He debated getting up and going over to say hi. Heather was cool. He liked how tall she was, how tough, too, in her own way. He liked her broad shoulders and the way she walked, straight-backed, even though he was sure she would have liked to be a few inches shorter – could tell from the way she wore only flats and sneakers with worn-down soles.

But if he got up, he'd have to talk to Natalie – and even looking at Nat from across the beach made his stomach seize up, like he'd been kicked. Nat wasn't exactly *mean* to him – not like some of the other kids at school – but she wasn't exactly nice, either, and that bothered him more than anything else. She usually smiled vaguely when she caught him talking to Heather, and as her eyes skated past him, through him, he knew that she would never, ever, actually look at him. Once, at the homecoming bonfire last year, she'd even called him Dave.

He'd gone just because he was hoping to see her. And then, in the crowd, he had spotted her; had moved toward her, buzzed from the noise and the heat and the shot of whiskey he'd taken in the parking lot, intending to talk to her, *really* talk to her, for the first time. Just as he was reaching out to touch her elbow, she had taken a step backward, onto his foot.

'Oops! Sorry, Dave,' she'd said, giggling. Her breath smelled like vanilla and vodka. And his stomach had opened up, and his guts went straight onto his shoes.

There were only 107 people in their graduating class, out of the 150 who'd started at Carp High freshman year. And she didn't even know his name.

So he stayed where he was, working his toes into the ground, waiting for the dark, waiting for the whistle to blow and for the games to begin.

He was going to win Panic.

He was going to do it for Dayna.
He was going to do it for revenge.

heather

'TESTING, TESTING. ONE, TWO, THREE.' THAT WAS DIGGIN, testing the megaphone.

The old quarry off Whippoorwill Road, empty since the late 1800s, had been flooded in the fifties to make a swimming hole. On the south side was the beach: a narrow strip of sand and stone, supposedly off-limits after dark, but rarely used before then; a dump of cigarette butts, crushed beer cans, empty Baggies, and sometimes, disgustingly, condoms, scattered limply on the ground like tubular jellyfish. Tonight, it was crowded – packed with blankets and beach chairs, heavy with the smell of mosquito repellent and booze.

Heather closed her eyes and inhaled. This was the smell of Panic – the smell of *summer*. At the edge of the water, there was a sudden explosion of color and sound, shrieks of laughter. Firecrackers. In the quick glare of red and green light, Heather saw Kaitlin Frost and Shayna Lambert laughing, doubled over, while Patrick Culbert tried to get a few more flares to light.

It was weird. Graduation had been only yesterday – Heather

had bailed on the ceremony, since Krista, her mom, wouldn't show, and there was no point in pretending there was some big glory in floating through four years of mandated classes. But already she felt years and years away from high school, like it had all been one long, unmemorable dream. Maybe, she thought, it was because people didn't change. All the days had simply blurred together and would now be suctioned away into the past.

Nothing ever happened in Carp. There were no surprises.

Diggin's voice echoed over the crowd.

'Ladies and gentlemen, I have an announcement: school's out for summer.'

It was starting. Everyone cheered. There was another *pop-pop-pop*, a burst of firecrackers. They were in the middle of the woods, five miles from the nearest house. They could make all the noise they wanted.

They could scream. No one would hear them.

Heather knew she should say something encouraging to Nat – Heather and Bishop were there for Natalie, to give her moral support. Bishop had even made a poster: *Go Nat*, he had written. Next to the words, he had drawn a huge stick figure – Natalie could tell it was supposed to be her, because the stick figure was wearing a pink sweatshirt – standing on a pile of money.

'How come Nat's not wearing any pants?' Heather had asked.

'Maybe she lost them during the Jump,' Bishop said. He turned, grinning, to Nat. Whenever he smiled like that, his eyes went from syrup brown to honey colored. 'Drawing was never my thing.'

Heather didn't like to talk about Matt in front of Bishop. She couldn't stand the way he rolled his eyes when she brought him up, like she'd just switched the radio to a bad pop station. But finally she couldn't help it. 'He's still not here.' Heather spoke in a low voice, so only Nat would hear her. 'Sorry, Nat. I know this isn't the time – I mean, we came for *you*—'

'It's okay.' Nat reached out and squeezed Heather's hand with both of her own. She pulled a weird face – like someone had just made her chug a limeade. 'Look. Matt doesn't deserve you. Okay? You can do better than Matt.'

Heather half laughed. 'You're my best friend, Nat,' she said. 'You aren't supposed to lie to me.'

Nat shook her head. 'I'm sure he'll be here soon. The game's about to start.'

Heather checked her phone again, for the millionth time. Nothing. She'd powered it down several times and rebooted it, just to make sure it was working.

Diggin's voice boomed out again: 'The rules of Panic are simple. Anyone can enter. But only one person will win.'

Diggin announced the pot.

$67,000.

Heather felt as though she'd been punched in the stomach. $67,000. That had to be the biggest pot ever. The crowd began to buzz – the number ran through them like an electric current, jumping from lip to lip. *Shit, man, you'd have to be crazy* not *to play.* Nat looked as though she'd just taken a large spoonful of ice cream.

Diggin plunged on, ignoring the noise, and explained the rules – a half-dozen events, spaced throughout the summer, conducted under conditions of strictest privacy; eliminations after every round; individual challenges for each contestant who made it past the halfway mark – but nobody was listening. It was the same speech as always. Heather had been watching

Panic since she was in eighth grade. She could have made the speech herself.

That number – 67,000 – wrapped itself around her heart and squeezed. Without meaning to, she thought of all she could do with the money; she thought of how far she could go, what she could buy, how long she could live. How many miles away from Carp she could get.

But no. She couldn't leave Matt. Matt had said he loved her. He was her plan. The grip on her heart eased a little, and she found she could breathe again.

Next to Heather, Natalie shimmied out of her jean shorts and kicked off her shoes. 'Can you believe it?' she said. She took off her shirt, shivering in the wind. Heather couldn't believe she'd insisted on that ridiculous bikini, which would fly off as soon as she hit the water. Natalie had only laughed. Maybe, she'd joked, that would earn her extra points.

That was Natalie: stubborn. Vain, too. Heather still couldn't understand why she'd even chosen to play. Nat was afraid of everything.

Someone – probably Billy Wallace – whistled. 'Nice ass, Velez.'

Nat ignored him, but Heather could tell she had heard and was pretending not to be pleased. Heather wondered what Billy Wallace would say if she tried to wear a scrap of fabric like that. *Whoa. Look at the size of that thing! Do you need a permit to carry that thing around, Heather?*

But Matt loved her. Matt thought she was pretty.

The noise on the beach swelled, grew to a roar: hoots and screams, people waving homemade banners and flags, fire-crackers exploding like a smattering of gunfire, and she knew it was time. The whistle would blow.

Panic was about to begin.

Just then Heather saw him. The crowd parted temporarily; she could see him, smiling, talking to someone; then the crowd shifted and she lost sight of him. 'He's here. Nat, he's *here*.'

'What?' Nat wasn't paying attention anymore.

Heather's voice dried up in her throat. Because the crowd had opened again, just as she'd started moving toward him, as though directed by gravity – relief welling in her chest, a chance to make things right, a chance to *do* things right, for once – and in that second she had seen that he was speaking to Delaney O'Brien.

Not just speaking. Whispering.

And then: kissing.

The whistle blew – sharp and thin in the sudden silence, like the cry of an alien bird.

Heather reached the top of the ridge just as Derek Klieg got a running start and hurled himself into the air, body contorted, shouting. A few seconds later, a cheer went up as he hit.

Natalie was crouching a few feet away from the edge, her face pale; for a second, Heather thought she heard her counting. Then Nat turned and blinked repeatedly, as though trying to bring Heather's face into focus. She opened her mouth and closed it again.

Heather's heart was beating hard and high. 'Hey, Nat,' she said, just as Natalie straightened up.

'What the hell are you doing?' Natalie spat out.

Now Heather registered everything, all at once: the ache in her hands and thighs, the pain in her fingers, the sharp bite of the wind. Natalie looked furious. She was shaking, although that might have been the cold.

'I'm going to jump,' Heather said, realizing, as she said it, how stupid it sounded – how stupid it *was*. All of a sudden, she thought she might puke.

I'll be cheering for you, Heather had said to Natalie. The guilt was there, throbbing alongside the nausea. But Matt's voice was bigger than everything. Matt's voice, and underneath it a vision of the water stains above her bed; the dull thud of music from the park; the smell of weed and cigarettes; the sounds of laughter, and later, someone screaming, *You dumb piece of* . . .

'You can't jump,' Nat said, still staring. '*I'm* jumping.'

'We'll jump together,' Heather said.

Natalie took two steps forward. Heather noticed she was balling her fists almost rhythmically. Squeeze, relax. Squeeze, relax. Three times.

'Why are you doing this?' The question was almost a whisper.

Heather couldn't answer. She didn't even know, not exactly. All she knew – all she could feel – was that this was her last chance.

So she just said, 'I'm going to jump now. Before I chicken out.'

When she turned toward the water, Natalie reached for Heather, as if to pull her back. But she didn't.

Heather felt as though the rock underneath her had begun to move, bucking like a horse. She had a sudden terror that she was going to lose her balance and go tumbling down the rocky slope, cracking her head in the shallows.

Panic.

She took small, halting steps forward, and still reached the edge far too quickly.

'Announce yourself!' Diggin boomed out.

Below Heather, the water, black as oil, was still churning

with bodies. She wanted to shout down – *move, move, I'm going to hit you* – but she couldn't speak. She could hardly breathe. Her lungs felt like they were being pressed between two stones.

And suddenly she couldn't think of anything but Chris Heinz, who four years ago drank a fifth of vodka before doing the Jump, and lost his footing. The sound his head made as it cracked against the rock was delicate, almost like an egg breaking. She remembered the way everyone ran through the woods; the image of his body, broken and limp, lying half submerged in the water.

'Say your name!' Diggin prompted again, and the crowd picked up the chant: *Name, name, name.*

She opened her mouth. 'Heather,' she croaked out. 'Heather Nill.' Her voice broke, got whipped back by the wind.

The chant was still going: *Name, name, name, name.* Then: *Jump, jump, jump, jump.*

Her insides were white; filled with snow. Her mouth tasted a little like puke. She took a deep breath. She closed her eyes.

She jumped.

SATURDAY, JUNE 25

heather

HEATHER HAD NEVER REGRETTED ANYTHING AS MUCH AS SHE regretted making the decision, on the beach, to enter the game. In the days that followed, it seemed to her like a kind of insanity. Maybe she'd inhaled too much booze-vapor on the beach. Maybe seeing Matt with Delaney had driven her temporarily psychotic. That happened, didn't it? Weren't whole defenses built on that kind of thing, when people went crazy and hacked their ex-wives to pieces with an ax?

But she was too proud to withdraw. And the date of the first official challenge kept drawing nearer. Despite the fact that the breakup made her want to go into permanent hiding, despite the fact that she was doing her best to avoid everyone who knew her even vaguely, the news had reached her: the water towers near Copake had been defaced, painted over with a date. Saturday. Sundown.

A message and invitation to all the players.

She moved as slowly as she could; spent her nights curled up on the couch watching TV with her sister, Lily; turned off

her phone when she wasn't obsessively checking it for calls
from Matt. She didn't want to deal with Bishop, who would
lecture her and tell her that Matt was an idiot anyway; and
Nat spent three days giving her the cold shoulder before admit-
ting, finally, that she wasn't that mad anymore.

Time tumbled, cascaded on, as though life had been set to
fast-forward.

Finally Saturday came, and she couldn't avoid it anymore.

She didn't even have to bother to sneak out. Earlier in the
evening, her mom and her stepdad, Bo, had gone over to some
bar in Ancram, which meant they wouldn't be stumbling home
until the early hours or, possibly, Sunday afternoon – bleary-
eyed, reeking of smoke, probably starving and in a foul mood.

Heather made mac 'n' cheese for Lily, who ate in sullen
silence in front of the TV. Lily's hair was parted exactly down
the middle, combed straight, and fixed in a hard knot at the
back of her head. Recently she had been wearing it like that,
and it made her look like an old woman stuck in an eleven-
year-old's body.

Lily was giving her the silent treatment, and Heather didn't
know why, but she didn't have enough energy to worry about
it. Lily was like that: stormy one minute, smiley the next.
Lately, she'd been more on the *stormy* side – more serious, too,
very careful about what she wore and how she fixed her hair,
quieter, less likely to laugh until she snorted milk, less likely
to beg Heather for a story before she went to bed – but Heather
figured she was just growing up. There wasn't that much to
smile about in Carp. There *definitely* wasn't much to smile
about in Fresh Pines Mobile Park.

Still, it made Heather's chest ache a little. She missed the
old Lily: sticky Dr Pepper hands, the smell of bubblegum

breath, hair that was never combed, and glasses that were always smudgy. She missed Lily's eyes, wide in the dark, as she rolled over and whispered, 'Tell me a story, Heather.'

But that was the way it worked – evolution, she guessed; the order of things.

At seven thirty p.m., Bishop texted her to say that he was on his way. Lily had withdrawn to the Corner, which was what Heather called their bedroom: a narrow, cramped room with two beds squeezed practically side by side; a chest of drawers missing a leg, which rocked violently when it was opened; a chipped lamp and a varnish-spotted nightstand; clothes heaped everywhere, like snowdrifts.

Lily was lying in the dark, blankets drawn up to her chin. Heather assumed she was sleeping and was about to close the door, when Lily turned to her, sitting up on one elbow. In the moonlight coming through the dirty windowpane, her eyes were like polished marbles.

'Where are you going?' she said.

Heather navigated around a tangle of jeans and sweatshirts, underwear and balled-up socks. She sat down on Lily's bed. She was glad that Lily wasn't asleep. She was glad, too, that Lily had decided to talk to her after all.

'Bishop and Nat are picking me up,' she said, avoiding the question. 'We're going to hang out for a little while.'

Lily lay down again, huddling in her blankets. For a minute, she didn't say anything. Then: 'Are you coming back?'

Heather felt her chest squeeze up. She leaned over to place a hand on Lily's head. Lily jerked away. 'Why would you say something like that, Billygoat?'

Lily didn't answer. For several minutes Heather sat there, her heart raging in her chest, feeling helpless and alone in the dark. Then she heard Lily's breathing and knew she had fallen asleep. Heather leaned over and kissed her sister's head. Lily's skin was hot and wet, and Heather had the urge to climb into bed with her, to wake her up and apologize for everything: for the ants in the kitchen and the water stains on the ceiling; for the smells of smoke and the shouting from outside; for their mom, Krista, and their stepdad, Bo; for the pathetic life they'd been thrust into, narrow as a tin can.

But she heard a light honk from outside, so instead she got up, closing the door behind her.

Heather could always tell Bishop was coming by the sound of his cars. His dad had owned a garage once, and Bishop was a car freak. He was good at building things; several years ago he'd made Heather a rose out of petals of copper, with a steel stem and little screws for thorns. He was always tinkering with rusted pieces of junk he picked up from God-knows-where. His newest was a Le Sabre with an engine that sounded like an old man trying to choke out a belt buckle.

Heather took shotgun. Natalie was sitting in the back. Weirdly, Natalie always insisted on sitting bitch, in the exact middle, even if there was no one else in the car. She'd told Heather that she didn't like picking sides – left or right – because it always felt like she was betting with her life. Heather had explained to her a million times that it was more dangerous to sit in the middle, but Nat didn't listen.

'I can't believe you roped me into this,' Bishop said when Heather got in the car. It was raining – the kind of rain that didn't so much fall as materialize, as though it was being exhaled by a giant mouth. There was no point in using an umbrella or rain jacket – it was coming from all directions at once, and got in collars and under shirtsleeves and down the back.

'Please.' She cinched her hoodie a bit tighter. 'Cut the holier-than-thou crap. You've always watched the game.'

'Yeah, but that was before my two best friends decided to go batshit and join.'

'We get it, Bishop,' Nat said. 'Turn on some music, will you?'

'No can do, my lady.' Bishop reached into the cup holder and handed Heather a Slurpee from 7-Eleven. Blue. Her favorite. She took a sip and felt a good freeze in her head. 'Radio's busted. I'm doing some work on the wiring—'

Nat cut him off, groaning exaggeratedly. 'Not *again*.'

'What can I say? I love the fixer-uppers.'

He patted the steering wheel as he accelerated onto the highway. The Le Sabre made a shrill whine of protest, followed by several emphatic bangs and a horrifying rattle, as if the engine were coming apart.

'I'm pretty sure the love is *not* mutual,' Nat said, and Heather laughed, and felt a little less nervous.

As Bishop angled the car off the road and bumped onto the narrow, packed-dirt one-laner that ran the periphery of the park, NO TRESPASSING signs were lit up intermittently in the mist of his headlights. Already, a few dozen cars were parked on the lane, most of them squeezed as close to the woods as possible, some almost entirely swallowed by the underbrush.

Heather spotted Matt's car right away – the old used Jeep he'd inherited from an uncle, its rear bumper plastered with half-shredded stickers he'd tried desperately to key off, as though he had backed up into a massive spiderweb.

She remembered the first time they'd ever driven around together, to celebrate the fact that he had finally gotten his license after failing the test three times. He'd stopped and started so abruptly she'd felt like she might puke up the doughnuts he'd bought her, but he was so happy, she was happy too.

All day, all week, she'd been both desperately hoping to see him and praying that she would never see him again.

If Delaney was here, she really *would* puke. She shouldn't have had the Slurpee.

'You okay?' Bishop asked her in a low voice as they got out of the car. He could always read her: she loved and hated that about him at the same time.

'I'm fine,' she said, too sharply.

'Why'd you do it, Heather?' he said, putting a hand on her elbow and stopping her. 'Why'd you really do it?'

Heather noticed he was wearing the exact same outfit he'd been wearing the last time she'd seen him, on the beach – the faded-blue Lucky Charms T-shirt, the jeans so long they looped underneath the heels of his Converse – and felt vaguely annoyed by it. His dirty-blond hair was sticking out at crazy angles underneath his ancient 49ers hat. He smelled good, though, a very Bishop smell: like the inside of a drawer full of old coins and Tic Tacs.

For a second, she thought of telling him the truth: that when Matt had dumped her, she had understood for the first time that she was a complete and total nobody.

But then he ruined it. 'Please tell me this isn't about Matthew Hepley,' he said. There it was. The eye roll.

'Come on, Bishop.' She could have hit him. Even hearing the name made her throat squeeze up in a knot.

'Give me a reason, then. You said yourself, a million times, that Panic is stupid.'

'Nat entered, didn't she? How come you aren't lecturing her?'

'Nat's an idiot,' Bishop said. He took off his hat and rubbed his head; his hair responded as though it had been electrified and promptly stood straight up. Bishop claimed that his super-power was electromagnetic hair. Heather's only superpower seemed to be the amazing ability to have one angry red pimple at any given time.

'She's one of your best friends,' Heather pointed out.

'So? She's still an idiot. I have an open-door idiot policy on friendship.'

Heather couldn't help it; she laughed. Bishop smiled too, so wide she could see the small overlap in his two front teeth.

Bishop shoved on his baseball hat again, smothering the disaster of his hair. He was one of the few boys she knew who was taller than she was – even Matt had been exactly her height, five-eleven. Sometimes she was grateful; sometimes she resented him for it, like he was trying to prove a point by being taller. Up until the time they were twelve years old, they'd been exactly the same height, to the centimeter. In Bishop's bedroom was a ladder of old pencil marks on the wall to prove it.

'I'm betting on you, Nill,' he said in a low voice. 'I want you to know that. I don't want you to play. I think it's totally idiotic. But I'm betting on you.' He put an arm over her shoulder and gave her a squeeze, and something in his tone of voice reminded her that once – ages and ages ago, it felt like – she had been briefly head over heels in love with him.

Freshman year, they'd had one fumbling kiss in the back of the Hudson Movieplex, even though she'd had popcorn stuck in her teeth, and for two days they'd held hands loosely, suddenly incapable of conversation even though they'd been friends since elementary school. And then he had broken it

off, and Heather had said she understood, even though she
didn't.

She didn't know what made her think of it. She couldn't
imagine being in love with Bishop now. He was like a brother –
an annoying brother who always felt the need to point out
when you had a pimple. Which you did, always. But just
one.

Already, she could hear faint music through the trees, and
the crackle and boom of Diggin's voice, amplified by the megaphone. The water towers, scrawled with graffiti and imprinted
faintly with the words COLUMBIA COUNTY, were lit starkly from
below. Perched on rail-thin legs, they looked like overgrown
insects.

No – like a *single* insect, with two rounded steel joints.
Because Heather could see, even from a distance, that a narrow
wooden plank had been set between them, fifty feet in the air.

The challenge, this time, was clear.

By the time Heather, Nat, and Bishop had arrived at the
place where the crowd was assembled, directly under the
towers, her face was slick. As usual, the atmosphere was
celebratory – the crowd was keyed up, antsy, although
everyone was speaking in whispers. Someone had managed
to maneuver a truck through the woods. A floodlight, hooked
up to its engine, illuminated the towers and the single wooden
plank running between them, and lit up the mist of rain.
Cigarettes flared intermittently, and the truck radio was going
– an old rock song thudded quietly under the rhythm of
conversation. They had to be quieter tonight; they weren't
far from the road.

'Promise not to ditch me, okay?' Nat said. Heather was glad
she'd said it; even though these were her classmates, people

she'd known forever, Heather had a sudden terror of getting lost in the crowd.

'No way,' Heather said. She tried to avoid looking up, and she found herself unconsciously scanning the crowd for Matt. She could make out a group of sophomores huddled nearby, giggling, and Shayna Lambert, who was wrapped in a blanket and had a thermos of something hot, as though she was at a football game.

Heather was surprised to see Vivian Trager, standing by herself, a little ways apart from the rest of the crowd. Her hair was knotted into dreadlocks, and in the moonlight, her various piercings glinted dully. Heather had never seen Viv at a single social event – she'd never seen her doing much of anything besides cutting classes and waiting tables at Dot's. For some reason, the fact that even Viv had showed made her even more anxious.

'Bishop!'

Avery Wallace pushed her way through the crowd and promptly catapulted herself into Bishop's arms, as though he'd just rescued her from a major catastrophe. Heather looked away as Bishop leaned down to kiss her. Avery was only five foot one, and standing next to her made Heather feel like the Jolly Green Giant on a can of corn.

'I missed you,' Avery said, when Bishop pulled away. She still hadn't even acknowledged Heather; she'd once overheard Heather call her 'shrimp-faced' and had obviously never forgiven her. Avery did, however, look somewhat shrimplike, all tight and pink, so Heather didn't feel that bad about it.

Bishop mumbled something in return. Heather felt nauseous, and heartbroken all over again. No one should be allowed to be happy when you were so miserable – especially not your best friends. It should be a law.

Avery giggled and squeezed Bishop's hand. 'Let me get my beer, okay? I'll be back. Stay right here.' Then she turned and vanished.

Immediately, Bishop raised his eyebrows at Heather. 'Don't say it.'

'What?' Heather held up both hands.

Bishop stuck a finger in her face. 'I know what you're thinking,' he said, and then jabbed at Nat. 'You too.'

Nat did her best innocent face. 'Unfair, Marks. I was just thinking what a lovely accessory she makes. So small and convenient.'

'The perfect pocket liner,' Heather agreed.

'All right, all right.' Bishop was doing a pretty good job of pretending to be angry. 'Enough.'

'It's a compliment,' Nat protested.

'I said, enough.' But after a minute, Bishop leaned over and whispered, 'I can't keep her in my pocket, you know. She bites.' His lips bumped against Heather's ear – by accident, she was sure – and she laughed.

The weight of nerves in her stomach eased up a little. But then someone cut the music, and the crowd got still and very quiet, and she knew it was about to begin. Just like that, she felt a numbing cold all over, as though all of the rain had solidified and frozen on her skin.

'Welcome to the second challenge,' Diggin boomed out.

'Suck it, Rodgers,' a guy yelled, and there were whoops and scattered laughs. Someone else said, 'Shhh.'

Diggin pretended he hadn't heard: 'This is a test of bravery and balance—'

'And sobriety!'

'Dude, I'm gonna fall.'

More laughter. Heather couldn't even smile. Next to her, Natalie was fidgeting – turning to the right and left, touching her hip bones. Heather couldn't even ask what she was doing.

Diggin kept plowing on: 'A test of speed, too, since all the contestants will be timed—'

'Jesus Christ, get on with it.'

Diggin finally lost it. He wrenched the megaphone from his mouth. 'Shut the hell *up*, Lee.'

This provoked a new round of laughter. To Heather it all felt off, like she was watching a movie and the sound was a few seconds too late. She couldn't stop herself from looking up now – at that single beam, a few bare inches of wood, stretched fifty feet above the ground. The Jump was a tradition, more for fun than for anything else, a plunge into water. This would be a plunge to hard earth, packed ground. No chance of surviving it.

There was a momentary stutter when the truck engine gave out. Everything went dark, and several people shouted in protest. When, a few seconds later, the engine gunned on again, Heather saw Matt: standing in the beam of the headlights, laughing, one hand in the back of Delaney's jeans.

Her stomach rolled over. Weirdly, it was that fact – the way he had his hand shoved up against her butt – more than even seeing them together, that made her sick. He had never once touched her in that way, had even complained that couples who stood like that, hand-to-butt, should be shot.

Maybe he'd thought she wasn't cute enough. Maybe he'd been embarrassed by her.

Maybe he had just been lying then, to spare her feelings.

Maybe she'd never really known him.

This thought struck her with terror. If she didn't know Matt

Hepley – the boy who'd once applauded after she burped the alphabet, who'd even, once, noticed that she had a little period blood on the outside of her white shorts and not made a big deal of it, and pretended not to be grossed out – then she couldn't count on knowing any of these people, or what they were capable of.

Suddenly she was aware of a stillness, a pause in the flow of laughter and conversation, as though everyone had drawn a breath at once. And she realized that Kim Hollister was inching out onto the plank, high above their heads, her face stark-white and terrified, and that the challenge had started.

It took Kim forty-seven seconds to make her way across, shuffling, keeping her right foot always in front of her left. When she reached the second water tower safely, she briefly embraced it with both arms, and the crowd exhaled as one.

Then came Felix Harte: he made it even faster, taking the short, clipped steps of a tightrope walker. And then Merl Tracey. Even before he'd crossed to safety, Diggin lifted the megaphone and trumpeted the next name.

'Heather Nill! Heather Nill, to the stage!'

'Good luck, Heathbar,' Natalie said. 'Don't look down.'

'Thanks,' Heather said automatically, even as she registered it as ridiculous advice. When you're fifty feet in the air, where else do you look but down?

She felt as though she were moving in silence, although she knew, too, that that was unlikely – Diggin couldn't keep his mouth off that stupid megaphone for anything. It was just because she was afraid; afraid and still thinking, stupidly, miserably, about Matt, and wondering whether he was watching her with his hand still shoved down the back of Delaney's pants.

As she began to climb the ladder that ran up one leg of the eastern water tower, her fingers numb on the cold, slick metal, it occurred to her that he'd be staring at her butt, and feeling Delaney's butt, and that was really sick.

Then it occurred to her that everyone could see her butt, and she had a brief moment of panic, wondering if her underwear lines were visible through her jeans, since she just couldn't stomach thongs and didn't understand girls who could.

She was already halfway up the ladder by then, and it further occurred to her that if she was stressing so hard about underwear lines, she couldn't truly be afraid of the height. For the first time, she began to feel more confident.

But the rain was a problem. It made the rungs of the ladder slick under her fingers. It blurred her vision and made the treads of her sneakers slip. When she finally reached the small metal ledge that ran along the circumference of the water tank and hauled herself to her feet, the fear came swinging back. There was nothing to hold on to, only smooth, wet metal behind her back, and air everywhere. Only a few inches' difference between being alive and not.

A tingle worked its way from her feet to her legs and up into her palms, and for a second she was afraid not of falling but of jumping, leaping out into the dark air.

She shuffled sideways toward the wooden beam, pressing her back as hard as she could against the tank, praying that from below she didn't look as frightened as she felt.

Crying out, hesitating – it would all be counted against her.

'Time!' Diggin's voice boomed out from below. Heather knew she had to move if she wanted to stay in the game.

Heather forced herself away from the tank and inched forward onto the wooden plank, which had been barely secured to the ledge by means of several twisted screws. She had a sudden image of wood snapping under her weight, a wild hurtle through space. But the wood held.

She raised her arms unconsciously for balance, no longer thinking of Matt or Delaney or Bishop staring up at her, or anything other than all that thin air, the horrible prickling in her feet and legs, an itch to jump.

She could move faster if she paced normally, one foot in front of the other, but she couldn't bring herself to break contact with the board; if she lifted a foot, a heel, a toe, she would collapse, she would swing to one side and die. She was conscious of a deep silence, a quiet so heavy she could hear the fizz of the rain, could hear her own breathing, shallow and quick.

Beneath her was blinding light, the kind of light you'd see just before you died. All the people had merged with shadow, and for a second she was afraid she *had* died, that she was all alone on a tiny, bare surface, with an endless fall into the dark on either side of her.

Inch by inch, going as fast as she could without lifting her feet.

And then, all at once, she was done – she had reached the second water tower and found herself hugging the tank, like Kim had done, pressing flat against it, letting her sweatshirt get soaked. A cheer went up, even as another name was announced: Ray Hanrahan.

Her head was ringing, and her mouth tasted like metal. Over. It was over. Her arms felt suddenly useless, her muscles weak with relief, as she made her way clumsily down the ladder, dropping the last few feet and taking two stumbling steps before righting herself. People reached out, squeezed her shoulders, patted her on the back. She didn't know if she smiled or not.

'You were amazing!' Nat barreled to her through the crowd. Heather barely registered the feel of Nat's arms around her neck. 'Is it scary? Were you freaked?'

Heather shook her head, conscious of people still watching her. 'It went quick,' she said. As soon as the words were out of her mouth, she felt better. It was over. She was standing in the middle of a crowd: the air smelled like damp fleece and cigarette smoke. Solid. Real.

'Forty-two seconds,' Nat said proudly. Heather hadn't even heard her time be announced.

'Where's Bishop?' Heather asked. Now she was starting to feel good. A bubbly feeling was working its way through her. Forty-two seconds. Not bad.

'He was right behind me . . .' Nat turned to scan the crowd, but the truck's headlights turned everyone into silhouettes, dark brushstroke-people.

Another cheer erupted. Heather looked up and saw that Ray had crossed already. Diggin's voice echoed out hollowly: 'Twenty-two seconds! A record so far!'

Heather swallowed back a sour taste. She hated Ray Hanrahan. In seventh grade, when she still hadn't developed boobs, he stuck a training bra to the outside of her locker and spread a rumor that she was taking medicine to turn into a boy. 'Got any chin hairs yet?' he'd say when he passed her in the halls. He only left her alone once Bishop threatened to tell the cops that Luke Hanrahan was selling weed from Pepe's, where he worked, slipping bags of pot under the slice if patrons asked for 'extra oregano.' Which he was.

It was Zev Keller's turn next. Heather forgot about looking

for Bishop. She watched, transfixed, as Zev moved out onto the plank. From the safety of the ground, it looked almost beautiful: the soft haze of rain, Zev's arms extended, a dark black shape against the clouds. Ray hadn't come down the ladder. He must have been watching too, although he had moved behind the water tank, so he was invisible.

It happened in a split second; Zev jerked to one side, lost his footing, and was falling. Heather heard herself cry out. She felt her heart rocket into the roof of her mouth, and in that second, as his arms pinwheeled wildly and his mouth contorted in a scream, she thought, *Nothing and none of us will ever be the same.*

And then, just as quickly, he caught himself. He got his left foot back onto the board, and his body stopped swaying wildly from right to left, like a loose pendulum. He straightened up.

Someone screamed Zev's name. And then the applause began, turning thunderous as he made his way, haltingly, the remaining few feet. No one heard the time that Diggin shouted. No one paid any attention to Ray as he came down the ladder.

But as soon as Zev was on the ground, he flew at Ray. Zev was smaller than Ray, and skinnier, but he tackled him from behind and the move was unexpected. Ray was on the ground, face in the dirt, in a second.

'You fucking asshole. You threw something at me.'

Zev raised his fist; Ray twisted, bucking Zev off him.

'What are you talking about?' Ray staggered to his feet, so his face was lit in the glare of the spotlight. He must have cut his lip on a rock. He was bleeding. He looked mean and ugly.

Zev got up too. His eyes were wild – black and full of hatred. The crowd was still, frozen, and Heather once again thought she could hear the rain, the dissolution of a hundred thousand different drops at once. Everything hung in the air, ready to fall.

'Don't lie,' Zev spat out. 'You hit me in the chest. You wanted me to fall.'

'You're crazy.' Ray started to turn away.

Zev charged him. And then they were down again, and all at once the crowd surged forward, everyone shouting, some pushing for a better view, some jumping in to pull the boys off each other. Heather was squeezed from all sides. She felt a hand on her back and she barely stopped herself from falling. She reached for Nat's hand instinctively.

'Heather!' Nat's face was white, frightened. Their hands were wrenched apart, and Nat went down among the blur of bodies.

'Nat!' Heather shoved through the crowd, using her elbows, thankful now to be so big. Nat was trying to get up, and when Heather reached her, she let out a scream of pain.

'My ankle!' Nat was saying, panicked, grabbing her leg. 'Someone stepped on my ankle.'

Heather reached for her, then felt a hand on her back: this time deliberate, forceful. She tried to twist around to see who had pushed her but she was on the ground, face in the mud, before she could. Feet churned up the dirt, splattered her face with moisture. For just one moment, Heather wondered whether this – the seething crowd, the surge – was part of the challenge.

She felt a break in the crowd, a fractional release.

'Come on.' She managed to stand up and hook Nat under the arm.

'It *hurts*,' Nat said, blinking back tears. But Heather got her to her feet.

Then a voice came blaring, suddenly, through the woods, huge and distorted.

'Freeze where you are, all of you . . .'

Cops.

Everything was chaos. Beams of light swept across the crowd, turning faces white, frozen; people were running, pushing to get out, disappearing into the woods. Heather counted four cops – one of them had wrestled someone to the ground, she couldn't see who. Her mouth was dry, chalky, and her thoughts disjointed. Her hoodie was smeared with mud, and cold seeped into her chest.

Bishop was gone. Bishop had the car.

Car. They needed to get out – or hide.

She kept a hand on Nat's arm and tried to pull her forward, but Nat stumbled. Tears welled up in her eyes.

'I can't,' she said.

'You have to.' Heather felt desperate. Where the hell was Bishop? She bent down to loop an arm around Nat's waist. 'Lean on me.'

'I can't,' Nat repeated. 'It hurts too bad.'

Then Dodge Mason came out of nowhere. He was suddenly next to them, and without pausing or asking permission, he put one of his arms around Nat's waist as well, so that she could be carried between them. Nat gave a short cry of surprise, but she didn't resist. Heather felt like she could kiss him.

'Come on,' he said.

They passed into the woods, stumbling, going as quickly as possible, moving away from the booming megaphone-voices, the screaming and the lights. It was dark. Dodge kept his cell phone out; it cast a weak blue light on the sodden leaves underneath them, the wet ferns and the shaggy, moss-covered trees.

'Where are we going?' Heather whispered. Her heart was pounding. Nat could barely put any weight on her left leg, so every other step, she leaned heavily into Heather.

'We have to wait until the cops clear out,' Dodge replied. He was short of breath.

A few hundred feet beyond the water towers, nestled in the trees, was a narrow pump house. Heather could hear mechanical equipment going inside it, humming through the walls, when they stopped so Dodge could shoulder the door open. It wasn't locked.

Inside, it smelled like mildew and metal. The single room was dominated by two large tanks and various pieces of rusted electrical equipment; the air was filled with a constant, mechanical *thrush*, like the noise of a thousand crickets. They could no longer hear shouting from the woods.

'Jesus.' Nat exhaled heavily and maneuvered onto the ground, extending her left leg in front of her, wincing. 'It hurts.'

'Probably sprained,' Dodge said. He sat down as well, but not too close.

'I swear I felt someone crack it.' Nat leaned forward and began touching the skin around her ankle. She inhaled sharply.

'Leave it, Nat,' Heather said. 'We'll get some ice on it as soon as we can.'

She was cold, and suddenly exhausted. The rush she'd felt from completing the challenge was gone. She was wet and hungry, and the last thing she wanted to do was sit in a stupid pump house for half the night. She pulled out her phone and texted Bishop. *Where r u?*

'How'd you know about this place?' Nat asked Dodge.

'Found it the other day,' Dodge said. 'I was scouting. Mind if I smoke?'

'Kind of,' Heather said.

He shrugged and replaced the cigarettes in his jacket. He kept his cell phone out, on the floor, so his silhouette was touched with blue.

'Thank you,' Nat blurted out. 'For helping me. That was really . . . I mean, you didn't have to.'

'No problem,' Dodge said. Heather couldn't see his face, but there was a weird quality to his voice, like he was being choked.

'I mean, we've never even spoken before . . .' Maybe realizing she sounded rude, Nat trailed off.

For a minute, there was silence. Heather sent another text to Bishop. *WTF?*

Then Dodge said abruptly, 'We spoke before. Once. At the homecoming bonfire last year. You called me Dave.'

'I did?' Nat giggled nervously. 'Stupid. I was probably drunk. Remember, Heather? We took those disgusting shots.'

'Mmmm.' Heather was still standing. She leaned up against the door, listening to the sound of the rain, which was drumming a little harder now. She strained to hear, underneath it, the continued sounds of shouting. She couldn't believe Bishop still hadn't texted her back. Bishop always responded to her messages right away.

'Anyway, I'm an idiot,' Nat was saying. 'Anyone will tell you that. But I couldn't very well forget a name like Dodge, could I? I wish I had a cool name.'

'I like your name,' Dodge said quietly.

Heather felt a sharp pain go through her. She had heard in Dodge's voice a familiar longing, a hollowness – and she knew then, immediately and without doubt, that Dodge liked Natalie.

For a second she had a blind moment of envy, a feeling that gripped her from all sides. Of course. Of course Dodge liked Nat. She was pretty and giggly and small and cute, like an animal you'd find in someone's purse. Like Avery.

The association arrived unexpectedly, and she dismissed it quickly. She didn't care about Avery, and she didn't care whether Dodge liked Nat, either. It wasn't her business.

Still, the idea continued to drum through her, like the constant patter of the rain: that no one would ever love her.

'How long do you think we should wait?' Nat asked.

'Not too much longer,' Dodge said.

They sat in silence for a few minutes. Heather knew she should make conversation, but she was too tired.

'I wish it wasn't so *dark*,' Nat said after a few minutes, rustling. Heather could tell from her voice she was getting impatient.

Dodge stood up. 'Wait here,' he said, and slipped outside.

For a while there was silence except for a tinny banging – something moving through the pipes – and the hiss of water on the roof.

'I'm going to go to L.A.,' Nat blurted out suddenly. 'If I win.'

Heather turned to her. Nat looked defiant, as though she expected Heather to start making fun of her. 'What for?' Heather asked.

'The surfers,' Nat said. Then she rolled her eyes. 'Hollywood, bean brain. What do you think for?'

Heather went over to her and crouched. Nat always said she wanted to be an actress, but Heather had never thought she was serious – not serious enough to do it, definitely not serious enough to play Panic for it.

But Heather just nudged her with a shoulder. 'Promise me

that when you're rich and famous, you won't forget the bean brains you knew back when.'

'I promise,' Nat said. The air smelled faintly like charcoal. 'What about you? What will you do if you win?'

Heather shook her head. She wanted to say: *Run until I burst. Build miles and miles and miles between me and Carp. Leave the old Heather behind, burn her to dust.* Instead, she shrugged. 'Go somewhere, I guess. Sixty-seven grand buys a lot of gas.'

Nat shook her head. 'Come on, Heather,' she said quietly. 'Why'd you really enter?'

Just like that, Heather thought of Matt, and how she had been so close to telling him that she loved him, and felt like she would cry. 'Did you know?' she said finally. 'About Matt, I mean, and Delaney.'

'I heard a rumor,' Nat said carefully. 'But I didn't believe it.'

'I heard she . . . with him . . .' Heather couldn't actually say the words. She knew she was probably a little prude, especially compared to Nat. She was embarrassed about it and proud of it at the same time: she just didn't see what was so great about fooling around. 'At the frigging Arboretum.'

'She's a whore,' Nat said matter-of-factly. 'Bet she gives him herpes. Or worse.'

'Worse than herpes?' Heather said doubtfully.

'Syphilis. Turns you into a moron. Puts holes in the brain, swiss-cheese-style.'

Heather sometimes forgot that Nat could always make her laugh. 'I hope not,' she said. She managed to smile. 'He wasn't that smart to begin with. I don't think he has a lot of brain to spare.'

'You hope so, you mean.' Nat mimed holding up a glass. 'To Delaney's syphilis.'

'You're crazy,' Heather said, but she was laughing full-on now.

Nat ignored her. 'May it turn Matt Hepley's brain to delicious, gooey cheese.'

'Amen,' Heather said, and raised her arm.

'Amen.' They pretended to clink.

Heather stood up again and moved to the door. Dodge was still not back; she wondered what he was doing.

'Do you think—' Heather took a deep breath. 'Do you think anyone will ever love me?'

'I love you,' Nat said. 'Bishop loves you. Your mom loves you.' Heather made a face, and Nat said, 'She does, Heathbar, in her own way. And Lily loves you too.'

'You guys don't count,' Heather said. Then, realizing how that sounded, she giggled. 'No offense.'

'None taken,' Nat said.

After a pause, Heather said, 'I love you, too, you know. I'd be a basket case without you. I mean it. I'd be carted off and, I don't know, drawing aliens in my mashed potatoes by now.'

'I know,' Nat said.

Heather felt as if all the years of their lives together, their friendship, were welling up there, in the dark: the time they'd practiced kissing on Nat's mom's sofa cushions; the first time they'd ever smoked a cigarette and Heather had puked; all the secret texts in classes, fingers moving under the desk and behind their textbooks. All of it was hers, hers and Nat's, and all those years were nestled inside them like one of those Russian dolls, holding dozens of tiny selves inside it.

Heather turned to Nat, suddenly breathless.

'Let's split the money,' she blurted out.

'What?' Nat blinked.

'If one of us wins, let's split it.' Heather realized, as soon as she said it, that she was right. 'Fifty-fifty. Thirty grand can still buy a lot of gas, you know.'

For a second, Nat just stared at her. Then she said, 'All right. Fifty-fifty.' Nat laughed. 'Should we shake on it? Or pinkie swear?'

'I trust you,' Heather said.

Dodge returned at last. 'It's clear,' he said.

Heather and Dodge supported Nat between them, and together they made their way underneath the water towers and into the clearing that had so recently been packed with people. Now the only evidence of the crowd was the trash left behind: stamped-out cigarette butts and joints, crushed beer cans, towels, a few umbrellas. The truck was still parked in the mud, but its engine was cut. Heather imagined the cops would bring out a tow for it later. The quiet was strange, and the whole scene felt weirdly creepy. It made Heather think that everyone had been spirited away into thin air.

Dodge gave a sudden shout. 'Hold on a second,' he said, and left Nat leaning on Heather. He moved several feet away and scooped something up from the ground – a portable cooler. Heather saw, when he angled his cell phone light onto it, that it still contained ice and beer.

'Jackpot,' Dodge said. He smiled for the first time all night.

He took the cooler with them, and when they reached Route 22, made a makeshift ice pack for Nat's ankle. There were three beers left, one for each of them, and they drank together on the side of the road, in the rain, while they waited for the bus to come. Nat got giggly after just a few sips, and she and Dodge joked about smoking a cigarette to make the bus come faster, and Heather knew she should be happy.

But Bishop's phone was still going straight to voice mail. Matt and Delaney were probably cozy and warm and dry somewhere together. And she kept remembering being high in the air, teetering on the flimsy wooden plank, and the itch in the soles of her feet, telling her to jump.

SUNDAY, JUNE 26

dodge

DODGE NEVER SLEPT MORE THAN TWO OR THREE HOURS AT A stretch. He didn't like to admit it, but he had nightmares. He dreamed of long, chalky roads that ended abruptly, leaving him to drop; and sometimes, of a dank basement where he was contained, with a low, dark ceiling crawling with spiders.

Plus, it was impossible to sleep past five a.m. once the garbage truck came rattling by on Meth Row. Impossible to nap, too, during the day, when the lunch crowd made a rush on Dot's Diner, and waiters hauled garbage in and out, and emptied grease traps, and rattled the Dumpsters past Dodge's window and into Meth Row for collection. Every so often, when the diner's back door opened, the swell of conversation carried the sound of Dodge's mom's voice.

More coffee, honey?

But the day after the challenge at the water towers, Dodge slept soundly, dreamlessly, all the way through the lunch rush, and didn't wake up until after two o'clock. He pulled on a pair of track pants, debated whether he should shower, then decided against it.

'Heya,' Dayna said when he wandered into the kitchen. He was starving. Thirsty, too. It was like the game was opening up a hunger inside him. 'How did it go?'

She was parked in the living room, where she could watch TV and look out the window onto the back of the diner. Gray light came weakly through the window, and dust motes floated in the air behind her. For a second, Dodge felt a rush of affection for the little room: the cracked TV stand, the thin, patchy rug, the lumpy sofa that had, for reasons unknown, been upholstered in denim.

And of course, for her. His Dayna.

Over the years, the resemblance between them had faded, especially in the last year, when she had put on a lot of weight in her face and chest and shoulders. Still, it was there, even though they didn't share a father, and she was much lighter than he was: in the dark brown hair, and the hazel eyes spaced far apart; the definite chins; and in their noses, which both curved almost imperceptibly to the left.

Dodge opened the refrigerator. His mom must have gone out last night; there were cartons of leftover Chinese. He opened them and sniffed. Chicken with broccoli and shrimp fried rice. Good enough. Dayna watched him as he piled it all onto a plate and, without bothering to nuke it, grabbed a fork and started eating.

'Well?' she prompted.

He had wanted to save the news, to torture her by not telling, but he had to talk. He had to share it with *someone*. He put the plate down, came into the living room, and sat on the couch, which he and Dayna had nicknamed the Butt. 'It was a bust,' he said. 'Cops came.'

She watched him carefully. 'Are you sure you want to do this, Dodge?' she said quietly.

'Come on, Dayna.' He was annoyed that she'd even asked. He hauled her legs into his lap. Massage was the only thing that would keep them from total atrophy, and he still insisted on working her calves every day, even though she'd been saying for a long time that it was useless. She'd seen a dozen different doctors. And she'd been going to physical therapy for well over a year now.

But there'd been no change. No improvement. She'd never walk again. Not without a miracle.

Despite the daily massages, Dayna's legs were thin – stalky and pale, like something that would grow on a plant. Even as her face had become rounder, the flesh of her arms looser, her legs continued to wither. Dodge tried not to think about how often, as a kid, those same legs had pumped her forward during a footrace, and propelled her into trees when they had climbing wars. She had always been strong – as hard as polished wood, scrappy and made of muscle. Stronger than most boys, and braver, too.

For Dodge's whole life, she had been his best friend, his partner in crime. She was two years older than him, and had been the de facto leader of whatever scheme or game they had invented. When he was five, they'd bottled their farts and tried to sell them. When he was seven, they'd spent a summer exploring their neighborhood in Dawson, Minnesota, looking for treasure, and wound up with a garden shed full of weird shit: an old top hat, a busted radio, two tire spokes, and the rusted frame of a bicycle. They'd found adventure in whatever shitty-ass town their mom had happened to dump them.

Now they would never have another adventure. She would never climb, or bike, or bet him five bucks she could still beat him in a footrace. She would always need help to bathe, to get on and off the toilet.

And it was all Luke Hanrahan's fault. He'd messed with Dayna's car, fucked with the steering in advance of the show-down, forcing her off the road. Dodge knew it.

'Mom went on a date last night,' Dayna said, obviously trying to change the subject.

'So?' Dodge said. He was still vaguely annoyed. Besides, everywhere they went, his mom found some new loser to date.

Dayna shrugged. 'She seemed into it. And she wouldn't tell me who.'

'She was probably embarrassed,' Dodge said. In the silence, he heard banging from outside – someone was going through the Dumpsters. Dayna leaned forward to look out the window.

'Shit,' she said.

'Little Kelly?' he said, and Dayna nodded. Little Bill Kelly had to be thirty and at least six foot five, but his dad, Bill Kelly, had been police chief for twenty years before his retirement, and everyone knew him as Big Kelly. Dodge had only ever seen Big Kelly once, and even then only for a second, when he'd accidentally biked out in front of Bill's car. Bill had leaned on the horn and shouted for Dodge to be careful.

Dodge sighed, eased Dayna's legs off his lap, and stood up. Through the window he could see Little Kelly balancing on a steel drum full of old grease, methodically sorting through one of the Dumpsters sandwiched up against the back of Dot's

Diner, just next to the kitchen door. It was the third time in a month he'd been picking garbage.

Dodge didn't bother putting on a shirt. He crossed the short concrete alley that divided their apartment from the diner, careful to avoid the broken glass. The kitchen boys drank beers during their shift sometimes.

'Hey, man,' Dodge said, deliberately loud, deliberately cheerful.

Little Kelly straightened up like he'd been electrocuted. He climbed down unsteadily from the steel drum. 'I'm not doing nothing,' he said, avoiding Dodge's gaze. Other than the stubble on his chin, Little Kelly had the face of an overgrown baby. He had once been a star athlete, a good student, too, but had gotten screwed in the head over in Afghanistan. Or Iraq. One of those. Now he rode the buses all day and forgot to come home. Once Dodge had passed Little Kelly sitting cross-legged at the corner of the road, crying loudly.

'You looking for something?' Dodge noticed that Little Kelly had made a small trash pile at the foot of the Dumpster, of tinfoil wrappers, metal coils, bottle caps, and a broken plate.

Little Kelly looked at him for a minute, jaw working, like he was trying to chew through leather. Then, abruptly, he pushed past Dodge and disappeared around the corner.

Dodge squatted and started to gather up all the crap Little Kelly had removed from the Dumpster. It was already hot, and the alley smelled. Just then he sensed motion behind him. Thinking Little Kelly had returned, he straightened and spun around, saying, 'You really shouldn't be back here—'

The words dried up in his throat. Natalie Velez was standing behind him, leaning her weight onto her good foot, looking

clean and showered and pretty and like she belonged anywhere
else but here.

'Hi,' she said, smiling.

His first, instinctive response was to walk past her, go into
the house, slam the door, and suffocate himself. But of course,
he couldn't. Holy shit. Nat Velez was standing in front of him,
and he was shirtless. And hadn't brushed his teeth. Or showered. And he was holding tinfoil from the trash.

'I was just cleaning up . . .' He trailed off helplessly.

Nat's eyes ticked down to his bare chest, then up to his hair,
which was in all probability sticking straight up.

'Oh my God.' Her face began to turn pink. 'I should have
called. I'm so sorry. Did you just get up or something?'

'No. No, not at all. I was just . . .' Dodge tried not to talk
too forcefully, or breathe too hard, in case his breath was rank.
'Look, can you give me a minute? Just wait here?'

'Of course.' Nat was even cuter when she blushed. She
looked like a cookie that had been iced for Christmas.

'One minute,' Dodge repeated.

Inside, Dodge sucked in a deep breath. Holy shit. Nat Velez.
He didn't even have time to worry about the fact that she was
seeing his house, his crappy little apartment, and had probably
had to walk past the grease traps being emptied, had gone in
her little sandals past the sodden bits of spinach that got trekked
out of the diner by the cooks, past the Dumpsters and their
smell.

In the bathroom, he brushed his teeth and gargled with
mouthwash. He smelled his underarms – not bad – and put
on deodorant just in case. He ran water through his hair and
pulled on a clean white T-shirt, one that showed just a bit of
the tattoo that covered most of his chest and wrapped around

his right shoulder and forearm. His hair was already sticking up again. He rammed on a baseball hat.

Good. Decent, at least. He sprayed on a bit of this man's body-spray thing his mom had gotten for free at Walmart, feeling like a douche, but thinking it was better to feel like a douche than to smell like an asshole.

Outside, Nat was doing a good job of pretending not to notice that Dodge lived in a falling-down apartment behind a diner.

'Hey.' She smiled again, big and bright, and he felt his insides do a weird turnover. He hoped Dayna wasn't watching out the window. 'Sorry about, like, barging up on you.'

'That's okay.'

'I was going to call,' she said. 'I texted Heather for your number. Sorry. But then I thought it might be better to talk in person.'

'It's totally fine.' Dodge's voice came out more harshly than he'd intended. Shit. He was screwing this up already. He coughed and crossed his arms, trying to look casual. Really it was because his hands suddenly felt like meat hooks at the end of his arms, and he had forgotten what to do with them. 'How's your ankle?' An Ace bandage was wrapped thickly around her ankle and foot; it made a funny contrast to her legs, which were bare.

'Sprained.' Nat made a face. 'I'll live, but . . .' For a brief second, her face spasmed, like she was in pain. 'Look, Dodge, is there someplace we can go? Like, to talk?'

There was no way he was taking her inside. Not an icicle's chance in hell. He didn't want Nat gaping at Dayna or, worse, trying too hard to be nice. 'How did you get here?' he asked, thinking she might have a car.

Again, she blushed. 'I had my dad drop me,' she said.

He didn't ask how she'd figured out where he lived. Like all things in Carp, it was usually just a question of asking around. The problem was where to take her. He couldn't go into the diner. His mom was working. That left Meth Row.

Nat walked slowly, still limping, although she seemed to be in less pain than she had been last night. But she took the first opportunity to sit down: on the rusted fender of an abandoned, wheel-less Buick. All its windows were shattered, and the seats were speckled with bird shit, the leather torn up by tiny animals.

'I wanted to thank you again,' Nat said. 'You were so . . . You were great. For helping me last night.'

Dodge felt vaguely disappointed, as he often felt when inter-acting with other people, when the reality failed to meet his expectations. Or in this case, his fantasies. Some part of him had been hoping she'd come over to confess that she'd fallen madly in love with him. Or maybe she'd skip the words al-together, and strain onto her tiptoes and open her mouth and let him kiss her. Except she probably couldn't stand on her toes with her ankle the way it was, which is one of the 2,037 ways his fantasy was unrealistic.

He said, 'It's not a problem.'

She twisted her mouth, like she'd swallowed something sour. For a second she didn't say anything. Then she blurted, 'Did you hear Cory Walsh and Felix Harte were arrested?'

He shook his head, and she clarified, 'Drunk and disorderly conduct. And trespassing.' She shifted her weight. 'You think Panic is over?'

'No way,' he said. 'The cops are too stupid to stop it, anyway.'

She nodded but didn't look convinced. 'So what do you think will happen next?'

'No idea,' he said. He knew that Nat was asking him for a hint. He swallowed back a bad taste in his mouth. She knew he liked her, and she was trying to use him.

'I think we can use each other,' she said abruptly, and it was this fact – the fact of her acknowledgment, her honesty – that made him want to keep listening.

'Use each other how?' he asked.

She picked at the hem of her skirt. It looked like it was made of terry cloth, which made him think of towels, which made him think of Nat in a towel. The sun was so bright, he was dizzy.

'We make a deal,' she said, looking up at him. Her eyes were dark, eager, and sweet, like the eyes of a puppy. 'If either of us wins, we split the cash fifty-fifty.'

Dodge was so startled, he couldn't say anything for a minute. 'Why?' he asked finally. 'Why me? You don't even – I mean, we hardly even know each other.' *What about Heather?* he almost said.

'It's just a feeling I have,' she said, and once again he found her honesty appealing. 'You're good at this game. You know things.' It seemed somehow surprising that Nat Velez, with her thick, perfect hair and slicked lip-gloss lips, would speak so frankly about a subject most people avoided. It was like hearing a supermodel fart: surprising and kind of thrilling. She plowed on: 'We can help each other. Share information. Team up against the others. We have more of a chance of getting to Joust that way. And then . . .' She gestured with her hands.

'Then we'll have to face off,' Dodge said.

'But if one wins, we both win,' Nat said, smiling up at him.

He had no intention of letting anyone else win. Then again, he didn't care about the money, either. He had a different goal in mind. Maybe she knew that, or sensed it somehow.

So he said, 'Yeah, okay. Partners.'

'Allies,' Nat said, and stuck out her hand, formally. It felt soft, and also slightly sweaty.

She stood up, laughing. 'It's settled, then.' She couldn't crane onto her tiptoes to kiss him, so she just grabbed his shoulders and planted a kiss on the side of his neck. She giggled. 'Now I have to do the other side, so you're even.'

And he knew then that he was going to fall totally head over heels for her this summer.

Afterward, no one knew who had posted the video online; it appeared on so many pages simultaneously, and spread to everybody else so quickly, it was impossible to determine its point of origin, although many people suspected it was Joey Addison or Charlie Wong, just because they were both dicks and two years ago had secretly filmed, and posted, videos of the girls' locker rooms.

It wasn't even that interesting – just a couple of jerky shots of Ray and Zev swinging at each other, shoulders butting up into the frame as a crowd formed; and then flashing lights, people screaming, a moment when the feed went dead. Then more images: sweeping lights and cops' distorted voices, tinny and harmless-sounding in the recording, and one close-up of Nat, mouth wide, with one arm around Heather and the other around Dodge. Then darkness.

Dodge still kept a copy on his hard drive, so he could freeze-frame on that final moment, when Nat looked so scared and he was helping support her.

Just a few hours later an email made the rounds as well. Subject line: blank. From an encrypted address: judgment@panic.com.

The message was simple, only two lines.

Loose lips sink ships.
Nobody tells. Or else.

TUESDAY, JUNE 28

heather

'YOU'RE SURE THIS IS LEGIT, RIGHT?' BISHOP WAS SITTING forward in the driver's seat, both hands on the wheel, maneuvering the car over a pitted one-lane dirt track. His hair looked even more exuberant than usual, as though he'd tried to style it with a vacuum cleaner. He was wearing his dad's old Virginia Tech sweatshirt, loose flannel pajama bottoms, and flip-flops. When he came for Heather he had announced, with a certain pride, that he had not yet showered. 'You're not going to get axed to death by some psychopath, right?'

'Shut up, Bishop.' Heather reached out to shove him and he jerked the wheel, nearly sending them into one of the ditches that ran along both sides of the road.

'That's no way to treat your driver,' he said.

'Fine. Shut up, *driver*.' There was an anxious feeling in Heather's stomach. The trees here were so thick, they almost completely blocked out the sun.

'Just looking out for you, m'lady,' Bishop said, smiling,

showing off the overlap in his teeth. 'I don't want my best girl to be turned into a lamp shade.'

'I thought Avery was your best girl,' Heather said. She'd meant it as a joke, but the words came out sounding bitter. Like a bitter, heartbroken, lonely spinster. Which she kind of was. Maybe not a spinster – you couldn't be a spinster at eighteen, she didn't think. But close.

'Come on, Heather,' Bishop said. He actually looked hurt. 'You've always been my best girl.'

Heather kept her face to the window. They would arrive any second. But she felt a little better now. Bishop had that effect on her – like a human anti-anxiety pill.

The day after the challenge at the water towers, Heather had overslept, waking only when an anonymous text pinged on her phone: *Quit now, before you get hurt.* She was so shaken, she'd spent fifteen minutes searching for her car keys before remembering she'd stashed them on the hook by the door, then got fired from Walmart when she showed up twenty minutes late for her shift. And suddenly she had found herself blubbering in the parking lot. A week and a half earlier, she'd had a boyfriend and a job – not a good job, but still a job. A little money in her pocket.

Now she had nothing. No boyfriend, no job, no money. And someone wanted to make sure she didn't play Panic.

Then, out of nowhere, she'd been attacked by a dog with the biggest tongue she'd ever seen. Maybe *attacked* was the wrong word, since the dog was just licking her – but still, she'd never been much of an animal person, and it had *seemed* like an attack. And some crazy old lady carrying a shit ton of grocery bags had offered her a job on the spot, even though

Heather had snot dripping from her nose and was wearing a tank top streaked with salad dressing, which she hadn't noticed in her rush to get out of the house.

The woman's name was Anne. 'Muppet's taken a shine to you,' she'd said. Muppet was the name of the dog with the long tongue. 'He doesn't usually get on with strangers. You seem like you're a natural with animals.'

Heather had stayed quiet. She didn't want to admit that for the most part she thought animals, like pimples, were best to ignore. If you fussed too much with them, it would backfire. The only time she'd tried to keep a pet, an anemic-looking goldfish she'd called Star, it had been dead within thirty-two hours. But she said yes when Anne asked if she'd be into doing some pet sitting and light chores. It was $150 a week, cash in the hand, which was roughly the same as she would have made working part-time for Walmart.

Suddenly the trees opened up and they arrived. Heather immediately felt relieved. She didn't know what she'd been expecting – maybe, after what Bishop said, a dingy barn full of rusting farm tools and machetes – but instead she saw a sprawling red farmhouse and a large circular parking area, neatly trimmed of grass. She could see a barn, too, but it wasn't dingy – and next to it, a series of whitewashed sheds.

As soon as she opened the door, several roosters came trotting toward her, and a dog – more than one dog? – began furiously barking. Anne emerged from the house and waved.

'Holy shit,' Bishop said. He actually looked impressed. 'It's a zoo.'

'See? Not a human lamp shade in sight.' Heather slid out of the car, then ducked so she could say good-bye. 'Thanks, Bishop.'

He saluted. 'Text when you need a pickup, ma'am.'

Heather closed the door. Anne crossed the yard toward her.

'Is that your boyfriend?' Anne said, shielding her eyes with one hand, as Bishop began to turn around.

This was so unexpected, Heather's face got hot. 'No, no,' she said quickly, angling her body away from the car, as though Bishop, in case he was still watching, would be able to read the conversation in her body language.

'He's cute,' Anne said matter-of-factly. She waved, and Bishop tapped the horn before pulling away. The blush grew to an all-over body inferno. Heather crossed her arms and then dropped them again. Fortunately, Anne didn't seem to notice.

'I'm glad you came.' Anne smiled, as though Heather had just dropped by for a social visit. 'Let me show you around.'

Heather was relieved that Anne seemed to approve of her choice of outfit: clean jeans, sneakers, and a soft, nubby henley shirt, which had belonged to Bishop before he accidentally shrank it. She hadn't wanted to look sloppy, but then again, Anne had told her to wear clothes she could muck up, and she hadn't wanted to look like she hadn't *listened*.

They started toward the house. The roosters were still running around like crazy, and Heather noticed a chicken pen on the other side of the yard, in which a dozen yellow-feathered chicks were strutting and pecking and preening in the sun. The dogs kept up their racket. There were three of them, including Muppet, pacing around a small enclosure, barking lustily.

'You have a lot of animals,' Heather pointed out, and then immediately felt like an idiot. She tucked her hands into her sleeves.

But Anne laughed. 'It's awful, isn't it? I just can't stop.'

'So is this, like, a farm?' Heather didn't see any farming equipment, but she didn't know anyone who kept chickens for fun.

Again, Anne laughed. 'Hardly. I give the eggs away to the pantry sometimes. But I don't pull up a damn thing besides bird poop, dog poop, poop of all kinds.' She held the door to the house open for Heather. Heather thought that she would probably spend the whole summer shoveling shit. 'My husband, Larry, loved animals,' Anne continued as she followed Heather into the house.

They entered the prettiest kitchen Heather had ever seen. Even Nat's kitchen didn't compare. The walls were cream and yellow; the cupboards tawny wood, bleached nearly white from the sun, which poured through two large windows. The counters were spotless. No ants here. Against one wall were shelves arranged with blue-and-white pottery and small porcelain figurines: miniature horses, cats, donkeys, and pigs. Heather was almost afraid to move, like one step in the wrong direction might cause everything to shatter.

'Tea?' Anne asked. Heather shook her head. She didn't know anyone who drank tea in real life – only British people in TV miniseries.

Anne filled a kettle and plunked it on the stove. 'We moved here from Chicago.'

'Really?' Heather burst out. The farthest she had ever been from Carp was Albany. Once on a school trip, and once when her mom had a court date because she'd been driving with a suspended license. 'What's Chicago like?'

'Cold,' Anne said. 'Freeze your balls off ten months out of the year. But the other two are pure joy.'

Heather didn't respond. Anne didn't seem like the type

who would say *balls*, and Heather liked her a little better for it.

'Larry and I worked in ad sales. We swore we'd make a change someday.' Anne shrugged. 'Then he died, and I did.'

Once again, Heather didn't say anything. She wanted to ask how Larry had died, and when, but didn't know if it was appropriate. She didn't want Anne to think she was obsessed with death or something.

When the water had boiled, Anne filled her mug and then directed Heather back through the door they had come. It was funny, walking across the yard with Anne, while the steam rose from her tea and mingled with the soft mist of morning. Heather felt like she was in a movie about a farm somewhere far away.

They rounded the corner of the house, and the dogs began to bark again.

'Shut it!' Anne said, but good-naturedly. They didn't listen. She kept up a nonstop stream of conversation as they walked. 'This one's the feed shed' – this, as she unlocked one of the small, whitewashed sheds, pushing it open with one hand – 'I try to keep everything organized so I don't end up throwing grain to the dogs and trying to force kibble on a chick. Remember to turn off the lights before you lock up. I don't even want to tell you what my electricity bills are like.

'This is where the shovels and rakes go' – they were at another shed – 'buckets, horseshoes, any kind of crap you find lying around that doesn't seem to fit anywhere else. Got it? Am I going too fast?'

Heather shook her head, and then, realizing Anne wasn't looking at her, said, 'No.'

She realized she wasn't nervous anymore. She liked the feel of the sun on her shoulders and the smell of dark, wet ground

everywhere. Probably some of what she was smelling was
animal shit, but it actually didn't smell that bad – just like
growth and newness.

Anne showed her the stables, where two horses stood quietly
in the half-dark, like sentinels guarding something precious.
Heather had never been so close to a horse before, and she
laughed out loud when Anne gave her a carrot and instructed
her to feed it to the black one, Lady Belle, and Heather felt its
soft, leathery muzzle and the gentle pressure of its teeth.

'They were race horses. Both injured. Saved 'em from being
shot,' Anne said as they left the stables.

'Shot?' Heather repeated.

Anne nodded. For the first time, she looked angry. 'That's
what happens when they're no good for running anymore.
Owner takes a shotgun to their head.'

Anne had saved all the animals from one gruesome fate or
another: the dogs and horses from death, the chickens and
roosters from various diseases, when no one else had cared
enough to spend the money to nurse them. There were turkeys
she had saved from slaughter, cats she had rescued from the
street in Hudson, and even an enormous potbellied pig named
Tinkerbell, which had once been an unwanted runt. Heather
couldn't imagine that it had ever been the runt of *anything*.

'All she wanted was a little love,' Anne said, as they passed
the pen where Tinkerbell was lolling in the mud. 'That, and
about a pound of feed a day.' She laughed.

Finally they came to a tall, fenced-in enclosure. The sun had
broken free of the trees, and refracted through the rising mist,
it was practically blinding. The fence encircled an area of at
least a few acres – mostly open land, patches of dirt, and high
grass, but some trees, too. Heather couldn't see any animals.

For the first time all morning, Anne grew quiet. She sipped her tea, squinting in the sun, staring off through the chain-link fence. After a few minutes, Heather couldn't stand it anymore.

'What are we waiting for?' she asked.

'Shhh,' Anne said. 'Look. They'll come.'

Heather crossed her arms, biting back a sigh. The dew had soaked through her sneakers. Her feet were too cold, and her neck was too hot.

There. There was movement by a small cluster of trees. She squinted. A large, dark mass, which she had taken for a rock, shook itself. Then it stood. And as it stood, another form emerged from the shadow of the trees, and the two animals circled each other briefly, and then loped gracefully into the sun.

Heather's mouth went dry.

Tigers.

She blinked. Impossible. But they were still there, and coming closer: two tigers, *tigers*, like you would find at a circus. Massive square heads and huge jaws, bodies muscled and rippling, coats glossy in the sun.

Anne whistled sharply. Heather jumped. Both tigers swung their heads toward the sound, and Heather lost her breath. Their eyes were flat, incurious, and *old* – impossibly old, as though instead of looking forward, their eyes saw back to a distant past.

They ambled up to the fence, so close that Heather stepped backward, quickly, terrified. So close she could smell them, feel the heat of their bodies.

'How?' she finally managed to ask, which was not quite what she meant, but good enough. A thousand thoughts were colliding in her head.

'More rescues,' Anne said calmly. 'They get sold on the black market. Sold, then abandoned when they're too big, or put down when there's no one to care for them.' As she spoke, she reached her hand through a gap in the fence and actually *petted* one of the tigers – like it was an overgrown house cat. When she saw Heather gaping, she laughed. 'They're all right once they've been fed,' she said. 'Just don't try and cuddle up when they're hungry.'

'I don't – I won't have to go in there, will I?' Heather was rooted to the ground, paralyzed with fear and wonder. They were so big, so close. One of the tigers yawned, and she could make out the sharp curve of its teeth, white as bone.

'No, no,' Anne said. 'Most of the time, I just chuck the food in through the gate. Here, I'll show you.'

Anne walked her to the padlocked gate, which to Heather looked alarmingly flimsy. On the other side of the fence, the tigers followed – languidly, as though by coincidence. Heather wasn't fooled, though. That's how predators were. They sat back and waited, lured you into feeling safe, and then they pounced.

She wished Bishop were here. She did *not* wish Nat were here. Nat would flip. She hated big animals of any kind. Even poodles made her jumpy.

When they turned their backs on the tigers' pen and returned to the house, Heather's stomach started to unknot, although she still had the impression the tigers were watching her, and kept picturing their sharp claws slotting into her back.

Anne showed her where she stored all the keys to the sheds, hanging from neatly labeled hooks in the 'mudroom', as she called it, where Heather could also find spare rubber boots like the kind Anne wore, mosquito repellent, gardening shears, and suntan and calamine lotions.

After that, Heather went to work. She fed the chickens while Anne instructed her how to scatter the feed, and laughed out loud when the birds piled together, pecking frantically, like one enormous, feathered, many-headed creature.

Anne showed her how to chase the roosters back in the pen before letting out the dogs to run around, and Heather was surprised that Muppet seemed to remember her, and immediately ran several times around her ankles, as though in greeting.

Then there was mucking the stables (as Heather had suspected, this involved horse poop, but it actually wasn't as bad as she'd thought), and brushing the horses' coats with special, stiff-bristled brushes. Then helping Anne prune the wisteria, which had begun to colonize the north side of the house. By this time, Heather was sweating freely, even with her sleeves rolled up. The sun was high and hot, and her back ached from bending over and straightening up again.

But she was happy, too – happier than she'd been in forever. She could almost forget that the rest of the world existed, that she'd ever been dumped by Matt Hepley or made the Jump in the first place. Panic. She could forget Panic.

She was surprised when Anne called an end to the day, saying it was almost one o'clock. While Heather waited for Bishop to return for her, Anne fixed her a tuna sandwich with mayonnaise she'd made herself and tomatoes she'd grown in her garden. Heather was afraid to sit down at the table, since she was so dirty, but Anne set a place for her, so she did. She thought it was the best thing she'd ever eaten.

'Hey there, cowgirl,' Bishop said when Heather slid into the car. He still hadn't changed out of his pajama pants. He made a big show of sniffing. 'What's that smell?'

'Shut up,' she said, and punched him in the arm. He

pretended to wince. As Heather rolled down her window, she caught a glimpse of herself in the side mirror. Her face was red and her hair was a mess and her chest was still wet with sweat, but she was surprised to find that she looked kind of . . . pretty.

'How was it?' Bishop asked as they began thumping down the drive again. He'd gotten her an iced coffee from 7-Eleven: lots of sugar, lots of cream, just how she liked it.

She told him – about the runt pig that had ballooned to a huge size, the horses, the chickens and roosters. She saved the tigers for last. Bishop was taking a sip of her coffee and nearly choked.

'You know that's totally illegal, right?' he said.

She rolled her eyes. 'So are the pants you're wearing. If you don't tell, I won't.'

'*These* pants?' Bishop pretended to be offended. 'I wore these just for you.'

'You can take them off just for me,' Heather said, and then blushed, realizing how it sounded.

'Anytime,' Bishop said, and grinned at her. She punched him again. She was still fizzy with happiness.

It was a twenty-minute ride back to downtown Carp, if the Motel 6, the post office, and the short string of greasy shops and bars could be counted as a downtown, but Bishop claimed to have figured out a shortcut. Heather went quiet when they turned onto Coral Lake, which couldn't have been more inaccurately named: there was no water in sight, nothing but fallen logs and patchy, burnt-bare stubs of trees, because of a fire that had raged there several years ago. The road ran parallel to Jack Donahue's property, and it was bad luck.

Heather had been on Coral Lake only a few times. Trigger-

Happy Jack was known for being consistently drunk, and half-insane, and for owning an arsenal of weapons. His property was fenced in and guarded by dogs and who knew what else. When his fence came into view, pushing right up to the road, she half-expected him to come banging out of his house and start taking potshots at the car. But he didn't. Several dogs came running across the yard, though, barking madly. These dogs were nothing like Anne's. They were skinny, snarling, and mean-looking.

They had almost passed the limits of Trigger-Happy Jack's property when something caught Heather's eye.

'Stop!' she nearly screamed. 'Stop!'

Bishop slammed on the brakes. 'What? Jesus Christ, Heather. What the hell?'

But she was already out of the car, jogging back toward a sagging scarecrow – at least, it *looked* like a scarecrow – dumped on the ground, leaning back against Donahue's fence. Her stomach was tight with fear, and she had the weirdest sense of being watched. There was something wrong with the dummy. It was too crudely made, too *useless*. There were no farms this side of Coral Lake, no reason for a scarecrow, especially one that looked like it had been dumped from the trunk of a car.

When she reached the scarecrow, she hesitated for a second, like it might suddenly come to life and bite her.

Then she lifted its head, which was slumped forward on a spindly stuffed neck.

In place of features, the scarecrow had words written neatly, in marker, on its blank canvas face.

FRIDAY, MIDNIGHT.
THE GAME MUST GO ON.

FRIDAY, JULY 1

dodge

THE CROWD WAS SMALLER ON FRIDAY NIGHT; THE atmosphere tense, unhappy. Nervous.

There was no beer, no music, no bursts of laughter. Just a few dozen people huddled silently fifty feet down the road from Trigger-Happy Jack's fence, massed together, lit up white-faced in the glare of the bouncing headlights.

When Bishop cut the engine, Dodge could hear the sound of Nat's ragged breathing. Dodge had spent the ride over trying to distract her by doing easy magic tricks, like making a joker appear in her jacket pocket and a penny vanish from her palm. Now he said, 'Just follow the plan, okay? Follow the plan and everything will be okay.'

Nat nodded, but she looked sick – like she might puke. She was deathly afraid of dogs, she had told him. Also: ladders, heights, darkness, and the feeling you get in the middle of the night when you check your phone and see no one has texted. As far as he could tell, she was pretty much afraid of everything. And yet, she had decided to play. This made him like her even more.

And she had chosen him, Dodge, as her ally.

Bishop said nothing. Dodge wondered what he was thinking. He'd always thought Bishop was nice enough, and book smart for sure, but just like a big dumb guy who followed Heather everywhere. But Dodge was starting to change his mind. During the drive, Bishop's eyes had clicked to his for a second in the rearview, and Dodge had detected some kind of warning there.

The night was clear and still. The moon was high and halfway to full, and turning everything to silhouette, drawing angles around the fence. Still, it was dark. A flashlight went on and off several times, a silent signal. Heather, Bishop, Nat, and Dodge walked toward it. Dodge had the urge to take Nat's hand, but Nat was hugging herself tightly.

At least Dodge had had time to plan, to prepare. If Nat hadn't told him about the dummy Heather had spotted on Tuesday, he might not have known about the newest challenge until this morning.

The email had come to all the players simultaneously from judgment@panic.com.

Location: Coral Lake Road
Time: Midnight
Goal: Take a prize from the house.
Bonus: Find the desk in the gun room and take what's hidden there.

'All right.' Diggin was speaking quietly as they drew up close to the group. They were late. 'Players, step forward.'

They did, detaching themselves from the people who had

come to watch. Fewer players, fewer spectators. After the bust, everyone was jumpy. And Coral Lake Road was bad luck. Trigger-Happy Jack was bad – all bad. A psycho and a drunk and worse.

Dodge knew he wouldn't think twice about shooting them.

The beam of a flashlight swept over each of the players in turn. It felt like the minutes were swelling into hours. The counting took forever. Dodge could see Ray Hanrahan, chewing gum loudly, standing on the outer edge of the circle of players. His face was concealed in shadow. Dodge felt a familiar clutch of anger. Strange how it didn't go away; over the past two years, it just seemed to be growing, like a cancer in his stomach.

'Walsh is missing,' Diggin said finally. 'So is Merl.'

'They're out, then,' someone said.

'It's midnight.' Diggin was still practically whispering. The wind lifted the trees, hissed at them, as though it knew they were trespassing. The dogs were still quiet, though. Sleeping, or waiting. 'The second challenge—'

'Second challenge?' Zev broke in. 'What about the water towers?'

'Invalidated,' Diggin said. 'Not everyone got to go.'

Zev spat on the ground, and Heather made a noise of protest. Diggin ignored them.

'When I say go,' he said.

He paused. For a moment, it seemed that everything went still. Dodge could feel the slow drum of his heart, beating in the hollow of his chest. And as they stood there in the dark, waiting, it occurred to him that here, somewhere in this crowd, were the judges – hiding behind familiar faces, maybe enjoying it.

'Go,' Diggin said.

'Go!' Dodge said to Heather and Nat, at the same time. Heather nodded and took Nat's hand; they vanished together into the dark, Nat moving stiff-legged, still limping slightly, like a broken doll.

Dodge made straight for the fence, like they'd agreed, like he'd scoped the place out and knew what he was doing. And as he predicted, a half-dozen people ran after him in silence, doubled over as though, even now, they were being watched.

But much of the group didn't move right away. They floated aimlessly to the fence, pacing it, watching, too scared to try to climb. They'd all be disqualified for doing nothing. Still, they stood there, watching the dark house, watching the shadow-people climb the fence, everything silent except for the occasional creak of metal, a muttered curse, and the wind.

Dodge was one of the first up the fence. There were other players around him – people grunting and breathing hard, bodies knocking into his – but he ignored them, focused on the bite of chain link on his palms and his breathing and the seconds running forward like water.

It was all about timing. Just like magic tricks: planning, mastery, staying calm under pressure. You could anticipate another person's response; you could know what people would do, or say, or how they would react, even before they did.

Dodge knew it wouldn't be long until Donahue came out with a rifle.

At the top of the fence, he hung back, even though his adrenaline was pumping, telling him to go. Several other people – it was too dark to make out faces – dropped and hit the ground first, and even though they barely made a sound, the explosion of barking came right away. Four dogs – no, five – tore out from the back of the house, barking like mad. Dodge felt every second like it had a different taste, a different texture from the second before it, like individual moments were ticking off in his head. Tick. Someone was screaming. There'd be points taken off for that. Tick. Only a few more seconds until the shooting would begin. Tick. Heather and Nat should have reached the hole in the fence by now.

Tick.

He was airborne, and then he felt the impact of the ground and he was up and fumbling for the Mace in his pocket. He didn't head for the front of the house directly but instead made a loop, circumnavigating the small crowd of players, the dogs going crazy, snarling and snapping. Some of the players were already climbing the fence again, trying to reach the safety of the other side. But Dodge kept going.

Tick.

A dog came at him. He almost didn't see it; it had its jaws practically around his arm before he pivoted and sprayed it, full-on, in the face. The dog dropped back, whimpering. Dodge kept going.

Tick.

Right on time, a light in the house clicked on. There was a roar – a sound that echoed out even over the chaos and the frantic sounds of barking – and something crashed to the ground. A black shape rocketed out the front door, into the night. Even from a distance of one hundred yards, Dodge could make out the stream of individual curses.

Goddamnmotherfuckingsonsofbitchesgetthehelloffmyyardyou piecesofshit . . .

Then Jack Donahue – paunchy, shirtless, wearing only a pair of saggy boxers – lifted his rifle and began to fire.

Pop. Pop. Pop. Shots exploded – louder, sharper than Dodge had expected, the first thing that had truly thrown him off guard. He'd never been so close to gunfire.

In the front yard, Trigger-Happy Jack was still screaming. *YoucocksuckersdeadasadoornailI'llburyyouallyoufuckers* . . .

Tick.

It wouldn't be long now. Donahue would call the cops at some point. He'd have to.

Dodge sprinted around the house. His breath was caught somewhere in his throat, like each time he inhaled he was taking in glass. He didn't know what had happened to the other players, where Ray was, whether anyone had made it inside yet. He thought he heard a whisper in the dark – he assumed Heather and Nat had taken up their positions, as planned.

At the back of the house was a half-rotten porch, cluttered with dark shapes – Dodge vaguely registered a refrigerator before he saw the distended screen door, barely hanging on its hinges. The shots were still cracking through the air. One two three four.

Tick.

He didn't stop to think. He flung open the door.

He was in.

heather

HEATHER AND NAT REACHED THE PLACE WHERE THE FENCE veered north, away from the road, just as the dogs began barking. Their timing was already all wrong. And Dodge was counting on them.

'You gotta move faster,' Heather said.

'I'm trying,' Nat said. Heather could hear the strain in her voice.

There was a volley of shouting from the yard – a cry of pain and the snarling of an enraged animal.

Heather felt her pulse beating frantically in her neck. Focus. Focus. Stay calm.

They had reached the portion of the fence they'd prepped yesterday. And no one had followed them. Good.

Dodge had cut a makeshift door in the fence. Heather gave it a solid push and it groaned open, giving her just enough room to squeeze through. Nat followed.

Suddenly Nat froze, her eyes wide, horrified.

'I'm stuck,' she whispered.

Heather whirled around, impatient. Nat's left sleeve was snagged on the fence. She reached out and tugged it free.

'You're unstuck,' she said. 'Come on.'

But Nat didn't move. 'I – I can't.' Her face was drawn, terrified. 'I'm not even.'

'You're not *what*?' Heather was losing it. Dodge would be going in any minute; he expected them to stand guard. They'd made a pact. He was helping them; Heather didn't know why, but she didn't care, either.

'I'm not even.' Nat's voice was high-pitched, hysterical. She was still standing, frozen, as though both legs had been rooted to the ground.

That's when Jack Donahue came blasting from the front door.

Goddamnmotherfuckingsonsofbitchesgetthehelloffmyyardyou piecesofshit . . .

'Come *on*.' Heather grabbed Nat's arm and pulled, hard, dragging her across the lawn toward the house, ignoring the sound of Nat's whimpering, the words she was muttering under her breath. Counting. She was counting up to ten, then down again. Heather dug her nails harder into Nat's arm, almost wanting to hurt her. Jesus. They were running out of time, and Nat was losing it. She didn't care about Nat's ankle, or that Nat was shaking, choking back sobs.

Pop. Pop. Pop.

Heather jerked Nat down and into the shadows as Donahue thundered off the porch, gun up, firing. The light on the porch was white, half-blinding, and made him look like a character from a movie. Heather's thighs were shaking. She didn't see Dodge. She couldn't see anyone – just shapes, blurring together in the darkness, and the small cone of light illuminating

Donahue's back, the curl of hair on his shoulders, his flab, the awful butt of his rifle.

Where was Dodge?

Heather could hardly breathe. She pressed up against the side of the house, rocking her weight back onto her heels, trying to think. There was too much noise.

And she didn't know if Dodge had made it into the house already. What if he hadn't? What if he'd screwed up?

'Stay here,' Heather whispered. 'I'm going in.'

'Don't.' Nat turned to her, eyes wide, frantic. 'Don't leave me here.'

Heather gripped her shoulders. 'In exactly one minute, if I'm not out yet, I want you to run back to the car. Okay? In exactly one minute.'

She didn't even know if Nat heard her – and almost didn't care, at this point. She straightened up. Her body felt bloated and clumsy. And suddenly she registered several things at once: that the shots had happened, and were no longer happening; that the front door had just opened and closed with a firm *click*. Someone had gone in.

Immediately, her body turned to ice. What if Dodge *was* inside? She, Heather, was supposed to have been watching. She was supposed to have whistled if Donahue approached.

But the front door had opened and closed. And she had not whistled.

She was no longer thinking. Instinctively, she pulled herself onto the porch and opened the front door and slipped inside, into the hall. It stank of BO and old beer, and it was pitch-dark. Donahue had turned on a light earlier – that she had noticed, a bad omen – so why had he turned it off? Her heart surged into her throat and she reached out with her hands, grazed both walls lightly with her fingertips, centering herself in the hallway. She swallowed.

She took several steps forward and heard a rustling, the creak of a footstep. She froze, expecting at any second for the lights to click on, for the barrel of a gun to shine directly at her heart. Nothing happened.

'Dodge?' she risked whispering into the dark.

Footsteps crossed quickly toward her. She fumbled along the wall and hit a doorknob. The door opened easily and she slipped out of the hall, closing the door as quietly as possible, holding her breath. But the footsteps kept going. She heard the front door creak open and close.

Was it Donahue? Dodge? Another player?

Here, moonlight filtered in through a large, curtainless window, and Heather suddenly sucked in a breath. The walls were covered with metal, glinting dully in the milky light. Guns. Guns mounted to the walls, hanging from upended deer hooves, crisscrossing the ceiling. The gun room. She thought it even smelled faintly like gunpowder, but she might have been imagining it.

The room was cluttered with workbenches and overstuffed chairs, bleeding stuffing onto the floor. Underneath the window was a large desk. Heather felt as if the air in the room were suddenly too thin; she felt breathless and dizzy, remembering the email she'd received that morning.

> *Bonus: Find the desk in the gun room and take what's hidden there.*

Heather moved across the room to the desk, navigating the clutter of objects. She began with the drawers on the sides – right, and then left. Nothing.

The shallow central drawer was loose, as though from frequent use. The gun was curled there, like an enormous black beetle, shiny, hard-backed.

The bonus.

She reached in, hesitated – then seized it quickly, like it might bite her. Heather felt nausea rising in her throat. She hated guns.

'What are you doing?'

Heather spun around. She could just see Dodge silhouetted in the doorway, although it was too dark to make out his face.

'Shhh,' Heather whispered. 'Keep your voice down.'

'What the hell are you *doing*?' Dodge took two steps across the room. 'You were supposed to keep watch.'

'I was.' Before Heather could explain further, Dodge cut her off.

'Where's Natalie?'

'Outside,' Heather said. 'I thought I heard—'

'Was this some kind of a trick?' Dodge spoke quietly, but Heather could hear the edge in his voice. 'You guys get me to do the dirty work, then sneak in and grab the bonus? So you could get ahead?'

Heather stared at him. '*What?*'

'Don't screw with me, Heather.' Two more steps and Dodge was there, directly in front of her. 'Don't lie to me.'

Heather fought for breath. Tears were pushing at the back of her eyes. She knew they were being too loud. Too loud. Everything was all wrong. The gun in her hand felt awful, cold but also alive, like some alien creature that might suddenly roar to life.

'What are *you* doing here?' she finally said. 'You were supposed to get proof for us and get out.'

'I *heard* something,' Dodge fired back. 'I thought it might be one of the other players—'

The lights came on.

Jack Donahue was standing in the doorway, eyes wild, chest slick with sweat. Then he was shouting and the barrel of the gun was swinging toward them and there was an explosion of glass, and Heather realized Dodge had just hurled a chair straight through the window. Everything was fracture, roar, blur.

'Go, go, go!' Dodge was shouting, pushing Heather toward the window.

Heather threw herself shoulder-first into the night. She heard a second explosion and felt a spray of soft wood as she went through the window, felt pain slice through her arm and an immediate dampness pooling in her armpit. Dodge hauled her to her feet and they were running, fleeing into the night, toward the fence, while Jack shouted after them and sent two more shots off into the dark.

Through the fence – gasping, panting – to the road, mostly empty of cars. There was the dazzle, the wide sweep of headlights. Heather recognized Bishop's car. Nat suddenly materialized in front of her, backlit, like a kind of dark angel.

'Are you okay?' Her voice was wild, urgent. 'Are you okay?'

'We're okay,' Heather answered for both of them. 'Let's go.'

Then they were in the car and moving quickly, bumping over the country roads. For several minutes they were quiet, listening to the distant sound of police sirens. Heather gritted her teeth every time they hit a rut. She was bleeding. A piece of glass had sliced the soft skin of her inner arm.

She still had the gun. Somehow, it had ended up in her lap. She kept staring at it, bewildered, half in shock.

'Jesus Christ,' Bishop finally said when they had put several miles behind them, and the noise of the sirens was lost beneath the quiet shushing of the wind through the trees. 'Holy shit. That was crazy.'

All of a sudden, the tension broke. Dodge started whooping and Nat began to cry and Heather rolled the windows down and laughed like a maniac. She was relieved, grateful, *alive* – sitting in the warm backseat of Bishop's car, which smelled like soda cans and old gum.

Bishop told them about nearly pissing himself when Trigger-Happy Jack came barreling out of the house; he told them that Ray had cracked one of the dogs with a huge rock and sent it whimpering off into the dark. But half the kids never even made it over the fence, and he thought Byron Welcher might have been mauled. It was hard to tell in the dark, with all the chaos.

Dodge told them about getting so close to Donahue; he thought for sure he'd be shot in the skull. But Donahue was enraged, and probably drunk. He wasn't aiming well. 'Thank God,' Dodge said, laughing.

Dodge had stolen three items from the kitchen – a butter knife, a saltshaker, and a shot glass shaped like a cowboy boot – to prove they'd all been in the house. He gave Nat the shot glass and Heather the butter knife, and kept the saltshaker for himself. He made Bishop pull over and placed the saltshaker on the dashboard, so he could get a good picture of it.

'What are you doing?' Heather asked. Her brain still felt like it was wrapped in a wet blanket.

Dodge passed over the phone wordlessly. Heather saw that Dodge had emailed the photo to judgment@panic.com, subject line: PROOF. Heather shivered. She didn't like thinking of the mysterious judges – invisible, watching, judging them.

'What about the gun?' Dodge said.

'The gun?' Nat repeated.

'Heather found it,' Dodge said neutrally.

'Dodge and I found it at the same time,' she said automatically. She didn't know why. She could feel Dodge staring at her.

'You should both get credit, then,' Nat said.

'*You* take the picture, Heather,' Dodge said. His voice was slightly gentler. 'You send it.'

Heather arranged the shot glass and the gun on her lap, clumsily, with one arm. Her stomach tightened. She wondered if the gun was loaded. Probably. So weird to have a weapon so close. So weird to see it *sitting* there. She'd been a year old when her dad shot himself – probably with a gun just like this one. She had a paranoid fear that it might go off on its own, exploding the night into noise and pain.

Once the picture was sent, Bishop asked, 'What are you going to do with the gun?'

'Keep it, I guess.' But she didn't like the idea of having a gun in her house, waiting, smiling its metal smile. And what if Lily found it?

'You can't *keep* it,' he said. 'You *stole* it.'

'Well, what *should* I do with it?' Heather felt panic welling inside her. She had broken into Donahue's house. She had stolen something that was worth a lot of money. People went to jail for shit like that.

Bishop sighed. 'Give it to me, Heather,' he said. 'I'll get rid of it for you.'

She could have hugged him. She could have kissed him. Bishop shut the gun in the glove box.

Now everyone was quiet. The dashboard clock glowed green. 1:42. The roads were all dark except for the sickly cone of the headlights. The land was dark too, on either side of them – houses, trailers, whole streets swallowed up by blackness, like they were traveling through an endless tunnel, a place with no boundaries.

It started to rain. Heather leaned her head against the window. At some point, she must have fallen asleep. She dreamed of falling into the dark, slick throat of an animal, and of trying to cut herself out of its belly with a butter knife, which turned into a gun in her hands, and went off.

SATURDAY, JULY 2

THE NEXT DAY, THE NOTICES WERE EVERYWHERE: PINK BETTING slips, papering the underpass, stuck to gas pumps and in the windows of the 7-Eleven and Duff's Bar, threaded between the gaps in the chicken-wire fences that lined Route 22.

The betting slips blew all the way to Fresh Pines Mobile Park, carried on the soles of muddy boots, snatched up by the metal underbelly of passing trucks before escaping on the wind. They found their way to Nat's quiet residential street. They appeared, half-sodden, sunk in the mud in Meth Row.

There were a third as many players now as there once had been. Only seventeen players had even made it over the fence – of those, ten had managed to get something from Donahue's house.

But there were other notices too: printed on large, glossy sheets of paper, inscribed with the crest of the Columbia County Police Department.

ANY INDIVIDUALS FOUND TO BE PARTICIPATING
IN THE GAME COMMONLY KNOWN AS PANIC WILL BE
SUBJECT TO CRIMINAL PROSECUTION.

In smaller letters, the pertinent criminal charges were enumerated: *reckless endangerment, destruction of private property, breaking and entering, intent to do grievous/bodily harm, drunken disorderliness.*

Someone had squealed, and it was obvious to everyone that it had either been Cory Walsh, after his arrest at the water towers, or Byron Welcher, who had, it turned out, been mauled pretty badly by one of Donahue's dogs, and was now in the hospital over in Hudson. There was no getting to Byron, at least not until he was released, so a few people took out their anger on Cory – and he ended up in the hospital too, his face beaten to the pulpy purple of a bruised and rotten tomato.

That was only a few hours before Ian McFadden found out from his older brother – a cop – that actually it hadn't been either Cory *or* Byron, but a quiet junior named Reena, whose boyfriend had just been eliminated from the competition.

By the time the sun was bleeding out over the horizon, all the windows in Reena's car had been smashed, and her house had been covered with a fine, trembling sheen of egg, so it looked as though it had been enclosed inside a membrane.

Nobody believed that Panic would stop, of course.

The game must go on.

The game always went on.

MONDAY, JULY 4

dodge

THE WEATHER STAYED BEAUTIFUL – FINE AND SUNNY, JUST HOT enough – for a whole week after the challenge at Donahue's house. The Fourth of July was no different, and Dodge woke to sunlight washing over his navy-blue blanket, like a slow surf of white.

He was happy. He was more than happy. He was psyched. He was hanging out with Nat today.

His mom was home, awake, and actually making breakfast. He leaned in the door frame and watched her crack eggs into a pan, break the yolks up with the edge of a wooden spatula.

'What's the occasion?' he said. He was still tired and his neck and back were sore; he'd worked two shifts stocking shelves after closing time at the Home Depot in Leeds, where his mom's ex-boyfriend Danny was manager. Dumb work, but it paid okay. He had a hundred dollars in his pocket and would be able to buy Nat something at the mall. Her birthday was still a few weeks away – July 29 – but still. Might as well get her something small a little early.

'I could ask you the same thing.' She let the eggs sizzle and came over to him, and gave him a big smack on the cheek before he could pull away. 'Why are you up so early?'

He could see traces of makeup. So. She'd been on a date last night. No wonder she was in a good mood.

'Didn't feel like sleeping anymore,' he said cautiously. He wondered whether his mom would admit to going out. Sometimes she did, if a date had gone really well.

'Just in time for eggs. You want eggs? You hungry? I'm making some eggs for Dayna.' She shook the scrambled eggs onto a plate. They were perfectly scrambled, trembling with butter. Before he could answer, she lowered her voice and said, 'You know all that therapy Dayna's been doing? Well, Bill says—'

'Bill?' Dodge cut in.

His mom blushed. Busted. 'He's just a friend, Dodge.'

Dodge doubted it, but he said nothing.

His mom went on, in a rush: 'He took me out to Ca'Mea in Hudson last night. Nice tablecloths and everything. He drinks wine, Dodge. Do you believe that?' She shook her head, amazed. 'And he knows someone, some doctor at Columbia Memorial who works with people like Day. Bill says Dayna's got to go more regular, like every day.'

'We can't—' Dodge started to say, but his mom understood and finished for him.

'I *told* him we couldn't afford it. But he said he could get us in, even with no insurance. Can you believe it? At the *hospital*.'

Dodge said nothing. They'd gotten their hopes up before – new doctor, new treatment, someone who could help. And something always went wrong. A pipe burst and the emergency fund would dry up replacing it; or the doctor would be a quack. The one time they'd managed to see someone in a real hospital, he'd looked at Dayna for five minutes, done nerve tests, banged on her knee and squeezed her toes, and straightened up.

'Impossible,' he'd said, sounding angry, like he was mad at them for wasting his time. 'Car accident, right? My advice is: apply for a better chair. No reason she should be wheeling around in this piece of junk.' And he'd toed the wheelchair, the five-hundred-dollar wheelchair Dodge had busted his ass for a whole autumn trying to purchase, while his mom cried, while Dayna lay curled up every night on her bed, fetal, vacant.

'So you want eggs or not?' his mom said.

Dodge shook his head. 'Not hungry.' He picked up Dayna's plate, grabbed a fork, and carried both into the living room. She had her head sticking out of the open window, and as he entered he heard her shout, 'In your dreams!' and then a burst of laughter from below.

'What's that about?' he asked her.

She snapped around to face him. Her face went red. 'Just Ricky, talking stupid,' she said, and took the plate from him. Ricky worked in the kitchen at Dot's, and he was always sending gifts up to Dayna – cheap flowers, purchased at the gas station; little teddy bear figurines. Ricky was all right.

'Why are you staring at me?' Dayna demanded.

'Not staring,' Dodge said. He sat next to her and pulled her feet into his lap, began working her calves with his knuckles, as he always did. So she could walk again. So she would keep believing it.

Dayna ate quickly, eyes on her plate. She was avoiding him. Finally, her mouth crooked into a smile. 'Ricky said he wants to marry me.'

'Maybe you should,' Dodge said.

Dayna shook her head. 'Freak.' She reached out and punched Dodge's shoulder, and he pretended it had hurt. He was over-whelmed, momentarily, with happiness.

It was going to be a good day.

He showered and dressed carefully – he'd even remembered to put his jeans in the wash, so they looked good, crisp and clean – and took the bus to Nat's neighborhood. It was only ten thirty, but the sun was already high, hovering in the sky like a single eye. As soon as Dodge turned onto Nat's street, he felt like he was stepping onto a TV set, like he was in one of those shows from the 1950s where someone was always washing a car in the driveway and the women wore aprons and said hello to the mailmen.

Except there was no movement here, no voices, no people hauling trash or banging doors. It was almost too quiet. That was one thing about living in the back of Dot's: someone was always yelling about *something*. It was kind of comforting, in a way, like a reminder that you weren't all alone in having problems.

Nat was waiting on her front stoop. Dodge's stomach bottomed out as soon as he saw her. Her hair was fixed low, in a side ponytail, and she was wearing a ruffled yellow jumper-type thing, with the shirt and shorts attached, that would have looked stupid on anyone else. But on her it looked amazing, like she was some kind of life-size, exotic Popsicle. He couldn't help but think that whenever she had to use the bathroom she'd have to get totally undressed.

She stood up, waving at him, as though he could *possibly* miss her, wobbling slightly on large wedge heels. She wasn't wearing her ankle brace anymore, even though he knew she'd screwed her ankle up again running away from Donahue's house. But she winced slightly when she walked.

'Bishop and Heather went to get iced coffees,' she said as he approached her, doing his best not to walk too quickly. 'I told them to get us some too. Do you drink coffee?'

'I'd shoot coffee, if I could,' he said, and she laughed. The sound made him warm all over, even though he still felt a weird, prickling discomfort standing on her property, like he was in a One-of-These-Things-Doesn't-Belong drawings. A curtain twitched in a ground-floor window, and a face appeared and disappeared too rapidly for Dodge to make out.

'Someone's spying on us,' he said.

'Probably my dad.' Nat waved dismissively. 'Don't worry. He's harmless.'

Dodge wondered what it would be like to have a dad like that – in the house, around, so taken-for-granted you could dismiss him with a wave of the hand. Dayna's dad, Tom, had actually been married to Dodge's mom – only for eighteen months, and only because Dodge's mom got pregnant, but still. Her dad sent emails to her regularly, and money every month, and sometimes even came for a visit.

Dodge had never heard a word from his father, not a single peep. All he knew was his dad worked construction and came from the Dominican Republic. He wondered, for just a split second, what his father was doing now. Maybe he was alive and well, back in Florida. Maybe he'd finally settled down and had a whole host of little kids running around, with dark eyes like Dodge's, with the same high cheekbones.

Or maybe, even better, he'd taken a big-ass tumble from a tall scaffold and split open his head.

When Bishop and Heather returned in another one of

Bishop's junkers – which rattled and shook so badly, Dodge was sure it would quit on them before they reached the mall – Dodge helped Nat to the back and opened the door for her.

'You're so sweet, Dodge,' she said, and kissed his cheek, looking almost regretful.

The ride to Kingston was good. Dodge tried to pay Bishop back for the iced coffee, but Bishop waved him off. Heather managed to coax a decent station out of the patchy radio, and they listened to Johnny Cash until Nat begged for something that had been recorded in *this century*. Nat made Dodge do magic tricks again, and this time she laughed when he made a straw materialize from her hair.

The car smelled like old tobacco and mint, like an old man's underwear drawer, and the sun came through the windows, and the whole state of New York seemed lit up by a special, interior glow. Dodge felt, for the first time since moving to Carp, for the first time maybe in his life, like he belonged somewhere. He wondered how different the past few years would have been if he had been hanging out with Bishop and Heather, if he'd been dating Nat, picking her up to drive her to the movies on Fridays, dancing with her in the gym at homecoming.

He fought down a wave of sadness. None of it would last. It couldn't.

Dodge had driven past the Hudson Valley Mall in Kingston but had never gone inside it. The ceiling was fitted with big skylights, which made the spotless linoleum floors seem to glow. The air smelled like body spray and the little bags of potpourri his mom put in her underwear drawer.

But mostly, it smelled like bleach. Everything was white, like a hospital, like the whole building had been dunked in

Clorox. It was still pretty early and the crowds were thin. Dodge's cowboy boots echoed loudly on the ground when he walked, and he hoped Nat wouldn't find it annoying.

Once inside, Nat consulted a small flyer she had pulled from her bag, and announced that she would meet up with the group in an hour or so, outside the Taco Bell in the food court.

'You're *leaving*?' Dodge blurted out.

Nat looked to Heather for help.

Heather jumped in: 'Nat has an audition.'

'An audition for what?' Dodge asked. He wished he didn't sound so upset. Immediately, Nat began to blush.

'You're going to make fun of me,' she said. His heart practically ripped open. Like he, Dodge Mason, would ever *dream* of making fun of Natalie Velez.

'I won't,' he said quietly. Bishop and Heather were already wandering off. Bishop pretended to shove Heather into the fountain. She yelped and walloped him with a fist.

Wordlessly, Nat passed him the flyer. It was badly designed. The font was practically illegible.

WANTED: MODELS AND ACTRESSES TO
SHOWCASE THE BEST AND THE BRIGHTEST AT DAZZLING GEMS!
COMMERCIAL AUDITIONS:
11:30 A.M. SATURDAY AT THE HUDSON VALLEY MALL.
MUST BE EIGHTEEN OR OLDER.

'Your birthday's on the twenty-ninth, right?' Dodge said, hoping he might get extra points for remembering.

'So? That's only three weeks away,' Nat said, and he remembered she was one of the youngest in their graduating class. He passed her the flyer, and she shoved it back into her bag as though she was embarrassed to have shown him. 'I thought I'd try, anyway.'

You're beautiful, Natalie, he wanted to say to her. But all he could say was, 'They'd be morons to take anyone else.'

She smiled so widely, he could see all of her perfect teeth, nestled in her perfect mouth, like small white candies. He was hoping she might kiss his cheek again, but she didn't.

'It won't take more than an hour or two,' she said. 'Probably less.'

Then she was gone.

Dodge was left in a foul mood. He wandered behind Bishop and Heather for a while, but even though both of them were perfectly nice, it was clear they wanted to be alone. They had their own language, their own jokes. They were constantly touching each other too – pushing and shoving, pinching and hugging, like kids flirting on a playground. Jesus. Dodge didn't know why they just didn't get it on already. They were obviously crazy about each other.

He made an excuse about wanting to get something for his sister and wandered outside, smoking three cigarettes in a row in the parking lot, which was beginning to fill up. He checked his phone a few times, hoping Nat had already texted. She hadn't. He began to feel like an idiot. He had all this money on him. He'd been planning to buy her something. But this wasn't a date. Was it? What did she *want* from him? He couldn't tell.

Inside, he wandered around aimlessly. The mall wasn't actually that big – only one floor – and there was no carousel, which disappointed him. One time he'd taken a carousel ride with Dayna at a mall in Columbus – or was it Chicago? They'd raced around, trying to ride every single horse before the music stopped playing, yelling like cowboys.

The memory made him happy and sad at the same time. It took him a moment to realize he'd accidentally stopped in front of a Victoria's Secret. A mom and her daughter were giving him weird looks. They probably thought he was a perv. He turned away quickly, resolving to go to Dazzling Gems and see whether Nat was done yet. It had been nearly an hour, anyway.

Dazzling Gems was all the way on the other side of the building. He was surprised to see a long line snaking out of the boutique – girls waiting to audition, all of them tanned and wearing next to nothing and perching like antelope on towering heels, and none of them close to as pretty as Nat. They were all cheesy-looking, he thought.

Then he saw her. She was standing just outside the boutique doors, talking to an old dude with a face that reminded Dodge of a ferret. His hair was greasy and thinning on top; Dodge could see patchy bits of his scalp. He was wearing a cheap suit, and even this, somehow, managed to look greasy and threadbare.

At that second, Nat turned and spotted Dodge. She smiled big, waving, and pushed toward him. Ferret melted into the crowd.

'How was it?' Dodge asked.

'Stupid,' she said. 'I didn't even make it through the doors. I waited on line for, like, an hour and barely moved three places. And then some woman came around and checked IDs.' She said it cheerfully, though.

'So who was that?' Dodge asked carefully. He didn't want her to think he was jealous of Ferret, even though he sort of was.

'Who?' Nat blinked.

'That guy you were just talking to,' he said. Dodge noticed Nat was holding something. A business card.

'Oh, that.' Nat rolled her eyes. 'Some modeling scout. He said he liked my look.' She said it casually, like it was no big deal, but he could tell she was thrilled.

'So . . . he just, like, goes around handing out cards?' Dodge said.

He could tell right away he'd offended her. 'He doesn't just hand them out to anyone,' she said stiffly. 'He handed one to *me*. Because he liked my face. Gisele got discovered in a mall.'

Dodge didn't think Ferret looked anything like a modeling agent – and why would an agent be scouting at the mall in Kingston, New York, anyway? – but he didn't know how to say so without offending her further. He didn't want her to think he thought she wasn't pretty enough to be a model, because he did. Except models were tall and she was short. But otherwise, definitely.

'Be careful,' he said, because he could think of nothing else to say.

To his relief, she laughed. 'I know what I'm doing,' she said. 'Come on. Let's go get something to eat. I'm starving.'

Nat didn't like to hold hands because it made her feel 'imbalanced', but she walked so close to him, their arms were almost touching. It occurred to him that anyone looking would assume they were together, like boyfriend-girlfriend, and he had a sudden rush of insane happiness. He had no idea how this had happened – that he was walking next to Nat Velez like he belonged there, like she was his girl. He thought, vaguely, it had something to do with Panic.

They found Bishop and Heather arguing about whether to go to Sbarro or East Wok. While they hashed it out,

Dodge and Nat agreed easily on Subway. He bought her lunch – a chicken sub, which she changed at the last second to a salad ('Just in case,' she said cryptically) – and a Diet Coke. They found an empty table and sat down while Heather and Bishop stood on line at Taco Bell, which they had at last agreed on.

'So what's up with them?' Dodge said.

'With Bishop and Heather?' Nat shrugged. 'Best friends, I guess.' She slurped her soda loudly. He liked the way she ate: unself-consciously, unlike some girls. 'I think Bishop has a crush on her, though.'

'Seems like it,' Dodge said.

Nat tilted her head, watching him. 'What about you?'

'What about me what?'

'Do *you* have a crush on anyone?'

He had just taken a big bite of his sandwich; the question was so unexpected he nearly choked. He couldn't think of a single thing to say that wasn't lame.

'I'm not . . .' He coughed and took a sip of his Coke. Jesus. His face was burning. 'I mean, I don't—'

'Dodge.' She cut him off. Her voice was suddenly stern. 'I'd like you to kiss me now.'

He had just been scarfing a meatball sub. But he kissed her anyway. What else could he do? He felt the noise in his head, the noise around them, swelling into a clamor; he loved the way she kissed, like she was still hungry, like she wanted to eat him. Heat roared through his whole body, and for one second he experienced a crazy shock of anxiety: he must be dreaming.

He put one hand on the back of her head, and she pulled away just long enough to say, 'Both hands, please.'

After that, the noise in his head quieted. He felt totally relaxed, and he kissed her again, more slowly this time.

On the way home, he barely said anything. He was happier than he'd ever been, and he feared saying or doing anything that would ruin it.

Bishop dropped Dodge off first. Dodge had promised to watch fireworks on TV with Dayna tonight. He wondered whether he should kiss Nat again – he was stressing about it – but she solved the problem by hugging him, which would have been disappointing except she was pressed up next to him in the car and he could feel her boobs against his chest.

'Thanks a lot, man,' he said to Bishop. Bishop gave him a fist bump. Like they were friends.

Maybe they were.

He watched the car drive off, even after he could no longer make out Nat's silhouette in the backseat, until the car disappeared beyond a hill and he could hear only the distant, guttural growl of the engine. Still, he stood there on the sidewalk, reluctant to head inside, back to Dayna and his mom and the narrow space of his room, piled with clothes and empty cigarette packs, smelling vaguely like garbage.

He just wanted to be happy for a little longer.

His phone buzzed. An email. His heart picked up. He recognized the sender.

Luke Hanrahan.

The message was short.

Leave us alone. I'll go to the police.

Dodge read the message several times, enjoying it, reading desperation between the lines. He'd been wondering whether Luke had received his message; apparently he had.

Dodge scrolled down and reread the email he had sent a week earlier.

> *The bets are in. The game is on.*
> *I'll make you a trade:*
> *A sister's legs for a brother's life.*

Standing in the fading sun, Dodge allowed himself to smile.

heather

IT HAD BEEN A GOOD DAY – ONE OF THE BEST OF THE WHOLE summer so far. For once, Heather wouldn't let herself think about the future, and what would happen in the fall, when Bishop went to college at SUNY Binghamton and Nat headed to Los Angeles to be an actress. Maybe, Heather thought, she could just stay on at Anne's house, as a kind of helper. Maybe she could even move in. Lily could come too; they could share a room in one of the sheds.

Of course that meant she'd still be stuck in Carp, but at least she'd be out of Fresh Pines Mobile Park.

She liked Anne, and she especially liked the animals. She'd been out to Mansfield Road three times in a week, and she was already looking forward to heading back. She liked the smell of wet straw and old leather and grass that hung over everything; she liked the way the dog Muppet recognized her, and the excited chittering of the chickens.

She decided she liked the tigers, too – from a distance, anyway. She was mesmerized by the way they moved, muscles rippling like the surface of water, and by their eyes, which looked so wise – so bleak, too, as though they had stared into the center of the universe and found it disappointing, a feeling Heather completely understood.

But she was happy to let Anne do the feeding. She couldn't believe the balls on the woman. It was a good thing Anne was too old for Panic. She would have nailed it. Anne actually went *inside* the pen, got within three feet of the tigers as they circled her, eyeing the bucket of meat hungrily – although Heather was sure they'd be just as happy to take a chomp of Anne's head. Anne insisted they wouldn't harm her, though. 'As long as I'm doing the feeding,' she said, 'they won't use me for feed.'

Maybe – just maybe – things would actually be okay.

The only bad part of the day was the fact that Bishop was constantly checking his phone, Heather assumed for texts from Avery. This reminded her that Matt hadn't texted her once since their breakup. Meanwhile, Bishop had Avery (Heather wouldn't think of her as a girlfriend), and Nat had Dodge hanging on her every word and was also still seeing a bartender over in Kingston, some sleazy guy who rode a Vespa, which Nat insisted was just as cool as a motorcycle. Right.

But after they dropped off Dodge, Nat asked, 'Is Avery coming tonight, Bishop?' and when Bishop said no, almost too quickly, Heather felt at peace with the world.

Nat made them detour so she could get a six-pack; then they headed to 7-Eleven and bought junky Fourth of July food: Doritos and dip, powdered doughnuts, and even a bag of pork cracklings, because it was funny and Bishop had bravely volunteered to eat some.

They headed to the gully: a steep, barren slope of gravel and broken-up concrete that bottomed out in the old train tracks, now red with rust and littered with trash. The sun was just starting to set. They picked their way carefully down the slope and across the tracks, and Bishop scouted the best place to light off the sparklers.

This was tradition. Two years ago, Bishop had even surprised Heather by buying two fifty-pound bags of mixed sand from Home Depot and making a beach. He'd even bought loopy straws and those paper umbrellas to put in their drinks, so she would feel they were somewhere tropical.

Today, Heather wouldn't have chosen to be anywhere else in the whole world. Not even the Caribbean.

Nat was already on her second beer, and she was getting wobbly. Heather had a beer too, and even though she didn't usually like to drink, she felt warm and happy. She stumbled over a loose slat in the tracks and Bishop caught her, looped an arm around her waist. She was surprised that he felt so solid, so strong. So warm, too.

'You okay there, Heathbar?' When he smiled, both of his dimples appeared, and Heather had the craziest thought: she wanted to kiss them. She banished the idea quickly. *That* was why she didn't drink.

'I'm fine.' She tried to pull away. He moved his arm to her shoulders. She could smell beer on his breath. She wondered if he, too, was a little drunk. 'Come on, get off me.' She said it jokingly, but she didn't feel like joking.

Nat was wandering up ahead of them, kicking at stones. Darkness was falling and her heart was beating hard in her chest and for a moment, she felt like she and Bishop were alone. He was staring at her with an expression she couldn't identify. She felt heat spreading through her stomach – she was nervous for no reason.

'Take a picture. It'll last longer,' she said, and gave him a push.

The moment passed. Bishop laughed and charged; she dodged him.

'Children, children. Stop fighting!' Nat called back to them.

They found a place to set off the sparklers. Nat's fizzled and sputtered out before they could get properly lit. Heather tried next. When she stepped forward with the lighter, there was a series of cracking sounds, and Heather jumped back, thinking confusedly she'd messed up. But then she realized that she hadn't even gotten the sparkler lit.

'Look, look!' Nat was bouncing up and down excitedly.

Heather turned just as a series of fireworks – green, red, a shower of golden sparks – exploded in the east, just above the tree line. Nat was laughing like a maniac.

'What the hell?' Heather felt dizzy with happiness and confusion. It wasn't even all-the-way dark yet, and there were never any fireworks in Carp. The nearest fireworks were in Poughkeepsie, fifty minutes away, at Waryas Park – where Lily would be with their mom and Bo right now.

Only Bishop didn't seem excited. His arms were crossed and he was shaking his head as they kept going: more gold, and now blue and red again, blooming and fading, sucked back into the sky, leaving tentacle-traces of smoke. And just as Nat started running, half-limping but still laughing, calling, 'Come on, come on!' like they could race straight through to the source, it hit Heather too: this wasn't a celebration.

It was a sign.

In the distance, sirens began to wail. The show stopped abruptly: ghostly fingers of smoke crept silently across the sky. At last Nat stopped running. Whipping around to face Heather and Bishop, she said, 'What? What is it?'

Heather shivered, even though it wasn't cold. The air smelled like smoke, and the wail of the fire trucks cut through her head, sharp and hot.

'It's the next challenge,' she said. 'It's Panic.'

It was just after eleven p.m. by the time Bishop dropped Heather off in front of the trailer. Now she wished she hadn't had the beer – she felt exhausted. Bishop had been quiet since Natalie got out of the car.

Now he turned to her and said, abruptly, 'I still think you should quit, you know.'

Heather pretended not to know what he was talking about. 'Quit what?'

'Don't play dumb.' Bishop rubbed his forehead. The light shining into the car from the porch lit up his profile: the straight slope of his nose, the set of his jaw. Heather realized that he really wasn't a boy anymore. Somehow, when she wasn't looking, he had become a guy – tall and strong, with a stubborn chin and a *girlfriend* and opinions she didn't share. She felt an ache in her stomach, a sense of loss and a sense of wanting. 'The game's just going to get more dangerous, Heather. I don't want you to get hurt. I'd never forgive myself if . . .' He trailed off, shaking his head.

Heather thought of that awful text message she'd received. *Quit now, before you get hurt.* Anger sparked in her chest. Why the hell was everyone trying to make sure she didn't compete? 'I thought you were rooting for me.'

'I am.' Bishop turned to face her. They were very close together in the dark. 'Just not like that.'

For a second, they continued staring at each other. His eyes were dark moons. His lips were a few inches away from hers. Heather realized that she was still thinking about kissing him.

'Good night, Bishop,' she said, and got out of the car.

Inside, the TV was on. Krista and Bo were lying on the couch, watching an old black-and-white movie. Bo was shirtless, and Krista was smoking. The coffee table was packed with empty beer bottles – Heather counted ten of them.

'Heya, Heather Lynn.' Krista stubbed out her cigarette. She missed the ashtray on her first try. She was glassy-eyed. Heather could barely look at her. She better not have been messed up and driving with Lily in the car; Heather would kill her. 'Where you been?'

'Nowhere,' Heather said. She knew her mom didn't really care. 'Where's Lily?'

'Sleeping.' Krista stuck a hand down her shirt, scratching. She kept her eyes on the TV. 'Big day. We saw fireworks.'

'Piss-packed with people,' Bo put in. 'There was a line for the goddamn porta-potties.'

'I'm going to sleep,' Heather said. She didn't bother trying to be nice; Krista was too drunk to lecture her. 'Keep the TV down, okay?'

She had trouble getting the door to the bedroom open; she realized that Lily had balled up one of her sweatshirts and shoved it in the crack between the door and the warped floorboards, to help keep out the noise and the smoke. Heather had taught her that trick. It was hot in the room, even though the window was open and a small portable fan was whirring rhythmically on the dresser.

She didn't turn on the light. There was a little moonlight coming through the window, and she could have navigated the room by touch, anyway. She undressed, piling her clothes on the floor, and climbed into bed, pushing her blankets all the way to the footboard, using only the sheet as cover.

She had assumed Lily was sleeping, but suddenly she heard rustling from the other twin bed.

'Heather?' she whispered.

'Uh-huh?'

'Can you tell me a story?'

'What kind of story?'

'A happy kind.'

It had been a long time since Lily had asked for a story. Now Heather told a version of one of her favorites, 'The Twelve Dancing Princesses', except instead of princesses, she made the girls normal sisters, who lived in a falling-down castle with a queen and king too vain and stupid to look after them. But then they found a trapdoor that led down to a secret world, where they *were* princesses, and where everyone fawned over them.

By the time she was done, Lily was breathing slowly, deeply. Heather rolled over and closed her eyes.

'Heather?'

Lily's voice was thick with sleep. Heather opened her eyes again, surprised.

'You should be sleeping, Billy.'

'Are you going to die?'

The question was so unexpected, Heather didn't answer for a few seconds. 'Of course not, Lily,' she said sharply.

Lily's face was half-mashed into her pillow. 'Kyla Anderson says you're going to die. Because of Panic.'

Heather felt a current of fear go through her – fear, and something else, something deeper and more painful. 'How did you hear about Panic?' she asked.

Lily mumbled something. Heather prompted her again. 'Who told you about Panic, Lily?' she asked.

But Lily was asleep.

The Graybill house was haunted. Everyone in Carp knew it, had been saying it for half a century, since the last of the Graybills had hanged himself from its rafters, just like his father and grandfather before him.

The Graybill curse.

No one had lived in the house officially in more than forty years, although occasionally there were squatters and runaways who risked it. No one *would* live there. At night, lights flickered on and off in the windows. Voices whispered in the mouse-infested walls, and ghosts of children ran down dust-covered hallways. Sometimes, locals claimed they heard a woman screaming in the attic.

Those were the rumors, at least.

And now, the fireworks: some of the old-timers, the ones who claimed they could still remember the day the last Graybill was found swinging by the neck, swore that the fireworks weren't set off by kids at all. They might not even *be* fireworks. Who knew what sort of forces leached out of that tumbledown house, what kind of bad juju, sizzling the night into fire and flame?

The cops thought it was just the usual Fourth of July prank. But Heather, Nat, and Dodge knew better. So did Kim Hollister and Ray Hanrahan and all the other players. Two days after the Fourth of July, their suspicions were confirmed. Heather had just gotten out of the shower when she booted up the ancient laptop and checked her email. Her throat went dry; her mouth turned itchy.

judgment@panic.com
Subject: Enjoy the fireworks?
The show will be even better this Friday at ten p.m.
See how long you can stand it. Remember: no calling for
help.

FRIDAY, JULY 8

heather

'IT'S TOO EASY,' HEATHER SAID AGAIN. SHE SQUEEZED THE steering wheel. She didn't really like to drive. But Bishop had been insistent. He wasn't going to make it to the challenge today, wasn't going to sit around and wait for hours while the players tried to outlast one another in a haunted house. And for once, she'd been able to use the car. Her mom and Bo were getting smashed with some friends in Lot 62, an abandoned trailer mostly used for partying. They'd crawl home around four, or possibly not until sunrise.

'They'll probably try and screw with us,' Nat said. 'They've probably rigged the whole house with sound effects and lights.'

'It's *still* too easy.' Heather shook her head. 'This is Panic, not Halloween.' Her palms were sweating. 'Remember the time we were kids, and Bishop dared you to stand on the porch for three minutes?'

'Only because *you* flaked,' Nat said.

'You flaked too,' Heather reminded her, sorry now that she had brought it up. 'You didn't make it for thirty seconds.'

'Bishop did, though,' Nat said, turning her face to the window. 'He went inside, remember? He stayed inside for five whole minutes.'

'I forgot about that,' Heather said.

'When was that?' Dodge spoke up unexpectedly.

'Years ago. We must have been ten, eleven. Right, Heather?'

'Younger. Nine.' Heather wished that Bishop had come. This was their first challenge without him, and her chest ached. Being with Bishop made her feel safe.

They turned the bend and the house became visible: the sharp peak of its roof silhouetted against the clouds knotted on the horizon, like something out of a horror movie. It rose crookedly out of the ground, and Heather imagined even from a distance she could hear the wind howling through the holes in the roof, the mice nibbling at the rotten wood floors. The only thing missing was a flock of bats.

There were a dozen cars parked on the road. Apparently most people felt the same way Bishop did, and most of the spectators had stayed home. Not all of them, though. Heather spotted Vivian Trager, sitting on the hood of her car, smoking a cigarette. A group of juniors huddled not far off, passing around a shared bottle of wine, looking solemn, as if they were attending a wake. For a second, before Heather turned the engine off, the rain misting through the headlights reminded her of thin slivers of glass.

Dodge climbed out of the car and opened the door for Nat. Heather reached for the bag she'd packed for the night: food, water, a big blanket. She would be here for as long as it took to win. Nat and Dodge, too.

Suddenly there was a muffled shout from outside. Heather looked up in time to see a dark shape rocket past the car.

Nat screamed. And people were suddenly rushing into the road.

Heather threw herself out of the car and ran around to the passenger side, in time to see Ray Hanrahan catch Dodge in the stomach with a shoulder. Dodge stumbled backward, bumping against the remains of a fence. A shower of wood collapsed behind him.

'I know what you're doing, you little freak,' he spat out. 'You think you can—'

He was cut off and grunted sharply. Dodge had stepped forward and grabbed Ray by the throat. There was a collective gasp. Nat cried out.

Dodge leaned in and spoke quietly into Ray's ear. Heather couldn't hear what he said.

Just as quickly, he stepped backward, releasing Ray, who stood, coughing and gagging in the rain. Dodge's face was calm. Nat moved as though to hug him – and then, at the last second, obviously thought better of it.

'Stay the hell away from me, Mason,' Ray said, when he had regained his breath. 'I'm warning you. You better watch it.'

'Come on, guys,' Sarah Wilson, another contestant, spoke up. 'It's pouring. Can we get started?'

Ray was still glowering at Dodge. But he said nothing.

'All right.' That was Diggin. Heather hadn't seen him in the crowd. His voice was suctioned away by the darkness and the rain. 'Rules are simple. The longer you make it in the house, the higher your score.'

Heather shivered. The night of the Jump, when Diggin was crowing into the megaphone, seemed like it had happened years ago: the radio, the beer, the celebration.

She suddenly couldn't remember how she had ended up

here – in front of the Graybill house, all its angles and planes wrong. A deformed place. Listing to one side as though it was in danger of collapse.

'No calling for help,' Diggin said, and his voice cracked a little. Heather wondered whether he knew something they didn't. 'That's it. Challenge is on.'

Everyone broke apart. Beams of light – flashlights, and the occasional blue glow of a cell phone – swept across the road, illuminated the crooked fence, the high grass, the remains of a front path, now choked with weeds.

Dodge was pulling his backpack out of the trunk. Nat was standing next to him. Heather pushed her way over to them.

'What was *that* about?' Heather asked.

Dodge slammed the trunk closed. 'No idea,' he said. In the dark, it was hard to decipher his expression. Heather wondered whether he knew more than he was telling. 'The guy's a psychopath.'

Heather shivered again as moisture seeped under the collar of her jacket, dampening her sweatshirt. She knew, like everyone did, that Dodge's older sister had gone up against Ray's older brother two years ago in Joust and been paralyzed. Heather hadn't been watching – she'd been babysitting Lily that night with Bishop. But Nat had said the car folded up like an accordion.

Heather wondered if Dodge blamed the Hanrahans. 'Let's stay away from Ray inside, okay?' she said. 'Let's stay away from *all* of them.' She didn't put it past Ray Hanrahan to sabotage them – jump out at them, grab them or take a swing.

Dodge turned to her and smiled. His teeth were very white, even in the dark. 'Deal.'

They trudged across the road and into the yard with the others. Heather's chest was heavy with something that wasn't fear, exactly – more like dread. It was too easy.

The rain made the mud suck at her shoes. It would be a shit night. She wished she'd thought to try and sneak a beer. She didn't even like the taste, but *that* would take the edge off, make the night go quicker.

She wondered whether the judges were here – maybe sitting in the front seat of one of the darkened cars, legs on the dash; or even standing in the road, jogging up and down, pretending to be normal spectators. That was the part of Panic she hated most of all: the fact that they were always being watched.

They were at the front porch too quickly. Zev Keller had just disappeared inside, and the door swung shut with a bang. Nat jumped.

'You okay?' Dodge asked her, in a low voice.

'Fine,' Nat spoke too loudly.

Once again, Heather wished Bishop had come along. She wished he were next to her, making stupid jokes, teasing her about being afraid.

'Here goes nothing.' Nat took a step forward and heaved open the door, which was hanging at a weird angle. She hesitated. 'It smells,' she said.

'As long as it doesn't shoot or bark, I'm fine with it,' Dodge said. He didn't seem afraid at all. He moved forward, in front of Nat, and stepped into the house. Nat followed. Heather was the last to enter.

Immediately, Heather smelled it too: mouse shit and mildew, rot, like the smell of a mouth closed up for years.

Jagged beams of light zigzagged across the halls and through dark rooms, as the other players slowly spread out, trying to stake out their own corners, their own hiding spots. Floorboards creaked and doors moaned open and closed; voices whispered in the dark.

The blackness was as thick and heavy as soup. Heather felt her stomach pooling, opening with fear. She fumbled in her pocket for her phone. Nat had the same idea. Nat's face was suddenly visible, lit up from underneath, her eyes deep hollows, her skin blue-tinged. Heather used the feeble light from her phone to cast a small circle on the faded wallpaper, the termite-eaten molding.

Suddenly a bright light flashed on.

'Flashlight app,' Dodge said, as Heather brought a hand to her eyes. 'Sorry. I didn't know it would be so strong.'

He directed the beam upward, to the ceiling, where the remains of a chandelier were swinging, creaking, in a faint wind. That was where three Graybill men had hanged themselves, if the rumors were true.

'Come on,' Heather said, trying to keep her voice steady. The judges might be anywhere. 'Let's move away from the door.'

They advanced farther into the house. Dodge took the lead. Footsteps rang out above them, on the second floor.

Dodge's flashlight cut a small, sharp blade through the blackness, and Heather was reminded of a documentary about the wreck of the *Titanic* she'd watched once with Lily – the way the recovery submersibles had looked, floating through all that dark space, crawling over the ruined wood and the old china plates, which were covered with mossy growth and underwater things. That was how she felt. As if they were at the bottom of the ocean. The pressure on her chest was squeezing,

squeezing. She could hear Nat breathing hard. From upstairs came muffled sounds of shouting: a fight.

'Kitchen,' Dodge announced. He swept the beam of light across a rust-pitted stove, a tile floor half ripped up. All the images were disjointed, bleached white, like in a bad horror film. Heather pictured insects everywhere, spiderwebs, horrible things dropping on her from above.

Dodge aimed his beam in the corner and Heather almost screamed: for a second she saw a face – black, pitted eyes, mouth leering.

'Can you stop pointing that thing at me?'

The girl raised her hand in front of her eyes, squinting, and Heather's heartbeat slowed. It was just Sarah Wilson, huddled in the corner. As Dodge angled the light down, Heather saw that Sarah had brought a pillow and a sleeping bag. It would be easier, far easier, if all the players could huddle together in one room, passing Cheetos and a bottle of cheap vodka someone had stolen from a parent's liquor cabinet.

But they were beyond that.

They passed out of the kitchen and down a short set of stairs, littered with trash, all of it lit up in starts and jerks: cigarette butts, brittle leaves, blackened Styrofoam coffee cups. Squatters.

Heather heard footsteps: in the walls, overhead, behind her. She couldn't tell.

'Heather' – Nat turned around, grabbed Heather's sweatshirt.

'Shhhh,' Dodge hushed them sharply. He shut off the flashlight.

They stood in darkness so heavy, Heather could taste it every time she inhaled: things moldering, rotting slowly; slippery, sliding, slithery things.

Behind her. The footsteps stopped, hesitated. Floorboards creaked. Someone was following them.

'Move,' Heather whispered. She knew she was losing it – that it was probably just another player exploring the house – but she couldn't stop a terrible fantasy that seized her: it was one of the judges, pacing slowly through the dark, ready to grab her. And not a human, either – a supernatural being with a thousand eyes and long, slick fingers, a jaw that would come unhinged, a mouth big enough to swallow you.

The footsteps advanced. One more step, and then another.

'Move,' she said again. Her voice sounded strangled, desperate in the dark.

'In here,' Dodge said. It was so dark, she couldn't even see him, though he must have been standing only a few feet away. He grunted; she heard the groaning of old wood, the whine of rusted hinges.

She felt Nat move away from her and she followed blindly, quickly, nearly tripping over an irregularity in the floor, which marked the beginning of a new room. Dodge swung the door closed behind her, leaning into it until it popped into place. Heather stood, panting. The footsteps kept coming. They paused outside the door. Her breath was shallow, as though she'd been underwater. Then the footsteps withdrew.

Dodge turned on the flashlight app again. In its glow, his face looked like a weird modern painting: all angles.

'What was that?' Heather whispered. She was almost afraid neither Dodge nor Nat had heard.

But Dodge said, 'Nothing. Someone trying to freak us out. That's all.'

He placed his phone on the floor so the beam of light was directed straight up. Dodge had a sleeping bag stuffed in his backpack; Heather shook out the blanket she'd brought. Nat sat down next to the cone of light, drawing the blanket around her shoulders.

All of a sudden, relief broke in Heather's chest. They were safe, together, around their makeshift version of a campfire. Maybe it *would* be easy.

Dodge squatted next to Nat. 'Might as well get comfortable, I guess.'

Heather paced the small room. It must have once been a storage area, or maybe a pantry, except that it was a little ways from the kitchen. It was probably no more than twenty feet square. High up against one wall was the room's single window, but the cloud cover was so thick, barely any light penetrated. On one wall were warped wooden shelves, which now contained nothing but a layer of dust and yet more trash: empty chip bags, a crushed soda can, an old wrench. She used the light of her cell phone to perform a quick exploration.

'Spiders,' she commented, as her phone lit up a web, perfectly symmetrical, glistening and silver, which extended between two shelves.

Dodge rocketed to his feet as though he'd been bit on the ass. 'Where?'

Heather and Nat exchanged a look. Nat cracked a small smile.

'You're afraid of spiders?' Heather blurted out. She couldn't help it. Dodge had shown no fear, ever. She would never have expected it.

'Keep your voice down,' he said roughly.

'Don't worry,' Heather said. She turned off her phone. 'It was just the web, anyway.' She didn't mention the small blurred lumps within it: insects, spun into the threads, waiting to be consumed and digested.

Dodge nodded and looked embarrassed. He turned away, shoving his hands in the pockets of his jacket.

'Now what?' Nat said.

'We wait,' Dodge replied, without turning around.

Nat reached over and popped open a bag of chips. A second later, she was crunching loudly. Heather looked at her.

'What?' Nat said with her mouth full. 'We're going to be here all night.' Except it came out, *'Weef gonna be hey all nife.'*

She was right. Heather went and sat down next to her. The floor was uneven.

'So waf do youf fink?' Nat said, which this time Heather had no trouble translating.

'What do I think about what?' She hugged her knees to her chest. She wished the cone of light were bigger, more powerful. Everything outside its limited beam was rough shadow, shape, and darkness. Even Dodge, standing with his face turned away from the light. In the dark, he could have been anyone.

'I don't know. Everything. The judges. Who *plans* all this?'

Heather reached out and took two chips. She fed them into her mouth, one from each hand. It was an unstated rule that no one spoke about the identity of the judges. 'I want to know how it got started,' she said. 'And why we've all been crazy enough to play.' It was meant to be a joke, but her voice came out shrill.

Dodge shifted and came to squat next to Natalie again.

'What about you, Dodge?' Heather said. 'Why did you agree to play?'

Dodge looked up. His face was a mask of hollows, and Heather was suddenly reminded of one summer when she'd

gone camping with some other Girl Scouts, the way the coun-
selors had gathered them around the fire to tell ghost stories.
They had used flashlights to turn their faces gruesome, and all
the campers were afraid.

For a second, she thought he smiled. 'Revenge.'

Nat started to laugh. 'Revenge?' she repeated.

Heather realized she hadn't misheard. 'Nat,' she said sharply.
Nat must have remembered, then, about Dodge's sister; her
smile faded quickly. Dodge's eyes clicked to Heather's.
She looked away. So he did blame Luke Hanrahan for what
had happened. She felt suddenly cold. The word *revenge* was
so awful: straight and sharp, like a knife.

As if he could tell what she was thinking, Dodge smiled. 'I
just want to cream Ray, that's all,' he said lightly, and reached
out to grab the bag of chips. Heather felt instantly better.

They tried to play cards for a while but it was too dark,
even for a slow-moving game; they had to keep passing the
flashlight around. Nat wanted to learn how to do a magic trick,
but Dodge resisted. Occasionally they heard voices from the
hall, or footsteps, and Heather would tense up, certain that
this was the beginning of the real challenge – spooky ghost
holograms or people in masks who would jump out at them.
But nothing happened. No one came barging in the door to
say *boo*.

After a while, Heather got tired. She balled up the duffel
bag she'd brought under her head. She listened to the low
rhythm of Dodge and Nat's conversation – they were talking
about whether a shark or a bear would win in a fight, and
Dodge was arguing that they had to specify a medium . . .

Then they were talking about dogs, and Heather saw two
large eyes (a tiger's eyes?) the size of headlights, staring at her

from the darkness. She wanted to scream; there was a monster here, in the dark, about to pounce . . .

And she opened her mouth, but instead of a scream coming out, the darkness poured in, and she slept.

dodge

DODGE WAS DREAMING OF THE TIME THAT HE AND DAYNA had ridden the carousel together in Chicago. Or maybe Columbus. But in his dream, there were palm trees, and a man selling grilled meats from a brightly colored cart. Dayna was in front of him, and her hair was so long it kept whipping him in the face. A crowd was gathered: people shouting, leering, calling things he couldn't understand.

He knew he was supposed to be happy – he was supposed to be having fun – but he wasn't. It was too hot. Plus there was Dayna's hair, getting tangled in his mouth, making it hard to swallow. Making it hard to breathe. There was the stench from the meat cart, too. The smell of burning. The thick clouds of smoke.

Smoke.

Dodge woke up suddenly, jerking upright. He'd fallen asleep straight on the floor, with his face pressed against the cold wood. He had no idea what time it was. He could just make out Heather's and Nat's entangled forms, the pattern of their breathing. For a second, still half-asleep, he thought they looked like baby dragons.

Then he realized why: the room was filling with smoke. It was seeping underneath the crack below the door, snaking its way into the room.

He stood up, then thought better of it, remembering that smoke rises, and dropped to his knees. There was shouting: screams and footsteps sounded from other parts of the house.

Too easy. He remembered what Heather had said earlier. Of course. Firecrackers exploded here on the Fourth of July; there would be a prize for the players who stayed in the house the longest.

Fire. The house was on fire.

He reached over and shook the girls roughly, not bothering to distinguish between them, to locate their elbows from their shoulders. 'Wake up. Wake up.'

Natalie sat up, rubbing her eyes, and then immediately began coughing. 'What—?'

'Fire,' he said shortly. 'Stay low. Smoke rises.' Heather was stirring now too. He crawled back to the door. No doubt about it: the rats were abandoning ship. There was a confusion of voices outside, the sound of slamming doors. That meant the fire must have already spread pretty far. No one would have wanted to bail right away.

He put his hand on the metal door handle. It was warm to the touch, but not scalding.

'Nat? Dodge? What's going on?' Heather was fully awake now. Her voice was shrill, hysterical. 'Why is it so smoky?'

'Fire.' It was Natalie who answered. Her voice was, amazingly, calm.

Time to get the hell out. Before the fire spread further. He had a sudden memory of some gym class in DC – or was it Richmond? – when all the kids had to stop, drop, and roll onto the foot-smelling linoleum. Even then, he'd known it was stupid. Like rolling would do anything but turn you into a fireball.

He grabbed the handle and pulled, but nothing happened. Tried again. Nothing. For a second, he thought maybe he was still asleep – in one of his nightmares, where he tried and tried to run but couldn't, or swung at some assailant's face and didn't even make a mark. On his third try, the handle popped off in his hand. And for the first time in the whole game, he felt it: panic, building in his chest, crawling into his throat.

'What's happening?' Heather was practically screaming now. 'Open the door, Dodge.'

'I can't.' His hands and feet felt numb. The panic was squeezing his lungs, making it hard to breathe. No. That was the smoke. Thicker now. He unfroze. He fumbled his fingers into the hole where the door handle had been, tugging frantically, and felt a sharp bite of metal. He jammed his shoulder against the door, feeling increasingly desperate. 'It's stuck.'

'What do you mean, *stuck*?' Heather started to say something else, and instead started coughing.

Dodge spun around, dropped into a crouch. 'Hold on.' He brought his sleeve to his mouth. 'Let me think.' He could no longer hear any footsteps, any shouting. Had everyone else gotten out? He could hear, though, the progress of the fire: the muffled snapping and popping of old wood, decades of rot and ruin slurped into flame.

Heather was fumbling with her phone.

'What are you doing?' Nat tried to swat at it. 'The rules said no calling for—'

'The rules?' Heather cut her off. 'Are you *crazy*?' She punched furiously at the keyboard. Her face was wild, contorted, like a wax mask that had started to melt. She let out a sound that was a cross between a scream and a sob. 'It's not working. There's no service.'

Think, think. Through the panic, Dodge carved a clear path in his mind. A goal; he needed a goal. He knew instinctively that it was his job to get the girls out safely, just like it was his job to make sure nothing bad ever happened to Dayna, his Dayna, his only sister and best friend. He couldn't fail again. No matter what.

The window was too high – he'd never reach it. And it was so narrow . . . But maybe he could give Natalie a boost . . . She might be able to fit. Then what? Didn't matter. Heather might be able to squeeze through too, although he doubted it.

'Nat.' He stood up. The air tasted gritty and thick. It was hot. 'Come on. You have to go through the window.'

Nat stared. 'I can't leave you guys.'

'You have to. Go. Take your phone. Find help.' Dodge steadied himself with one hand on the wall. He was losing it. 'It's the only way.'

Dodge barely saw her nod in the dark. When she stood up, he could smell her sweat. For a crazy second, he wished he could hug her, and tell her it would be okay. But there was no time. An image of Dayna popped into his head, the mangled ruin of her car, her legs shriveling slowly to pale-white stalks.

His fault.

Dodge bent down, gripped Nat by the waist, helped her climb onto his shoulders. She drove a foot into his chest by accident, and he nearly lost it and fell. He was weak. It was the goddamn smoke. But he managed to steady himself and straighten up.

'The window!' Nat gasped. And Heather, somehow, understood. She fumbled for the wrench she'd spotted earlier and passed it upward. Nat swung. There was a tinkling. A rush of air blew into the room, and after just a second a whooshing sound, as the fire – beyond the door, edging closer – sensed that air, felt it, and surged toward it, like an ocean thundering toward the beach. Black smoke poured underneath the door.

'Go!' Dodge shouted. He felt Nat kick his head, his ear; then she was outside.

He dropped to his knees again. He could barely see. 'You next,' he said to Heather.

'I'll never fit.' She said it in a whisper, but somehow he heard. He was relieved. He didn't really think he had the strength left to lift her.

His head was spinning. 'Lie down,' he said, in a voice that didn't sound like his own. She did, pressing flat against the ground. He was glad to lie down too. Lifting Nat that small distance had exhausted him. It was as though the smoke was a blanket . . . as though it was covering him, and telling him to sleep . . .

He was back on the carousel again. But this time the spectators were screaming. And it had started to rain. He wanted to get off . . . the ride was whirling faster and faster . . . lights were spinning overhead . . .

Lights, spinning, voices shouting. Sirens screaming.

Sky.

Air.

Someone – Mom? – saying, 'You're okay, son. You're going to be okay.'

SATURDAY, JULY 9

heather

WHEN HEATHER WOKE UP, SHE IMMEDIATELY KNEW SHE WAS in a hospital, which was kind of disappointing. In movies, people were always groggy and confused and asking where they were and what had happened. But there was no mistaking the smell of disinfectant, the clean white sheets, the *beep-beep-beep* of medical equipment. It was actually kind of pleasant – the sheets were clean and crisp; her mom and Bo weren't shouting; the air didn't reek of old booze. She'd slept better than she had in a long time, and for several minutes she kept her eyes closed, breathing deeply.

Then Bishop was speaking, quietly. 'Come on, Heather. We know you're faking. I can tell by the way your eyelid is twitching.'

Heather opened her eyes. Joy surged in her chest. Bishop was sitting in a chair drawn up to the bed, leaning forward, as close as he could get without crawling into the cot with her. Nat was there too, eyes swollen from crying, and she rocketed straight at Heather.

'Heather.' She started sobbing again. 'Oh my God, Heather. I was so scared.'

'Hi, Nat.' Heather had to speak through a mouthful of Nat's hair, which tasted like soap. She must have showered.

'Don't suffocate her, Nat,' Bishop said. Nat drew back, still sniffling, but she kept a grip on Heather's hand, as though she were worried Heather might float away. Bishop was smiling, but his face was sheet white and there were dark circles under his eyes. Maybe, Heather thought, he had been sitting by her bed all night, worried she might be dying. The idea pleased her.

Heather didn't bother asking what had happened. It was obvious. Nat had gotten help, somehow, and Heather must have been carted off to the hospital when she was passed out. So she asked, 'Is Dodge okay? Where is he?'

'Gone. He got up a few hours ago and walked out. He's okay,' Nat said all in a rush. 'The doctor said you'd be okay too.'

'You won the challenge,' Bishop said, his face expressionless. Nat shot him a look.

Heather inhaled again. When she did, she felt a sharp pain between her ribs. 'Does my mom know?' she asked.

Nat and Bishop exchanged a quick glance.

'She was here,' Bishop said. Heather felt her chest seize again. *She was here* meant she'd left. Of course. 'Lily, too,' he rushed on. 'She wanted to stay. She was hysterical—'

'It's all right,' Heather said. Bishop was still looking at her weirdly, like someone had just forced a handful of Sour Patch Kids into his mouth. It occurred to her that she must look like crap, probably smelled like crap too. She felt her face heat up. Great. Now she'd look like crap warmed over. 'What?' she said, trying to sound annoyed without breathing too hard. 'What is it?'

'Listen, Heather. Something happened last night, and you—'

The door swung open, and Mrs Velez came into the room, balancing two cups of coffee and a sandwich filmed in plastic, obviously from the cafeteria. Mr Velez was right behind her, carrying a duffel bag Heather recognized as belonging to Nat.

'Heather!' Mrs Velez beamed at her. 'You're awake.'

'I told my parents,' Nat said unnecessarily, under her breath.

'It's all right,' Heather said again. And secretly, she was pleased that Mr and Mrs Velez had come. She was suddenly worried she might cry. Mr Velez's hair was sticking straight up, and he had a grass stain on one of the knees of his khakis; Mrs Velez was wearing one of her pastel cardigans, and both of them were looking at Heather as though she had come back from the dead. Maybe she had. For the first time she realized, really *realized*, how close she had come. She swallowed rapidly, willing back the urge to cry.

'How are you feeling, sweetheart?' Mrs Velez set the coffees and sandwich on the counter and sat down on Heather's bed. She reached out and smoothed back Heather's hair; Heather imagined, just for a second, that Mrs Velez was her real mother.

'You know.' Heather tried, and failed, to smile.

'I had my dad bring some stuff,' Nat said. Mr Velez hitched the duffel bag a little higher, and it occurred to Heather that she had lost her own bag – left it in the Graybill house. It was probably ashes by now. 'Magazines. And that fuzzy blanket from my basement.'

The way Nat was talking made it seem as if Heather was actually going to be *staying* here. 'I'm really fine.' She sat up a little higher in bed, as though to prove it. 'I can go home.'

'The doctors need to make sure there's no damage inside,' Mrs Velez said. 'It might be a little while.'

'Don't worry, Heather,' Bishop said quietly. He reached out and took her hand; she was startled by the softness of his touch, by the slow warmth that radiated from his fingertips through her body. 'I'll stay with you.'

I love you. She thought the words suddenly; this urge, like the earlier urge to cry, she had to will down.

'Me too,' Nat said loyally.

'Heather needs to rest,' Mrs Velez said. She was still smiling, but the corners of her eyes were creased with worry. 'Do you remember what happened last night, honey?'

Heather tensed. She wasn't sure how much she should say. She looked to Nat and Bishop for cues, but both of them avoided her eyes. 'Most of it,' she said cautiously.

Mrs Velez was still watching her extra carefully, as if she were worried Heather might suddenly crack apart, or begin bleeding from the eyeballs. 'And do you feel up to talking about it, or would you rather wait?'

Heather's stomach began to twist. Why wouldn't Bishop and Nat look at her? 'What do you mean, talking about it?'

'The police are here,' Bishop blurted out. 'We tried to tell you.'

'I don't get it,' Heather said.

'They think that the fire wasn't an accident,' Bishop said. Heather felt like he was trying to communicate a message to her with his eyes, and she was too stupid to get it. 'Someone burned the house down on purpose.'

'But it *was* an accident,' Nat insisted.

'For God's sake, both of you.' Mrs Velez rarely lost her temper; Heather was surprised even to hear her say 'God'. 'Stop it. You're not doing anybody any good by lying. This is because of that game – Panic, or whatever you call it. Don't try to pretend it isn't. The police know. It's all over. Honestly, I would have expected better. Especially from you, Bishop.'

Bishop opened his mouth, then closed it again. Heather wondered whether he'd been about to defend himself. But that would mean selling out Heather and Nat. She felt horribly ashamed. Panic. The word seemed awful spoken out loud, here, in this clean white place.

Mrs Velez's voice turned gentle again. 'You'll have to tell them the truth, Heather,' she said. 'Tell them everything you know.'

Heather was starting to freak. 'But I don't know anything,' she said. She pulled her hand away from Bishop's; her palm was starting to sweat. 'Why do they need to talk to me? I didn't do anything.'

'Someone is dead, Heather,' Mrs Velez said. 'It's very serious.'

For a second, Heather was sure she'd misheard. 'What?'

Mrs Velez looked stricken. 'I thought you knew.' She turned to Nat. 'I was sure you would have told her.'

Nat said nothing.

Heather turned to Bishop. Her head seemed to take a very long time to move on her neck. 'Who?' she said.

'Little Bill Kelly,' Bishop said. He tried to find her hand again, but she pulled away.

Heather couldn't speak for a moment. The last time she'd seen Little Bill Kelly, he was sitting at a bus stop, feeding pigeons from the cup of his hands. When she'd smiled at him, he waved cheerfully and said, 'Hiya, Christy.' Heather had no idea who Christy was. She'd barely known Little Kelly – he was older than she was, and had been away for years in the army.

'I don't—' Heather swallowed. Mr and Mrs Velez were listening closely. 'But he wasn't . . .'

'He was in the basement,' Bishop said. His voice broke. 'Nobody knew. You couldn't have known.'

Heather closed her eyes. Color bloomed behind her eyelids. Fireworks. Fire. Smoke in the darkness. She opened her eyes again.

Mr Velez had gone into the hall. The door was partly open. She heard murmured voices, the squeak of someone's shoes on the tile floor.

He poked his head back in the room. He looked almost apologetic. 'The police are here, Heather,' he said. 'It's time.'

MONDAY, JULY 11

dodge

'CAN I HAVE SOME WATER, PLEASE?'

Dodge wasn't really thirsty, but he wanted a second to sit, catch his breath, and look around.

'Sure thing.' The cop who had greeted Dodge and ushered him into a small, windowless office – OFFICER SADOWSKI, read his name tag – hadn't stopped smiling, like he was a teacher and Dodge was his favorite student. 'You just sit tight. I'll be right back.'

Dodge sat very still while he waited, just in case someone was watching. He didn't have to turn his head to take in nearly everything: the desk, piled high with manila file folders; the shelves stacked with more papers; an ancient telephone, unplugged; photographs of several fat, smiling babies; a desk fan. It was a good thing, he thought, that Sadowski hadn't brought him into an interrogation room.

Sadowski was back in only a minute, carrying a Styrofoam cup full of water. He was on a mission to seem friendly. 'You comfortable? Happy with the water? You don't want a soda or anything?'

'I'm fine.' Dodge took a sip of the water and nearly choked. It was piss-warm.

Sadowski either didn't notice, or pretended not to. 'Really glad you decided to come down and talk to us. Dan, right?'

'Dodge,' Dodge said. 'Dodge Mason.'

Sadowski had taken a seat behind his desk. He made a big show of shuffling around some papers, grinning like an idiot, twirling a pen and leaning back in his chair. All casual. But Dodge noticed that he had Dodge's name written down on a piece of white paper.

'Right. Right. Dodge. Hard to forget. So what can I do you for, Dodge?'

Dodge wasn't buying the village idiot act, not for a second. Officer Sadowski's eyes were narrow and smart. His jaw was like a right triangle. He'd be a mean old bastard when he felt like it.

'I'm here to talk about the fire,' Dodge said. 'I figured you'd want to talk to me eventually.'

It had been two days since Dodge had woken up in the hospital. Two days of waiting for the knock on the door, for the cops to show up and start grilling him. The waiting, the ticking feeling of anxiety, was worse than anything.

So earlier that morning he'd woken with a resolution: he wouldn't wait anymore.

'You're the young man who left the hospital on Saturday morning, aren't you?' Right. As though he'd forgotten. 'We just missed talking to you. Why'd you run off in such a hurry?'

'My sister . . . needs help.' He realized, belatedly, he

shouldn't have mentioned his sister. It would only lead to bad places.

But Sadowski seized on it. 'What kind of help?'

'She's in a wheelchair,' Dodge said, with some effort. He hated saying the words out loud. It made them seem more real, and final.

Sadowski nodded sympathetically. 'That's right. She was in a car accident a few years ago, wasn't she?'

Dick. So the village idiot thing *was* a trick. He'd done his homework. 'Yup,' Dodge said.

He thought Sadowski would ask him more about it, but he just shook his head and muttered, 'Shame.'

Dodge started to relax. He took a sip of water. He was glad he'd come. It probably made him look confident. He *was* confident.

Then Sadowski said, abruptly, 'You ever heard of a game called Panic, Dodge?'

Dodge was glad he'd already finished swallowing, so he couldn't choke. He shrugged. 'I don't know. I never had too many friends around here.'

'You have a few friends,' Sadowski said. Dodge didn't know what he was getting at. He consulted his page of notes again. 'Heather Nill. Natalie Velez. Someone must have invited you to that party.'

That was the story that had gone around: a party in the Graybill House. A bunch of kids getting together to smoke weed, drink booze, freak one another out. Then: a stray spark. An accident. The blame was spread around that way, couldn't be pinned to anyone specific.

Of course, Dodge knew it was all bullshit. Someone had lit the place up, deliberately. It was part of the challenge.

'Well, yeah. Them. But they're not *friends* friends.' Dodge felt himself blushing. He wasn't sure whether he'd been caught in a lie.

Sadowski made a noise in the back of his throat Dodge didn't know how to interpret. 'Why don't you tell me all about it? In your own words, at your own pace.'

Dodge told him, speaking slowly, so he wouldn't screw it up, but not too slowly, so he wouldn't seem nervous. He told Sadowski he'd been invited by Heather; there'd been rumors of a keg party, but when he got there he found out it was pretty lame, and there was hardly any booze at all. He definitely hadn't been drinking. (He congratulated himself on thinking of this – he wouldn't get busted for anything, period.)

Sadowski interrupted him only once. 'So why the closed room?'

Dodge was startled. 'What?'

Sadowski only pretended to glance down at the report. 'The fire chiefs had to break down the door to get to you and the girl – Heather. Why'd you go off with her if the party was raging somewhere else?'

Dodge kept his hands on his thighs. He didn't even blink. 'I told you, the party was lame. Besides, I was kind of hoping . . .' He trailed off suggestively, raising his eyebrows.

Sadowski got it. 'Ah. I see. Go on.'

There wasn't much else to tell; Dodge told him he must have fallen asleep next to Heather. The next thing he knew, they heard people running and smelled smoke. He didn't mention Nat. No need to explain how she'd known to direct the firemen to the back of the house, unless he was asked.

For a while after Dodge finished talking, they sat in silence.

Sadowski appeared to be doodling, but Dodge knew this, too, was an act. He'd heard everything.

Finally Officer Sadowski sighed, set down his pen, and rubbed his eyes. 'It's tough shit, Dodge. Tough shit.'

Dodge said nothing.

Sadowski went on. 'Bill Kelly was – is – a friend. He was on the force. Little Kelly went to Iraq. Do you know what I'm saying?'

'Not really,' Dodge said.

Sadowski stared at him. 'I'm saying we're going to figure out exactly what happened that night. And if we find out the fire was started on purpose . . .' He shook his head. 'That's homicide, Dodge.'

Dodge's throat was dry. But he forced himself not to look away. 'It was an accident,' he said. 'Wrong place, wrong time.'

Sadowski smiled. But there was no humor in it. 'I hope so.'

Dodge decided to walk home. He was out of cigarettes and in a bad mood. Now he wasn't so sure that going to the cops had been a good idea. The way Sadowski looked at him made him feel like the cops thought *he'd* started the damn fire.

It was the judges – had to be, whoever they were. Any one of the players could squeal about the game, and that would be the end of that.

If Panic ended . . .

Dodge had no plans beyond winning Panic – beating Ray in the final round of Joust, and making sure it was a hard, bloody win. He hadn't thought of his life beyond that moment at all. Maybe he'd be arrested. Maybe he'd go out in a blaze. He didn't care either way.

Dayna, his Dayna, had been destroyed, ruined forever, and someone had to pay.

But for the first time he was seized with the fear that the game would actually end, and he would never get his chance. And then he would just have to live with the new Dayna on her plant-stalk legs, live with the knowledge that he'd been unable to save her. Live with knowing Ray and Luke were fine, going through the world, breathing and grinning and shitting and probably crapping on other people's lives too.

And that was impossible. Unimaginable.

The sun was bright and high. Everything was still, gripped in the hard light. There was a bad taste in Dodge's mouth; he hadn't eaten yet today. He checked his phone, hoping Nat might have called: nothing. They'd spoken the day before, a halting conversation, full of pauses. When Nat said her dad needed her downstairs and she had to get off the phone, he was sure she'd been lying.

Dodge circumnavigated Dot's Diner, checking instinctively to see whether he could spot his mom behind the smudgy glass windows. But the sun was too bright and turned everyone to shadow.

He heard a burst of laughter from inside the house. He paused with his hand on the door. If his mom was home, he wasn't sure he could deal. She'd been practically hysterical when he came home with a hospital bracelet, and since then she'd been giving him the fish-eye and grilling him every 0.5 seconds about how he was feeling, like she couldn't trust him even to pee without risking death. Plus, the news about Little Kelly was all over Dot's Diner, and when she wasn't demanding whether Dodge thought he had a fever, she was gossiping about the tragedy.

But then the laughter sounded again, and he realized it wasn't his mom laughing – it was Dayna.

She was sitting on the couch, a blanket draped over her legs. Ricky was sitting in a folding chair across from her; the chessboard was positioned on the coffee table. When Dodge entered, there were only a few inches between them.

'No, no,' she was saying, between fits of giggling. 'The bishop moves *diagonally*.'

'Diag-on-ally,' Ricky repeated, in his heavily accented English, and knocked over one of Dayna's pawns.

'It's not your turn!' She snatched her pawn back and let out another burst of laughter.

Dodge cleared his throat. Dayna looked up.

'Dodge!' she cried. Both she and Ricky jerked backward several inches.

'Hey.' He didn't know why they both looked so guilty. He didn't know why he felt so awkward, either – like he'd interrupted them in the middle of something far more intense than a game of chess.

'I was just teaching Ricky how to play,' Dayna blurted. Her cheeks were flushed and her eyes were bright. She looked better, prettier, than she had in a while. Dodge thought she might even be wearing makeup.

He suddenly felt angry. He was out busting his ass for Dayna, almost dying, and she was at home *playing chess* with Ricky on the old marble board his mom had bought on Dodge's eleventh birthday, and that Dodge had schlepped everywhere they'd moved since then.

Like she didn't even care. Like he wasn't playing Panic just for her.

'Want to play, Dodge?' she asked. But he could tell she didn't mean it. For the first time Dodge looked, really looked, at

Ricky. Could he be serious about marrying Dayna? He was probably twenty-one, twenty-two, tops.

Dayna would never do it. The guy barely spoke any English, for Christ's sake. And she would have told Dodge if she liked him. She'd always told Dodge everything.

'I just came in to get a drink,' Dodge said. 'I'm going out again.'

In the kitchen, he filled a glass with water and kept the sink running while he drank, to drown out the sound of muffled conversation from the next room. What the hell were they talking about? What did they have in common? When he shut off the sink, the voices fell abruptly into silence again. Jesus. Dodge felt like he was trespassing in his own house. He left without saying good-bye. Almost as soon as he shut the door, he heard laughter again.

He checked his phone. He had a response from Heather, finally. He'd texted her earlier: *Heard anything?*

Her text read simply: *Game over.*

Dodge felt a surge of nausea riding up from his stomach to his throat. And he knew, then, what he had to do.

Dodge had been to the Hanrahans' house only once before, two years earlier, when Dayna was still in the hospital – when, briefly, it had seemed like she might not wake up. Dodge hadn't budged from the chair next to her bed except to pee and smoke cigarettes in the parking lot and get coffee from the cafeteria. Finally Dodge's mom had convinced him to go home and get some rest.

He had gone home, but not to rest. He had stopped in only long enough to remove the butcher's knife from the kitchen and the baseball bat from the closet, along with a pair of old ski gloves that had never, as far as he knew, been used by anyone in his family.

It took him a while to find Ray and Luke's house on his bike, in the dark, half-delirious from the heat and no sleep and the rage that was strangling him, coiled like a snake around his gut and throat. But he did, finally: a two-story structure, all dark, that might have been nice one hundred years ago.

Now it looked like a person whose soul had been sucked out through his asshole: collapsed and desperate, wild and wide-eyed, sagging in the middle. Dodge felt a flash of pity. He thought of the tiny apartment behind Dot's, how his mom put daffodils in old pickle jars on the windowsills and scrubbed the walls with bleach every Sunday.

Then he remembered what he had come to do. He left his bike on the side of the road, slipped on his gloves, removed the baseball bat and knife from his duffel bag.

He stood there, willing his feet to move. A swift kick to the door, the sound of screaming. The knife flashing in the dark, the whistle of the bat cutting through the air. He was after Luke, and Luke alone.

It would be easy. Quick.

But he hadn't managed it. He'd stood there with his legs numb, heavy, useless, for what felt like hours, until he began to fear that he'd never move again – he'd be frozen in this position, in the darkness, forever.

At some point the porch light had clicked on, and Dodge had seen a heavy woman, with a face like a pulpy fruit, wearing a tentlike nightgown and no shoes, maneuver her bulk out onto the porch and light up a cigarette. Luke's mother.

All at once, Dodge could move again. He had stumbled toward his bike. It wasn't until he was four blocks away that he realized he was still holding the knife and he had dropped the baseball bat, probably on the lawn.

It had been two whole years, almost to the day. Ray's house looked even more run-down in the daylight. The paint was shedding like gray dandruff. On the porch were two tires, a few smelly armchairs, and an old porch swing hanging on rusty chains, which looked like it would collapse under the slightest pressure.

There was a doorbell, but it was disconnected. Instead Dodge banged loudly on the frame of the screen door. In response, the TV inside was abruptly muted. For the first time, it occurred to Dodge that it might not be Ray who answered the door, but that pulpy-faced woman from two years ago – or a father, or someone else entirely.

But it was Ray. He was wearing only basketball shorts. For a split second, he hesitated, obviously startled, just behind the screen.

Before Dodge could say anything, Ray kicked open the screen door. Dodge had to jump back to avoid it. He lost his footing.

'What the fuck are you doing here?'

The sudden motion had screwed Dodge up. He was already off balance when Ray grabbed him by the shirt and then shoved him. Dodge stumbled down the porch stairs and landed in the dirt on his elbows. He bit down on his tongue.

And Ray was above him, in a rage, ready to pounce. 'You must be out of your mind,' he spat out.

Dodge rolled away from him and scrambled to his feet. 'I'm not here to fight.'

Ray let out a bark of laughter. 'You don't have a choice.'

He took a step forward, swinging; but Dodge had regained his balance and sidestepped him.

'Look.' Dodge held up a hand. 'Just listen to me, okay? I came to talk.'

'Why the hell would I want to talk to you?' Ray said. His hands were still balled into fists, but he didn't try and swing again.

'We both want the same thing,' Dodge said.

For a second, Ray said nothing. His hands uncurled. 'What's that?'

'Panic.' Dodge wet his lips. His throat was dry. 'Both of us need it.'

There was an electric tension in the air, hot and dangerous. Ray took another quick step forward.

'Luke told me about your little threats,' Ray said. 'What kind of game do you think you're playing?'

Ray was so close, Dodge could smell cornflakes and sour milk on his breath. But he didn't step back. 'There's only one game that matters,' he said. 'You know it. Luke knew it too. That's why he did what he did, isn't it?'

For the first time, Ray looked afraid. 'It was an accident,' he said. 'He never meant—'

'Don't.'

Ray shook his head. 'I didn't know,' he said. Dodge knew he was lying.

'Are you going to help me, or not?' Dodge asked.

Ray laughed again: an explosive, humorless sound. 'Why should I help you?' he asked. 'You want me dead.'

Dodge smiled. 'Not like this,' he said. And he meant it, 100 percent. 'Not yet.'

Sometime around midnight, when Carp was quiet, dazzling in a light sheen of rain, Zev Keller woke in the dark to rough hands grabbing him. Before he could scream, he was gagging on the taste of cotton in his mouth. A sock. And then he was lifted, carried out of bed and into the night.

His first, confused, thought was that the cops had come to take him away. If he'd been thinking clearly, he would have realized that his assailants were wearing ski masks. He would have noticed that the trunk they forced him into belonged to a navy-blue Taurus, like the kind his brother drove. That it *was* his brother's car, parked in its usual spot.

But he wasn't thinking clearly. He was panicked.

Kicking out, watching the sky narrow to a sliver as the trunk closed over him, Zev felt something wet and realized that, for the first time since he was five years old, he'd peed himself.

At last he realized too that despite everything, the game was ongoing. And that he had just lost.

WEDNESDAY, JULY 13

heather

THE WAR MEETING TOOK PLACE AT BISHOP'S HOUSE. IT HAD to. Heather's trailer was too small, Dodge wouldn't have invited them to his place, and Nat's parents were home all day doing a garage-clean. Heather had to bring Lily. Lily had nothing to do now that school was over, and most days took the bus by herself a half-hour to Hudson, where the library was.

But the library was closed for renovations. For once, Lily was in a good mood, even though she was dirty and sweaty and stank like horses; in the morning, she'd helped Heather at Anne's. She sang a song about tigers all the way to Bishop's house, and made waves with her arm out the window.

Bishop lived in the woods. His father had once owned an antique store and pawnshop, and Bishop liked to say his dad 'collected' things. Heather always threatened to sign them up for that TV show about hoarders. The house, and the yard around it, was littered with stuff, from junky to bizarre: at least two to three old cars at all times, in various states of repair; crates of spray paint; rusted slides; stacks of timber; old furniture, half-embedded in the soil. Lily ran off, yelling, weaving through the old piles.

Heather found Nat and Bishop behind the house, sitting on an old merry-go-round, which no longer turned. Bishop looked as though he hadn't slept in days. He pulled Heather into a hug as soon as he saw her, which was weird.

She tensed up; she probably smelled like stables.

'What's up with you?' Heather said when he pulled away. The circles under his eyes were as dark as a bruise.

'Just glad to see you,' he said.

'You look like crap.' She reached out to smooth down his hair, an old habit. But he caught her wrist. He was staring at her intensely, like he wanted to memorize her face.

'Heather—' he started to say.

'Heather!' Nat called out at the same time. She, at least, seemed unaffected by Bill Kelly's death. 'I mean, it's not like we knew him,' she'd said days earlier, when Heather had told her how guilty she felt.

Heather didn't wait for Nat to speak, although Nat had called the meeting. 'I'm out,' she said. 'I'm not playing anymore.'

'We have to wait for Dodge,' Nat said.

'I don't have to wait for anyone,' Heather said. She was annoyed by Nat's calm. She was blinking happily, sleepily, in the sun – as though nothing had happened. 'I'm not playing anymore. It's as simple as that.'

'It's sick,' Bishop said fiercely. 'Sick. Anyone in their right minds—'

'The judges aren't in their right minds, though, are they?' Nat said, turning to him. 'I mean, they can't be. You heard about Zev?'

'That wasn't—' Bishop abruptly stopped speaking, shaking his head.

'I, for one, don't plan on losing my chance at sixty-seven thousand dollars,' Nat said, still with that infuriating calm. Then she shook her head. 'It isn't right to start without Dodge.'

'Why?' Heather fired back. 'Why are you so worried about Dodge? *I* made the deal with you, remember?'

Nat looked away, and then Heather knew. A bitter taste rushed into her throat. 'You made a deal with him, too,' she said. 'You lied to me.'

'No.' Nat looked at her, eyes wide, pleading. 'No. Heather. I never planned on cutting him in.'

'What are you guys talking about?' Bishop asked. 'What do you mean, "cutting him in"?'

'Stay out of it, Bishop,' Heather said.

'I'm in it,' he said. He dragged a hand through his hair, and in that instant, Heather felt they would never get back to normal: to making fun of Bishop's hair, to loading it with gel and twisting to make it stick straight up. 'You're at my house, remember?'

'This isn't a game anymore,' Heather said. Everything was spiraling out of control. 'Don't you get it? Someone's *dead*.'

'Jesus.' Bishop sat down heavily, rubbing his eyes, as though Heather saying the words had made them real.

'Why did you play, Heather?' Nat stood up when Bishop sat down. Her arms were crossed, and she made little clicking noises with her tongue. Rhythmic. A pattern. 'If you didn't want the risk, if you couldn't handle it, why did you play? Because Matt-stupid-Hepley dumped you? Because he was sick of getting blue-balled by his girlfriend?'

Heather lost her breath. She was conscious of the air going out of her at once, escaping in a short hiss.

Bishop looked up and spoke sharply: 'Nat.'

Even Natalie looked surprised, and immediately guilty. 'I'm sorry,' she said quickly, avoiding Heather's eyes. 'I didn't mean—'

'What did I miss?'

Heather turned. Dodge had just appeared, emerging from the glittering maze of junk and scrap metal. She wondered what they looked like to him: Nat flushed and guilty; Bishop awful-white, wild-eyed; and Heather blinking back tears, still sweaty from the stables.

And all of them angry: you could feel it in the air, a physical force among them.

Suddenly Heather realized that this, too, was a result of the game. That it was part of it.

Only Dodge seemed unaware of the tension. 'Mind if I smoke?' he asked Bishop. Bishop shook his head.

Heather broke in. 'I'm out. I said I was out and I meant it. The game should have ended—'

'The game never ends,' Dodge said. Nat turned away from him and for a moment, just a moment, he looked uncertain. Heather was relieved. Dodge had changed this summer. He wasn't the slope-shouldered weirdo, the outsider, who had sat for three years in silence. It was as though the game was *feeding* him somehow – like he was growing on it. 'You heard about Zev?' He exhaled a straight stream of smoke. 'That was me.'

Nat had turned back to him. 'You?'

'Me, and Ray Hanrahan.'

There was a moment of silence.

Heather finally managed to speak. 'What?'

'We did it.' Dodge took a final drag and ground out the cigarette butt underneath the heel of his cowboy boot.

'That's against the rules,' Heather said. 'The judges set the challenges.'

Dodge shook his head. 'It's Panic,' he said. 'There are no rules.'

'Why?' Bishop tugged at his left ear. He was furious and trying not to show it; that was his tell.

'To send a message to the judges. The players, too. The game will go on, one way or another. It has to.'

'You don't have the right,' Bishop said.

Dodge shrugged. 'What's right?' he said. 'What's wrong?'

'What about the cops? And the fire? What about Bill?'

No one said anything. Heather realized she was shaking.

'I'm done,' she said. She spun around and nearly collided with a rust-spotted furnace, which, along with an overturned bike, marked the beginning of the narrow path that wound through the landscape of litter and junk to the house, and around to the front yard. Bishop called out to her, but she ignored him.

She found Lily crouching in a bit of yard uncluttered by junk, marking the bare grass with bright-blue spray paint she had unearthed somewhere.

'Lily.' Heather spoke sharply.

Lily dropped the paint and stood up, looking guilty.

'We're going,' Heather said.

Lily's frown reappeared, as did the small pucker between her eyebrows. Immediately, she seemed to shrink and age. Heather thought of the night Lily had whispered, 'Are you going to die?' and felt a fist of guilt hit her hard in the stomach. She didn't know whether she was doing the right thing. She felt like nothing she did was right.

But what had happened to Bill Kelly was wrong. And pretending it hadn't happened was wrong too. That, she knew.

'What's the matter with you?' Lily said, sticking out her lower lip.

'Nothing.' Heather seized her wrist. 'Come on.'

'I didn't get to say hi to Bishop,' Lily whined.

'Next time,' Heather said. She practically dragged Lily to the car. She couldn't hear Nat or Bishop or Dodge anymore; she wondered whether they were talking about her. She couldn't get out of there fast enough. She drove in silence, gripping the wheel as though it was in danger of slipping suddenly from her hands.

WEDNESDAY, JULY 20

heather

THE WEATHER TURNED FOUL, COLD AND WET, AND THE GROUND turned to sludge. For two days, Heather heard nothing from Nat. She refused to be the one to call first. She texted back and forth with Bishop but avoided seeing him, which meant that to go to work she had to bus it to the 7-Eleven and walk three quarters of a mile in the driving rain, arriving wet and miserable just to stand for more hours in the rain, chucking the chickens soggy feed and hauling equipment into the sheds so it wouldn't rust.

Only the tigers seemed more miserable than she was; she wondered, as they huddled underneath a canopy of maple trees, watching her work, whether they dreamed of other places as much as she did. Africa, burnt grasses, a vast round sun. For the first time it struck her as selfish that Anne kept them here, in this craptastic climate of blistering heat, followed by rain, followed by snow and sleet and ice.

There were rumors that the police had turned up evidence of arson at the Graybill house. For a whole day, Heather waited in agony, certain that the evidence had to do with her duffel bag, positive that the police would haul her off to jail. What would happen to her, if she were accused of murder? She was eighteen. That meant she would go to real jail, not juvie.

But when several more days passed and no one came looking for her, she relaxed again. She hadn't been the one to light the stupid match. Really, when you thought about it, this was all Matt Hepley's fault. *He* should be arrested. And Delaney, too.

About Panic, there was not a single whisper. Dodge's move had, apparently, failed to rouse the judges to action. Heather wondered whether he would try again, then reminded herself it was no longer her business.

Still, it rained: this was mid-July in upstate New York, lush and green and wet as a rain forest.

Krista got sick from the humidity and the wet in the air, saying it made her lungs feel clotty. Heather refrained from pointing out that her lungs might feel better if she stopped smoking a pack of menthol cigarettes a day. Krista called in sick to work and instead lay on the couch in a daze of cold medicine, like something dead and bloated dragged up by the ocean.

At least Heather could use the car. The library had reopened. She dropped Lily there.

'Want me to pick you up later?' she asked.

Lily was back to being snotty. 'I'm not a baby,' she said as she slid out of the car, not even bothering with the umbrella Heather had brought for her. 'I'll bus it.'

'What about—?' Before Heather could remind her to take the umbrella, Lily had slammed the door and was dashing for the library entrance through a slow ooze of dark puddles.

Despite the rain, Heather was in a decent mood. Lily was

almost twelve. It was *normal* for her to be a brat. It was maybe even a good thing. It showed she was growing up okay, the way that everyone else did – that maybe she wouldn't be messed up just because she'd grown up in Fresh Pines with ants parading all over the spoons and Krista fumigating the house.

And there were still no police knocking on her door, still not a single, solitary breath about Panic.

Work was hard: Anne wanted her to muck the stables, and afterward they had to recaulk a portion of the basement, where the rain was coming in and the walls were speckled with mold. Heather was shocked when Anne stopped her for the day. It was nearly five p.m., but Heather hadn't noticed time passing, had barely looked up. The rain was worse than ever. It came down in whole sheets, like the quivering blades of a giant guillotine.

While Anne was preparing her a cup of tea, Heather checked her phone for the first time in hours, and her stomach went to liquid and pooled straight down to her feet. She'd missed twelve calls from Lily.

Her throat squeezed up so tight she could hardly breathe. She punched Lily's number immediately. Her cell phone went straight to voice mail.

'What's the matter, Heather?' Anne was standing at the oven, her gray hair frizzing around her face, like a strange halo.

Heather said, 'I have to go.'

Afterward, she didn't remember getting into the car or backing it down the driveway; she didn't remember the drive to the library, but suddenly she was there. She parked the car but left the door open. Some of the puddles were ankle deep, but she hardly noticed. She sprinted to the entrance; the library had been closed for an hour.

She called Lily's name, circled the parking lot, searching for her. She scanned the streets as she drove, imagining all the terrible things that might have happened to Lily – she'd been hurt, snatched, killed – and trying to stop herself from losing it, throwing up or breaking down.

Finally, she had no choice but to go home. She'd have to call the police.

Heather fought back another wave of panic. This was it, the real thing.

The road leading to Fresh Pines was full of ruts, sucking black mud, deep water. Heather bumped through it, tires spinning and grinding. The place looked sadder than usual: the rain was beating fists on the trailers, pulling down wind chimes, and overflowing outdoor fire pits.

Heather hadn't even stopped the car when she spotted Lily: huddled underneath a skinny birch tree missing most of its leaves, only fifteen feet away from the trailer steps, arms wrapped around her legs, shivering. Heather must have parked because all of a sudden she was rocketing out of the car, splashing through the water, taking Lily in her arms.

'Lily!' Heather couldn't hug her sister tight enough. Here, here, here. Safe. 'Are you okay? Are you all right? What happened?'

'I'm cold.' Lily's voice was muffled. She spoke into Heather's left shoulder. Heather's heart seized up; she would have spun the world in reverse for a blanket.

'Come on,' she said, pulling away. 'Let's get you inside.'

Lily reared back, like a bucking horse. Her eyes went huge, wild. 'I won't go in there,' she said. 'I don't want to go in there!'

'Lily.' Heather blinked rain out of her eyes, crouching down so she was eye level with her sister. Lily's lips were ringed with blue. God. How long had she been out here? 'What's going on?'

'Mom told me to go away,' Lily said. Her voice had turned small, broken. 'She – she told me to play outside.'

Something inside Heather cracked, and in that moment she was conscious that all her life she had been building up walls and defenses in preparation for something like this; behind them, the pressure had been mounting, mounting. Now the dam broke, and she was flooded, drowning in rage and hate.

'Come on,' she said. She was surprised she still sounded the same, when inside of her was a sucking blackness, a furious noise. She took Lily's hand. 'You can sit in the car, okay? I'll turn on the heat. You'll be nice and dry.'

She brought Lily to the car. There was an old T-shirt in the back – Krista's, reeking of smoke – but it was dry, at least. She helped Lily wriggle out of her wet shirt. She untied Lily's shoes for her, and peeled off her wet socks, then made Lily press her feet up to the vents where the heat had begun to blow. The whole time Lily was limp, obedient, as if all the life had been washed out of her. Heather moved mechanically.

'I'll be right back,' she told Lily. She felt detached from the words, as though she wasn't the one speaking. The anger was drumming out the knowledge of everything else.

Boom, boom, boom.

There was music coming from the trailer, practically shaking the walls. The lights were on too, although the blinds were down; she could see a figure swaying in silhouette, maybe dancing. She hadn't noticed before because she'd been too worried about Lily. She kept seeing her sister huddled underneath the pathetic birch, practically the single tree that Fresh Pines boasted.

Mom told me to go away. She told me to play outside.
Boom, boom, boom.

She was at the door. Locked. From inside, she heard a shriek of laughter. Somehow she fit the key in the lock; that must mean she wasn't shaking. *Strange,* she thought, and also: *Maybe I could have won Panic after all.*

She pushed the door open and stepped inside.

There were three of them: Krista, Bo, and Maureen, from Lot 99. They froze, and Heather froze too. She was seized momentarily by the sense that she'd entered a play and had forgotten all her lines – she couldn't breathe, didn't know what to do. The lights were high, bright. They looked like actors, all three of them – actors you see too close. They were too made up. But the makeup was horrible. It looked as though it was beginning to melt, slowly deforming their faces. Their eyes were bright, glittering: doll eyes.

Heather took in everything at once: the blue haze of smoke. The empty beer bottles, the overflowing cups used as ashtrays, the single bottle of Georgi vodka, half-empty.

And the small blue plastic plate on the table, still faintly outlined with the imprint of the *Sesame Street* characters – Lily's old plate – now covered with thin lines of fine white powder.

All of it hit Heather like a physical blow, a quick sock to the stomach. Her world went black for a second. The plate. Lily's plate.

Then the moment passed. Krista brought a cigarette unsteadily to her lips, nearly missing. 'Heather Lynn,' she slurred. She patted her shirt, her breasts, as though expecting to find a lighter there. 'What are you doing, baby? Why are you staring at me like I'm a—'

Heather lunged. Before her mother finished speaking, before

she could think about what she was doing, all of the rage traveled down into her arms and legs and she picked up the blue plate, crisscrossed with powder like it had been scarred by something, and threw.

Maureen screamed and Bo shouted. Krista barely managed to duck. She tried to right herself and, staggering backward, managed to land on Maureen's lap, in the armchair. This made Maureen scream even louder. The plate collided against the wall with a thud, and the air was momentarily full of white powder, like an indoor snow. It would have been funny if it weren't so horrible.

'What the hell?' Bo took two steps toward Heather and for a moment, she thought he might hit her. But he just stood there, fists clenched, red-faced and enraged. 'What the *hell*?'

Krista fought to her feet. 'Who in the goddamn do you think you are?'

Heather was glad that they were separated by the coffee table. Otherwise, she wasn't sure what she would do. She wanted to kill Krista. Really kill her. 'You're disgusting.' Her voice sounded mangled, like something had wrapped around her vocal cords.

'Get out.' The color was rising in Krista's face. Her voice, too, was rising, and she was shaking as though something awful was going to detonate inside her. 'Get out! Do you hear me? Get out!' She reached for the vodka bottle and threw it. Fortunately, she was slow. Heather sidestepped it easily. She heard shattering glass and felt the splash of liquid. Bo got his arms around Krista. He managed to restrain her. She was still shrieking, writhing like an animal, face red and twisted and awful.

And suddenly all of Heather's anger dissipated. She felt

absolutely nothing. No pain. No anger. No fear. Nothing but disgust. She felt, weirdly, as if she were floating above the scene, hovering in her own body.

She turned and went to her bedroom. She checked her top drawer first, in the plastic jewelry box where she kept her earrings. Everything was gone but forty dollars. Of course. Her mom had stolen it.

This didn't bring a fresh wave of anger, only a new kind of disgust. Animals. They were animals, and Krista was the worst of them.

She pocketed the twenties and moved quickly through the room, stuffing things in Lily's backpack: shoes, pants, shirts, underwear. When the backpack was full, she bundled things up in one of the comforters. They would need a blanket, anyway. And toothbrushes. She remembered reading in a magazine once that toothbrushes were the number one item travelers forgot to pack. But she wouldn't forget. She was calm, thinking straight. She had it all together.

She slid the backpack onto one of her shoulders – it was so small, she couldn't fit it correctly. Poor Lily. She wanted to get food from the kitchen, but that would mean walking past her mom and Bo and Maureen. She'd have to skip it. There probably wasn't much she could use, anyway.

At the last second she took the rose off her dresser, the one Bishop had made her from metal and wire. It would be good luck.

She hefted the blanket in her arms, now heavy with all the clothing and shoes it contained, and shuffled sideways out of the bedroom door. She'd been worried her mom would try and stop her, but she shouldn't have been. Krista was sitting on the couch, crying, with Maureen's arms around her. Her

hair was a stringy mess. Heather heard her say, '. . . did everything . . . on my own.' Only half the words were audible. She
was too messed up to speak clearly. Bo was gone. He'd probably split, since the drugs were nothing but carpet crumbs
now. Maybe he'd left to get more.

Heather pushed out the door. It didn't matter. She'd never
see Bo again. She'd never see her mother, or Maureen, or the
inside of that trailer again. For one second, she could have
sobbed, going down the porch steps. Never again – the idea
filled her with a relief so strong, it almost turned her knees to
water and made her trip.

But she couldn't cry, not yet. She had to be strong for Lily.

Lily had fallen asleep in the front seat, her mouth open, her
hair feathering slightly in the heat. Finally her lips weren't blue
anymore, and she was no longer shivering.

She didn't open her eyes until they were just bouncing out
of the entrance to the Pines and onto Route 22.

'Heather?' she said in a small voice.

'What's up, Billy?' Heather tried to smile and couldn't.

'I don't want to go back there.' Lily turned and rested her
forehead against the window. In the glass's reflection, her face
was narrow and pale, like a tapered flame.

Heather tightened her fingers on the wheel. 'We're not going
back there,' she said. Weirdly, the words made the taste of sick
come up. 'We're never going back, okay? I promise.'

'Where will we go?' Lily asked.

Heather reached over and squeezed Lily's knee. Her jeans
had finally dried. 'We'll figure something out. Okay? We're
going to be just fine.' The rain was still coming down in sheets;
the car carved waves in the road, sending liquid rivers sloshing
toward the gutters. 'You trust me, right?' Heather asked.

Lily nodded without turning her face away from the window.

'We're going to be fine,' Heather repeated, and returned both hands to the wheel, gripping tightly.

They couldn't, she realized, go to Bishop's or Nat's. She'd taken her mom's car and had no intention of returning it, which counted as stealing. And her friends' houses would be the first place her mom would think of looking when she sobered up and realized what had happened.

Would she call the police? Would they track Heather down? Maybe her mom would convince them that Heather was a delinquent, and they would try to pin the fire on her.

But there was no point in worrying about that yet.

No one could know. It came down to that. She and Lily would have to be very, very careful for the next few weeks. As soon as they had enough money to leave Carp, they would. And until then, they had to hide. They'd have to hide the car, too, and use it only at night.

The idea came to her suddenly: Meth Row. The whole road was cluttered with old cars and abandoned houses. No one would notice one more shitty car parked there.

Lily had fallen asleep again and was snoring quietly. Meth Row looked even bleaker than usual. The rain had turned the pitted road to sludge, and Heather had trouble just keeping the wheel from jerking under her hands. It was hard to tell which houses were occupied and which weren't, but she finally found a spot next to a storage shed and an old Buick, stripped nearly to its metal frame, where she could angle the car so it was mostly unseen from the road.

She turned off the engine. No point in wasting gas. They'd have to be careful about wasting anything now.

They'd be more comfortable in the backseat, but since Lily

was already asleep and Heather doubted she would sleep at all – it wasn't even six o'clock – she reached into the back and shook out all the things from the comforter. Stuff that had only an hour ago been littering their beds, the floor of their bedroom. Their home.

Homeless. It was the first time the word occurred to her, and she pushed it out of her mind. It was an ugly word, a word that smelled.

Runaways was better, a little more glam.

She spread the comforter over Lily, careful not to wake her. She found a hoodie in the back and put it on over her shirt, pulled up the hood, cinched the drawstrings tight. Thankfully it was summer and wouldn't get *too* cold.

It occurred to her that she should turn her cell phone off too, to conserve battery power. But before she did, she typed out a text to Nat and Dodge. She included Bishop too. Like he'd said, he was in it, one way or another.

Changed my mind, she wrote. *I'm back in.*

She was playing for keeps now. For Lily. Forget the promise she'd made to Nat. The money would be hers, and hers alone.

That night, long after Heather had finally drifted off, head back in the front seat of the Taurus – when Nat was curled up in bed with her computer, searching for funny videos – when even the bars were shutting down and the people who wanted to drink were forced to do it outside, or in the parking lot of 7-Eleven – Ellie Hayes was woken up by two masked figures. They hauled her roughly to her feet and handcuffed her wrists in front of her body, as if she were a convict.

Her parents were gone for the week – the players knew what they were doing. Her older brother, Roger, heard the noise and the scuffling and burst into the hall, holding a base-ball bat. But Ellie managed to cry out to him.

'It's Panic!' she said.

Roger lowered the baseball bat, shook his head, returned to his room. He, too, had played.

Ellie's biggest fear, other than floods, was enclosure, and she was relieved when instead of being packed in the trunk, she was guided roughly into the backseat of a car she didn't recognize.

They drove for what seemed like forever – long enough that she began to get bored and fell asleep. Then the car stopped, and she saw a vast, empty parking lot, and a fence enclosed by barbed wire. Before the headlights cut, she saw a weathered sign tacked to a sad, saggy-looking building.

WELCOME TO THE DENNY SWIMMING POOL.
HOURS 9 A.M.–DUSK, MEMORIAL DAY TO LABOR DAY.

The padlock on the gates had been left undone. Ellie remem-bered, as they passed through it, that Ray Hanrahan had done maintenance at the Denny Swimming Pool last summer. Could he be in on this?

Across the wet grass, the squelching mud, to the edge of the pool, which sat glimmering slickly in the moonlight, faintly lit up from below, electric and improbable.

The fear came rushing back all at once. 'You have to be kidding me.' She was at the edge of the deep end, trying to backpedal. But she couldn't move. They had her tightly. Something metal bit into the palm of her hands, and she curled her fingers instinctively around it, too frightened to think or wonder what it was. 'How do you expect me to—?'

She didn't get to finish before she was pushed, roughly, headfirst into the water.

Flood. A flood of water everywhere: mouth, eyes, nose.

She was underwater for a little more than a minute before she was hauled roughly to the surface, but she would afterward swear it was at least five, or seven. Endless seconds of her heartbeat thudding in her ears, her lungs screaming for air, her legs kicking for purchase. So many seconds of panic – so complete, so all-consuming, it wasn't until she was once again in the open air, taking deep, grateful breaths, she realized that all along she had been clutching tightly to the small metal key that fitted her handcuffs.

Dodge's gamble at last paid off. In the morning, the story of Ellie spread, and by noon the betting slips had once again appeared. This time, they were passed from hand to hand, secretively, cautiously. Zev Keller and Ellie Hayes had both failed their individual challenges. They were out of the game. Colin Akinson, too. He'd been the first to flee the Graybill house – rumor was he hadn't stopped running until he was almost to Massachusetts.

Dodge, Ray, Heather, and Nat were still in. So were Harold Lee, Kim Hollister, and Derek Klieg.

Only seven players left.

WEDNESDAY, JULY 27

dodge

THERE WAS NO JOY LEFT IN THE GAME – NO LIGHTNESS OR humor at all. Panic, as far as Dodge knew, had never been this serious. It had never been played with so much secretiveness, either. This was about more than getting busted for continuing a game. The cops were still trying to pin the fire at the Graybill house, and Little Bill's death, on someone.

Even the judges had, apparently, lost their sense of humor. The next email that arrived, several days after Ellie had been eliminated from the game, was bleakly to-the-point.

Malden Plaza, I-87. 9:00 p.m. Wednesday.

Bishop drove. It felt almost routine: Heather sat shotgun, Nat and Dodge were in the back. Nat spent the whole drive tapping the window with a knuckle, unconsciously beating out her own private rhythm. Dodge could almost believe they were just heading on some kind of late-night adventure to the mall. Except that Heather looked exhausted, and kept yawning, and Bishop hardly said a word except to ask her, in a low voice, what was wrong.

'What do you *think* is wrong?' Heather replied. Dodge didn't want to eavesdrop, but he couldn't help it.

'Your mom called,' Bishop said after a pause. 'She said you haven't been home.'

'I'm just staying at Anne's for a few days. I'm fine.'

'She said you took the car.'

'So now you're on her side?'

Bishop must have gone to Little Bill's funeral. Dodge recognized the folded memorial pamphlet, featuring a winged angel, now hanging on a ribbon from his rearview mirror. Like a charm, or a talisman. Weird that he'd felt the need to hang it. Bishop didn't strike Dodge as superstitious. Then again, Dodge didn't really get Bishop. He didn't, for example, understand why he seemed to feel he was part of the game, why he seemed to feel guilty for Bill Kelly's death.

When they passed the Columbia County water towers, Dodge looked out and remembered the night of the first raid, when he, Nat, and Heather had hid from the cops. He felt a sudden wrench of grief, for the way time always goes forward, relentlessly. It was like floodwater: it left only clutter in its wake.

The sky was choked with masses of dark clouds, but it had stopped raining at last. Impossible to tell, actually, where the sun was coming from. A thick beam of light, singular and strange, cut across the road. But the drive to Malden Plaza was long – they had to loop around to get to the northbound side – and before they'd arrived, the sun had set.

There were a few dozen cars in the lot, most of them hugging up as close to the McDonald's as possible, plus a couple of eighteen-wheelers, trucks that must have been on a run from Albany to Canada. From the opposite side of the lot, Dodge watched a family emerging from the big swinging doors, carrying paper bags of fast food and large soda cups. He wondered where they were off to. Somewhere better than here, probably.

The players had parked as far from the building as possible, at the edge of the lot, where the trees were creeping close to the pavement and it was much darker. Seven players left and only two dozen spectators. Dodge was kind of surprised that Diggin had bothered to show up. Standing under the tall, stiff-necked streetlamps, he looked kind of green, as if he was in danger of puking.

'Rules are simple.' Diggin practically had to shout over the roar of traffic behind him. I-87, separated from the parking lot by only a flimsy, shin-high divider, was a six-lane mega-highway. 'Each of you has to cross. The five who cross fastest move on. The other two don't.'

'I'll go first.' Ray stepped forward. He had avoided even glancing at Dodge. There was something like a truce between them, at least temporarily. It was funny. Ray was probably the guy Dodge hated most in the world, besides Luke. And yet Ray was the guy who knew more of Dodge's secrets than anyone. 'I want to get this over with.'

'Wait.' Diggin extracted a strip of black fabric from his pocket and shook it out. He truly looked miserable. 'You have to wear this.'

'What is that?' Ray asked, even though it was obviously a blindfold.

Nat and Heather exchanged a look. Dodge knew what they

were thinking without having to ask. There was always a twist. The game was never easy.

Diggin hesitated. For a second, it looked as though he was going to attempt to tie the blindfold on Ray himself.

Ray scowled at him. 'Give me that,' he said, and snatched the blindfold from Diggin. Diggin backed off quickly, obviously relieved. Ray put the fabric over his eyes and knotted it behind his head.

'Happy now?' he said, to no one in particular.

Dodge stepped forward, so he was standing directly in front of Ray. He threw a punch, stopping a few inches short of Ray's nose. Nat gasped and Diggin shouted. But Ray didn't even flinch.

'It's all right,' Dodge said. 'He can't see shit.'

'Don't trust me, Mason?' Ray's mouth curled into a smile.

'Not even a little,' Dodge said.

Diggin had to help guide Ray to the divider that separated the parking lot from the narrow patch of grass and gravel that ran along the highway. Trucks were thundering past, spitting exhaust and roaring heat. A car blew its horn as Ray fumbled over the divider, and Dodge imagined a sudden swerve, the headlights swollen, freezing Ray in place, the shudder of the impact.

But that would come later.

'Time,' Diggin shouted. He had his phone out. For the first time, he noticed that Bishop was standing some ways apart, his lips moving as though in silent prayer. His face was incredible: anguished, twisted.

And in that moment, Dodge had a suspicion. More like an intuition.

But he dismissed the thought quickly. Impossible.

'Ten seconds down,' Diggin announced. Dodge turned his eyes back to the highway. Ray was still hesitating, swaying like a drunk, like he was hoping momentum would unglue his feet. A truck blasted a horn, and he jerked backward. The sound rolled and echoed through the night air, distorted by distance to an alien cry. Motion was noise: Dodge closed his eyes and heard the fizz of the tires on the road, the thud of bass and music, engines grinding and spitting, the rush of air when a car blew by. He opened his eyes again.

'Twenty seconds!' Diggin's voice had gone shrill.

There was a sudden break in the traffic. Four, five seconds – in all six lanes, the road was clear. Ray sensed it and ran. He barreled straight into the divider on the other side of the road and nearly face-planted. But it didn't matter. He'd done it. He whipped off the blindfold and waved it above his head, victorious. The whole thing had taken him twenty-seven seconds.

He had to wait for another break in the traffic to cross, but this time he did so at a jog. He was showing off.

'Who's next?' Diggin said. 'Let's get this over with before—' Another truck blasted by, whipping away the rest of his words.

'I'll go.' Dodge stepped forward. Ray dangled the blindfold from one hand. For a second, their eyes met. They were joined now, more than ever.

'Don't choke,' Ray said in a low voice. Dodge snatched the blindfold from him.

'Don't worry about me,' he said.

The cloth was thick and totally opaque, like something you'd fashion a tarp out of. Once Dodge put it over his eyes, he was completely blind, and for a moment he felt a tightness in his chest, the overwhelming sense of disorientation and dizziness, like when you wake up from a nightmare in an unfamiliar place. He focused on the sounds: trucks, music, the fizz of the tires, and gradually he could map out the space in his mind. Funny how just being without sight could leave him feeling so exposed, raw. Anyone could rush at him and he'd never know.

He felt two soft hands slip around his wrist.

'Be careful,' Nat whispered.

He didn't answer, just fumbled to touch her face, hoping he wouldn't accidentally get her boob instead. Kind of hoping he would, too.

'All right,' he announced in what he hoped was Diggin's direction. 'I'm ready.'

As he had done with Ray, Diggin took his arm and guided him to the low metal divider, and instructed him to climb it. Then Dodge was standing blind on the side of the road, while cars and semis roared past him. The wind blew hot and stinking with exhaust, and the ground trembled from the motion of the crushing wheels. Horns screamed out and faded.

Dodge's heart was going hard and his mouth was dry. He hadn't expected to be so afraid. His ears were full of a pounding rhythm – he couldn't tell if it was noise from the highway or the echo of his heart. He barely heard Diggin call time. Shit. He couldn't hear – how was he going to know when to cross?

What if he tripped? His legs felt liquid and unstable – if he tried to walk, they would collapse, get tangled up. He pictured Nat's hands, the way she'd tilted her face to his when he kissed her. He imagined Dayna, imagined her chair pushed next to the window, the sun flooding the room, her legs growing, thickening, sprouting again into strong, muscled calves.

The pounding in his ears receded. He could breathe again. And suddenly he realized it was quiet. No fizz of tires, no honking, no roar of an engine bearing down on him. A break.

He ran.

Pavement, and then a narrow strip of grass, which marked the space that divided the different sides of the highway. He should have stopped and listened again, just to be sure, but he couldn't – if he stopped, he'd never go again. He had to keep moving. The wind was rushing in his ears and his blood was on fire. Suddenly he felt a searing pain in his shins and he jerked forward. He'd reached the divider on the other side.

He'd passed.

He ripped off the blindfold and turned around. He thought Nat and Heather were cheering, but he wasn't sure – two cars went by him, a twin blur, and although he could tell they were shouting, he couldn't hear what they said. Underneath the streetlamp, they looked like actors on a stage, or tiny figurines, set up for display – and the cars, shining as they passed through the light, like toy models of the real thing.

He still felt kind of dizzy. He waited for another break in the traffic, then crossed back at a slow jog. He wanted to move faster, but his legs resisted. He could barely lift them to climb over the divider.

Diggin patted him on the shoulder and Heather grabbed his arm. He was glad. Otherwise he might have collapsed.

'Nineteen seconds!' Diggin said.

And Heather kept saying, 'Awesome. Awesome.'

Heather volunteered to go next. Something had happened to her in the past few days – something had changed. She'd always been pretty, Dodge thought – sturdy-looking and dependable, like someone in an advertisement about deodorant.

A little awkward, too – always holding herself really carefully, like she was worried if she didn't pay attention she'd knock someone or something over. He hadn't gone to prom, but he'd seen pictures on Facebook, and Heather had stood out; slouching a little so she wouldn't be too much taller than Matt, wearing some ruffled pink thing that didn't suit her at all, and trying to smile through her discomfort.

But there was nothing awkward about her now. She was serious, straight-backed, focused. She barely hesitated at the edge of the road. As soon as there was a break, she ran. Nat gasped.

'There's a car—' she said. Her fingers tightened on Dodge's arm.

There *was* a car – northbound traffic, speeding toward her. It must have caught her in its headlights just as she crossed into the lane, because the driver sounded his horn, three quick blasts.

'Jesus.' Bishop was frozen, white-faced.

'Heather!' Nat screamed.

But Heather kept moving, and she reached safety just as the car blew over the spot where she'd been standing only a few seconds earlier. The driver gave four more furious blasts on the horn. Heather whipped off the blindfold and stood, chest heaving, at the side of the road. For a while she was lost to view in a surge of sudden traffic: two trucks passing simultaneously from opposite directions, a stream of cars.

When Heather crossed back, Diggin threw an arm around her shoulders. 'Seventeen seconds!' he crowed. 'Fastest one yet. You're safe.'

'Thanks,' she said. She was out of breath. As she passed under the streetlamp, she looked truly beautiful: hair long and tangled down her back, high cheekbones and glittering eyes.

'Good job,' Dodge said.

Heather nodded at him.

'Heathbar! I was so scared for you! That car.' Nat threw her arms around Heather's neck. She had to stand on her tiptoes.

'It's not that bad, Nat,' Heather said. For a second, she kept her eyes on Dodge. Something passed between them. He thought it was a warning.

Kim Hollister went next, and she was unlucky. As soon as she took her place blindfolded at the side of the road, there was a blast of traffic from both directions. But even after it cleared, she stayed where she was, hesitating, obviously afraid.

'Go!' Diggin shouted. 'You're fine! Go.'

'No fair,' Ray said. 'No fair. That's fucking cheating.'

They started to argue, but it didn't matter anyway; Kim still hadn't moved. Finally she screeched, 'Be quiet! Please. I can't hear anything. Please.'

It took a few more seconds before she shuffled onto the road, and almost immediately she backed up again.

'Did you hear that?' Her voice was shrill in the quiet. 'Is that a car?'

By the time she made it across, eighty-two seconds had elapsed.

It was Natalie's turn next. Suddenly she turned to him, eyes shining. He realized she was on the verge of tears.

'Do you think he's watching?' Nat whispered. Dodge thought she must be talking about God.

'Who?' he said.

'Bill Kelly.' A spasm passed over her face.

'There's no one watching us,' Dodge said. 'No one but the judges, anyway.'

His eyes met Bishop's across the lot. And again, just for a minute, he wondered.

FRIDAY, JULY 29

dodge

DODGE HAD BEEN HOPING NAT'S BIRTHDAY PARTY WOULD BE small, and he was disappointed when he pulled his bike up to Bishop's house and saw a dozen cars fitted together like Tetris pieces in the only part of the yard not dominated by junk. There was music playing from somewhere, and lanterns had been placed all around the yard, perched on various objects like metallic fireflies settling down to rest.

'You came!' Nat weaved toward him, holding a paper cup. Beer sloshed on his shoe, and he realized she was already drunk. She was wearing lots of makeup and a tiny dress, and she looked frighteningly beautiful, like someone much older. Her eyes were bright, almost like she was on something. He was aware that she had just been talking to a group of guys he didn't know – they, too, looked older, and were now staring at him – and felt suddenly uncomfortable.

She saw him looking and waved a hand. 'Don't worry about them,' she said. Her words were slurring together. 'Some guys

I know from a bar in Kingston. I only invited them because they brought the booze. I'm so glad you're here.'

Dodge had Nat's present wrapped in tissue paper in his pocket. He wanted to give it to her but not here, while people were watching. He wanted to tell her, too, that he was sorry about Panic. Nat had frozen up at the side of the highway and taken a little over a minute to cross. Just like that, the game was over for her.

On the way home from the highway challenge, Nat had barely said a word, just sat stiffly next to him with tears running down her face. No one had spoken. Dodge had been annoyed at Bishop and Heather. They were her best friends. They were supposed to know what to say to make her feel better.

He had felt helpless, as frightened as he had while standing on that highway with the blindfold.

But Nat was already hauling him off toward the back of the house. 'Come get a drink, okay? And say hi to everyone.'

At the back of the house a large grill was letting off thick clouds of smoke that smelled like meat and charcoal. An old dude was pushing around some burgers on it, holding a beer in one hand. Dodge thought it might have been Bishop's dad – they had the same nose, the same floppy hair, although the man's was gray – and was surprised. In school he'd always thought of Bishop as kind of a dork, well-meaning but just too nice to be interesting. He'd imagined Bishop's family would be of the mom-dad-sister-older-brother-picket-fence variety. Not some guy with a beer grilling in the middle of towers of rusting junk.

But that was another thing you learned when playing Panic: people would surprise you. They would knock you on your ass. It was practically the only thing you could count on.

Kids from school were standing around in little groups, or using some of the old furniture and gutted car frames as makeshift chairs. They were all staring at Dodge, some with curiosity and some with open hostility, and it wasn't until then that he realized none of the other Panic players had been invited, except for Heather. That's when it hit him that there really weren't many Panic players left. Just five.

And he was one of them.

The two things – the fact that Nat was holding his hand, and the fact that he was getting so close – sent a thrill up his spine.

'The keg's over there, behind the old motorcycle.' Nat giggled. She gestured with her cup, sending another bit of beer sloshing over the rim, and he remembered suddenly the time she'd called him Dave at homecoming last year. His stomach tightened. He hated parties, never felt comfortable at them. 'I'll be back, okay? I have to circulate. It's kinda my party, after all.'

She kissed him – on the cheek, he noticed, and of course then again on the other cheek – and quickly disappeared, blending into a knot of people standing around the keg. Without Nat next to him, he felt like he was back in the halls at school, except this time, instead of everyone ignoring him, everyone was staring. When he spotted Heather, he could have run up and kissed her.

She saw him at the same time and waved him over. She was sitting on the hood of what Dodge could only imagine was one of Bishop's projects: a Pinto junker, wheel-less and propped up on cinder blocks. He could count a half-dozen cars, in various states of construction and deconstruction, just from where he was standing.

'Hey.' Heather was drinking a Coke. She looked tired. 'I didn't know you would be here.'

Dodge shrugged. He wasn't sure what that meant. Maybe Nat had only invited him at the last minute? 'Didn't want to miss the big birthday,' was all he said.

'Nat's trashed already,' Heather said with a short laugh. She looked away, squinting. Again he was struck by the change that had come over her this summer. She was thinning out, sharpening, and her beauty was becoming more pronounced. Like she'd been wearing an invisibility cloak her whole life, and now it was coming off.

Dodge leaned against the hood and fumbled in his pocket for his cigarettes. He didn't even feel like smoking – he just wanted something to do with his hands. 'How's Lily?' he asked.

She looked at him sharply. 'She's fine,' she said slowly. Then: 'She's inside, watching TV.'

Dodge nodded. The day before he'd been smoking a cigarette in Meth Row when he'd heard the sound of someone singing behind the shed where he usually kept his bike. Curious, he circled around to the back.

And there was Heather.

Butt-naked.

She'd shouted and he'd turned quickly away, but not before he noticed she was washing herself with the hose from Dot's Diner, the one the kitchen boys used to spray down the alley in the evenings. He saw a car, her car, with clothes drying on its hood; and a girl who must have been Heather's sister, sitting in the grass, reading.

'Don't tell,' Heather had said.

Dodge had kept his back to her. One of the pairs of underwear had blown off the hood and onto the ground; he kept his eyes fixed on it. It was full-butt underwear, patterned with strawberries, faded. Next to it, he'd seen two toothbrushes and a curled-up tube of toothpaste sitting on an overturned bucket, and several pairs of shoes lined up neatly in the dirt. He wondered how long they'd been camping out there.

'I won't,' he had said without turning around.

And he wouldn't. That was another thing Dodge liked about secrets: they bonded people together. 'How long you think you can keep it up?' he asked now.

'As long as it takes to win,' she replied.

He looked at her – face so serious, so dead set – and felt a sudden surge of something like joy. Understanding. That's what it was; he and Heather understood each other.

'I like you, Heather,' he said. 'You're all right.'

She briefly scanned his face, as if to verify that he wasn't laughing at her. Then she smiled. 'Right back at you, Dodge.'

Nat reappeared, carrying a bottle of tequila. 'Take a shot with me, Heather.'

Heather made a face. 'Tequila?'

'Come on,' Nat said, pouting. Her words were more slurred than ever, but her eyes kept their strange, unnatural brightness – like something not quite human. 'It's my birthday.'

Heather shook her head. Nat laughed.

'I don't believe it.' Her voice was getting louder. 'You'll play Panic, but you're afraid of taking a shot.'

'Shhhh.' Heather's face turned red.

'She wasn't even supposed to play,' Nat said, pointing the bottle at Heather, as though addressing an audience. And people *were* listening. Dodge saw that they were turning in Heather's direction, smirking, whispering.

'Come on, Nat. You're not supposed to talk about the game, remember?' he said, but Nat ignored him.

'I was gonna play,' Nat announced. 'I did play. Not anymore. She – you – sabotaged me. You sabotaged me.' She turned to Heather.

Heather stared at her for a second. 'You're drunk,' she said matter-of-factly, then slid off the hood of the car.

Nat tried to grab her. 'I was just kidding,' she said. But Heather kept walking. 'Come on, Heath. I was just fucking around.'

'I'm going to find Bishop,' Heather said without turning.

Nat leaned up against the car, next to Dodge. She uncapped the bottle of tequila, took a sip, and made a face. 'Some birthday,' she muttered.

Dodge could smell her skin, the alcohol on her breath and strawberry shampoo in her hair. He was aching to touch her. Instead he shoved his hands in his pocket and felt for the gift. He knew he had to give it to her now, before he chickened out or she got even drunker.

'Look, Nat. Is there somewhere we could go? I mean, to be alone for a minute?' Realizing she might think he was going to try to feel her up or something, he rushed on: 'I have something for you.' And he showed her the little tissue-paper-wrapped box, hoping she wouldn't care that it had gotten squashed in his pocket.

Her face changed. She smiled huge, showing off her perfect little white teeth, and set the bottle of tequila down. 'Dodge, you didn't have to,' she said. And then: 'Come on, I know somewhere we can go.'

Just beyond the back porch was an area dedicated to what looked like lawn decorations: towering limestone statues of various mythical figures Dodge should probably know but didn't; limestone benches and birdbaths full of standing water, moss, and leaves. Because of the statues and the porch it was concealed from view, and as they entered the semicircular enclosure, the music was muffled.

'Go ahead,' he said, passing her the box. 'Open it.'

He thought he might puke. What if she hated it? Finally she got the wrapping off, and she opened the little box and stood there staring at it: a dark cord of velvet and a small, crystal butterfly charm, light dazzling from its wings, resting neatly on a bunch of cotton.

She stared at it for so long, he thought she must hate it, and then he thought he really would be sick. The necklace had cost him three full days of the cash he got stocking shelves.

'If you want to return it . . . ,' he started to say. But then she looked up and he saw that she was crying.

'It's beautiful,' she said. 'I love it.' And before he knew what was happening, she reached for him and drew him down to her and kissed him. Her lips tasted like salt and tequila.

When she pulled back, he felt dizzy. He'd kissed girls before but not like that. Usually he was too stressed about what their tongue was doing or whether he was using too much pressure or too little. But with Nat he forgot to think, or even breathe, and now his vision was clouded with black spots. 'Listen,' he blurted out. 'I want you to know I'll still honor the split. If I win, I mean. You can still take your share of the money.'

She stiffened suddenly, almost as if he'd slapped her. For a second she stood there, rigid. Then she shoved the jewelry box back at him. 'I can't take this,' she said. 'I can't accept it.'

Dodge felt like he'd just inhaled a bowling ball. 'What do you mean?'

'I mean I don't want it,' she said, and forced the box into his hand. 'We're not together, okay? I mean, I like you and all but . . . I'm seeing someone else. It isn't right.'

Cold, cold: washing through his whole body. He was freezing, confused and furious. He didn't feel like himself, didn't sound like himself either, as he heard himself say, 'Who is it?'

She had turned away from him. 'It doesn't matter,' she said. 'No one you know.'

'You kissed me,' he said. 'You kissed me, you made me think—'

She shook her head. She still wouldn't look at him. 'It was for the game. Okay? I wanted you to help me win. That's all.'

That voice he didn't recognize came out of his mouth again. 'I don't believe you.' The words sounded thin and flimsy.

She kept speaking, almost as if he wasn't there. 'But I don't need Panic. I don't need you. I don't need Heather. Kevin says I've got potential in front of the camera. He says—'

'Kevin?' Something clicked in Dodge's brain, and his stomach opened up. 'That scumbag you met at the mall?'

'He's not a scumbag.' Now she turned around to face him. She was shaking. Her fists were balled and her eyes were bright and there was wetness on her cheeks and it broke his heart. He still wanted to kiss her. He hated her. 'He's legit. He believes in me. He said he would help me . . .'

The cold in Dodge's chest had turned into a hard fist. He could feel it beating against his ribs, threatening to explode out through his skin. 'I'm sure he did,' he said, practically spitting. 'Let me guess. All you had to do was show him your tits—'

'Shut up,' she whispered.

'Maybe let him feel you up for a while. Or did you have to spread your legs, too?' As soon as he said it, he wished the words back into his mouth.

Nat stiffened as though a shock had run through her. And he could tell from her face – the guilt and the sadness and the sorrow – that she did, she had.

'Nat.' He could barely say her name. He wanted to say he was sorry, and he *was* sorry for her too, for what she'd done. He wanted to tell her that he believed in her and thought she was beautiful.

'Go away,' she whispered.

'Please.' He started to reach for her.

She stumbled backward, nearly tripping on the grass. 'Go,' she said. Her eyes locked on his for a minute. He saw two dark holes, like wounds; then she whirled around and was gone.

heather

BISHOP HAD A TRAMPOLINE; OR AT LEAST, HE HAD A TRAMPOLINE frame. The nylon had long ago disintegrated and been replaced with a heavy canvas tarp, stretched taut. Heather wasn't surprised to find him there, hiding out from the rest of the guests. He'd never been super social. She wasn't either. It was one of the things that bonded them.

'Having a good time?' she asked, as she maneuvered onto the canvas next to him. Bishop smelled like cinnamon, and a little like butter.

He shrugged. When he smiled, his nose crinkled. 'So-so. You?'

'So-so,' she admitted. 'How's Lily doing?' Heather had had no choice but to bring her. They'd installed her in the den, and Bishop had volunteered to check in on her when he went inside for more plastic cups.

'She's fine. Watching a marathon of some celebrity show. I made her popcorn.' He leaned back, so he was staring at the sky, and motioned for Heather to do the same.

When they were little, they had sometimes slept out here, side by side in sleeping bags, surrounded by empty packages of chips and cookies. One time, she had woken up and found a raccoon sitting on her chest. Bishop had yelled to startle it away – but not before getting a picture. It was one of her favorite memories from childhood.

She could still remember what it felt like to wake up next to him, with dew covering their sleeping bags and soaking the canvas, their breath steaming in the air – they were so warm next to each other. Like they were in the only safe, good place in the world.

Now she unconsciously moved her head onto the hollow space between his chest and shoulder, and he wrapped one arm around her. His fingers grazed her bare arms, and her body felt suddenly fizzy and warm. She wondered how they must look from above: like two pieces of a puzzle, fitted neatly together.

'Are you going to miss me?' Bishop asked suddenly.

Heather's heart gave a huge, awful thump, like it wanted to leap out of her throat.

She'd been trying all summer to ignore the fact that Bishop was going away to college. Now they had less than a month left. 'Don't be an idiot,' she said, nudging him.

'I'm serious.' He shifted, withdrawing his arm from under her head, rolling over onto one elbow to face her. Casually, he slung his other arm over her waist. Her shirt was riding up and his hand was on her stomach – his tan skin against her pale, freckled belly – and her lungs were having trouble working properly.

It's Bishop, she reminded herself. It's just Bishop.

'I'm gonna miss you so bad, Heather,' he said. They were

so close, she could see a bit of fuzz clinging to one of his eyelashes; she could see individual spirals of color in his eyes. And his lips. Soft-looking. The perfect imperfectness of his teeth.

'What about Avery?' Heather blurted. She didn't know where the words came from. 'Are you going to miss her, too?'

He drew back an inch, frowning. Then he sighed and shoved a hand through his hair. As soon as he wasn't touching Heather anymore, she would have given anything to have his touch back. 'I'm not with Avery anymore,' he said carefully. 'We broke up.'

Heather stared. 'Since when?'

'Does it matter?' Bishop looked annoyed. 'Look, it was never a real thing, okay?'

'You just liked hooking up with her,' Heather said. She suddenly felt angry, and cold, and exposed. She sat up, tugging down her shirt. Bishop was leaving her behind. He would find new girls – pretty, tiny girls like Avery – and he would forget all about her. It happened all the time.

'Hey.' Bishop sat up too. Heather wouldn't look at him, so he reached out and forced her chin in his direction. 'I'm trying to talk to you, okay? I . . . I had to break up with Avery. I like . . . someone else. There's someone else. That's what I'm trying to tell you. But it's complicated . . .'

He was staring at her so intensely; Heather could feel the warmth between them.

She didn't think. She just leaned in and closed her eyes and kissed him.

It was like taking a bite of ice cream that's been sitting out just long enough: sweet, easy, perfect. She wasn't worried about whether she was doing it right, as she had been all those years ago in the movie theater, when she could only think of the popcorn in her teeth. She was simply there, inhaling the smell of him, of his lips, while the music thudded softly in the background and the cicadas swelled an accompaniment. Heather felt little bursts of happiness in her chest, as though someone had set off sparklers there.

Then, abruptly, he pulled away. 'Wait,' he said. 'Wait.'

And instantly, the sparklers in her chest were extinguished, leaving only a smoking black place. Just that one word, and she knew: she'd made a mistake.

'I can't . . .' Suddenly he looked different – older, full of regret, like someone she barely knew. 'I don't want to lie to you, Heather.'

She felt her face begin to burn. It wasn't her. He was in love with someone else. And she'd just shoved her tongue down his throat like a lunatic.

She had to crab-walk backward, away from him, to the edge of the trampoline. 'Stupid,' she said. 'It was stupid. Just forget it, okay? I don't know what I was thinking.'

For a second, he looked hurt. But she was too embarrassed to care. And then he frowned, and he just looked tired and a little irritated, like she was an unruly child and he was a patient father. She realized suddenly that that was how Bishop saw her: like a kid. A kid sister.

'Will you just sit down?' he said in his tired-dad voice. His hair was sticking straight up – the hair equivalent of a scream.

'It's getting late,' Heather said, which it wasn't. 'I have to take Lily home. Mom will get worried.' Lie on top of lie. She didn't know why she said it. Maybe because in that moment she really wished for it – wished that she was heading back to a real home with a normal mom who cared, instead of back to the car and the parking spot on Meth Row. Wished that she was small and delicate, like a special Christmas ornament that needed to be handled correctly. Wished that she was someone else.

'Heather, please,' he said.

The world was breaking up, shattering into colors – and she knew if she didn't get out of there, she would start to cry. 'Forget about it,' she said. 'Seriously. Would you? Just forget it ever happened.'

She only made it a few steps away before the tears started. She swiped them away quickly with the heel of a hand; she had to pass through a dozen old classmates to get to the house, including Matt's best friend, and she would rather die than be the girl crying at her best friend's birthday party. Everyone would probably think she was wasted. Funny how people could be around you for so many years, and be so off the mark.

She went in through the back door, taking a second inside to stand, inhaling, trying to get control of herself. Weirdly, although Bishop's whole property was a junkyard, the house was clean, sparsely furnished, and always smelled like carpet cleaner. Heather knew that Mr Marks's longtime girlfriend, Carol, considered the yard a lost cause. But the home was her place, and she was always scrubbing and straightening and yelling at Bishop to take his dirty feet off the coffee table, for God's sake. Even though the house hadn't been remodeled since the seventies, and still sported shag carpet and weird orange-and-white-checkered linoleum in the kitchen, it looked spotless.

Heather's throat tightened again. Everything was so familiar here: the Formica dining room table; the crack running along the kitchen countertop; the curled photographs stuck to the fridge with magnets advertising dentists' offices and hardware stores. They were as familiar to her as any she had ever called her own.

They were hers, and Bishop had been hers, once.

But no more.

She could hear running water, and muffled TV sounds from the den, where Lily was watching. She stepped into the darkened hall and noticed the bathroom door was partly open. A wedge of light lay thickly on the carpet. Now she could hear crying, over the sound of the water. She saw a curtain of dark hair appear and disappear quickly.

'Nat?' Heather swung the door open carefully.

Water gushed from the faucet, and steam was drumming up from the porcelain bowl. The water must have been scalding, but Nat was still scrubbing her hands, and sniffling. Her skin was raw and red and shiny, like it had been burned.

'Hey.' Heather forgot, for the moment, about her own problems. She took a step into the bathroom. Instinctively, she reached out and shut off the faucet. Even the taps were hot. 'Hey. Are you okay?'

It was a stupid thing to say. Nat was obviously not okay.

She turned to Heather. Her eyes were puffy, and her whole face looked weird and swollen, like bread that was rising wrong. 'It's not working anymore,' she said in a whisper.

'What isn't?' Heather asked. She felt suddenly on hyperalert. She noticed the *drip-drip-drip* of the faucet, and Nat's monstrously red hands, hanging like deflated balloons by her side. She thought of the way that Nat always liked things even, straight down the middle. How sometimes she showered more than once a day. The taps and tongue clicks. Stuff she'd mostly ignored, because she was so used to it. Another blind spot between people.

'That's why I froze on the highway, you know,' Nat went on. 'I just . . . glitched.' Her eyes were watery again. 'Nothing's working.' Her voice wavered. 'I don't feel safe, you know?'

'Come here,' Heather said. She drew Nat into a hug and Nat continued crying, drunk, against her chest. She gripped Heather tightly as if she worried she might fall. 'Shhh,' Heather murmured, again and again. 'Shhh. It's your birthday.'

But she didn't say it would be okay. How could she? She knew that Nat was right.

None of them was safe.

No more. Never again.

dodge

DODGE HEARD VOICES IN THE LIVING ROOM AS SOON AS HE opened the door and immediately regretted coming home directly. It was just after eleven, and his first thought was that Ricky was over again. He wasn't in the mood to deal with Ricky grinning like an idiot and Dayna blushing and trying to make things not awkward and all the time shooting Dodge dagger eyes, like *he* was the one intruding.

But then his mom called, 'Come in here, Dodge!'

A man was sitting on the couch. His hair was graying, and he was wearing a rumpled suit, which matched his rumpled face.

'What?' Dodge said, barely looking at his mom. He didn't even try to be polite. He wasn't going to play nice with one of his mom's dates.

His mom frowned.

'Dodge,' she said, drawing out his name, like a warning bell. 'You know Bill Kelly, don't you? Bill came over for a little bit of company.' She was watching Dodge closely, and he read a dozen messages in her eyes at once: *Bill Kelly just lost his son, so if you're rude to him, I swear you'll be sleeping on the streets . . .*

Dodge felt suddenly like his whole body was made of angles and spikes, and he couldn't remember how to move it correctly. He turned jerkily to the man on the couch: Big Bill Kelly. Now he could see the resemblance to his son. The straw-colored hair running, in the father's case, to gray; the piercing blue eyes and the heavy jaw.

'Hi,' Dodge said. His voice was a croak. He cleared his throat. 'I was – *am* – I mean, we're all sorry to hear—'

'Thank you, son.' Mr Kelly's voice was surprisingly clear. Dodge was glad he'd been interrupted, because he didn't know what else he would have said. He was so hot he felt like his face was about to explode. He had the sudden, hysterical impulse to shout out: *I was there. I was there when your son died. I could have saved him.*

He took a deep breath. The game was wearing on him. He was starting to crack.

After what seemed like forever, Mr Kelly's eyes passed away from Dodge, back to his mother. 'I should go, Sheila.' He stood up slowly. He was so tall he nearly grazed the ceiling with his head. 'I'm going to Albany tomorrow. Autopsy's done. I don't expect any surprises, but . . .' He made a helpless gesture with his hands. 'I want to know everything. I *will* know everything.'

Sweat was pricking up underneath Dodge's collar. It might have been his imagination, but he was sure Mr Kelly's words were directed at him. He thought of all the Panic betting slips he'd been collecting this summer. Where were they? Had he put them in his underwear drawer? Or left them out on his bedside table? Jesus. He had to get rid of them.

'Of course.' Dodge's mom stood too. Now all three of them were standing, awkwardly, like they were in a play and had forgotten their lines. 'Say good night to Mr Kelly, Dodge.'

Dodge coughed. 'Yeah. Sure. Look, I'm sorry again—'

Mr Kelly stuck out his hand. 'God's works,' he said quietly. But Dodge felt that when Mr Kelly shook his hand, he squeezed just a little too hard.

That was the night Diggin went to a party down at the gully and ended up with a cracked rib, two black eyes, and one of his teeth knocked out. Derek Klieg was drunk; that was the excuse he gave afterward, but everyone knew it was deeper than that, and once the swelling in Diggin's face went down, he told anyone who would listen how Derek had jumped him, threatened him, tried to get him to cough up the names and identities of the judges, and wouldn't listen when Diggin insisted he didn't know.

It was an obvious violation of one of Panic's many unspoken rules. The announcer was off-limits. So were the judges.

Derek Klieg was immediately disqualified. He had forfeited his spot in the game, and his name was struck from the betting slips by morning.

And Natalie, the last player eliminated, was back on.

SATURDAY, JULY 30

heather

HEATHER WAS WOKEN BY SOMEONE RAPPING ON THE WINDOW. She sat up, rubbing her eyes, startled and momentarily disoriented. Sun was streaming through the windows of the Taurus. Dodge was watching her through the windshield.

Now that she was awake, everything came into sudden focus: the kiss with Bishop and its botched end; Natalie crying in the bathroom; and now Dodge watching her, taking in the rumpled sheet and beaten-up cups from Dairy Queen in the passenger seat, the chip bags and the flip-flops and the scattered clothing in the backseat.

Outside, Lily was barefoot and dressed in a bathing suit.

Heather opened the door and got out of the car. 'What are you doing here?' She was furious with him. He had violated an unspoken agreement. When she had said, *Don't tell,* she had also meant *Don't come back.*

'I tried calling you. Your phone was off.' If he could see she was angry, he didn't seem to care.

Her phone. She'd been powering down her phone as much

as she could, since she could only charge it when she worked at Anne's house. Besides, she didn't need to see the texts from her mom. But she realized she'd brought it into Bishop's kitchen last night to charge, and never retrieved it. Shit. That meant going back for it.

Heather had slept in her clothes – the same clothes she'd worn to Nat's party, including a tank top with sequins. She crossed her arms over her chest. 'What's up?'

He passed her a folded piece of paper. The newest betting slip. 'Nat's back on. Derek was disqualified.'

'Disqualified?' Heather repeated. She'd only heard of someone being disqualified from Panic once before, years earlier – one of the players was sleeping with a judge. It later turned out that the guy, Mickey Barnes, *wasn't* a judge, just pretending to be one so he could get laid. But it was too late. The player was replaced.

Dodge shrugged. Behind him, Lily had overturned their bucket of water and was making rivers out of the dirt. Heather was glad she wasn't listening.

'Are you gonna tell her?' he asked.

'You can,' she said.

He looked at her again. Something shifted in his eyes. 'No, I can't.'

They stood there for a second. Heather wanted to ask him what had happened, but she felt too weird. She and Dodge weren't exactly close – not like that, anyway. She didn't know what they were. Maybe she wasn't close with anyone.

'The deal's off,' he said after a minute. 'No splits.'

'What?' Heather was shocked to hear Dodge say it. That meant he knew she knew about his deal with Nat. Did he know about the deal she and Nat had made?

His eyes were almost gray, like a storm sky.

'We play the game how it was meant,' he said, and for the first time she was almost afraid of him. 'Winner takes the pot.'

'Why can't I come in and see Bishop?' Lily was in a bad mood. She'd been whining since she got up. She was too hot. She was dirty. The food that Heather had for her – more tinned stuff, and a sandwich she'd bought at the 7-Eleven – was gross. Heather guessed that the adventure of being without a home (she couldn't bring herself to think the word *homeless*), the newness of it, was wearing off.

Heather gripped the wheel, squeezing out her frustration through her palms. 'I'm just running in for a second, Lilybelle,' she said, forcing herself to sound cheerful. She wouldn't snap, she wouldn't scream. She would keep it together – all for Lily. 'And Bishop's busy.' She didn't know if this was true – she hadn't been able to call and see whether Bishop was even home, and part of her was hoping he wasn't. She kept flashing back to the kiss, the moment of warmth and rightness . . . and then the way he had pulled away, like the kiss had physically hurt him. *I don't want to lie to you, Heather.*

Never had she been so humiliated in her life. What on earth had possessed her? Thinking about it made her want to drive all the way to the ocean and keep gunning straight into it.

But she needed her phone. She was going to have to suck it up and risk seeing him. Maybe she could even do damage control, explain that she hadn't meant to kiss him – so he wouldn't think she was in love with him or something.

Her stomach gave another lurch into her throat. She wasn't in love with Bishop.

Was she?

'I'll be back in ten,' she said. She'd parked a little ways down the driveway, so if Bishop was outside, he wouldn't see her car and all the evidence that she was living inside it. The last thing she wanted was more pity from him.

There was still evidence of the party in the yard: a few plastic cups, cigarette butts, a pair of cheap sunglasses swimming in a birdbath filled with mossy water. But everything was quiet. Maybe he wasn't home.

But before she could even make it to the front door, Bishop appeared, carrying a trash bag. He froze when he saw her, and Heather felt the last flicker of hope – that things would be normal, that they could pretend last night had never happened – fizzle out.

'What are you doing here?' he blurted out.

'I just came to get my phone.' Her voice sounded weird, like it was being replayed on a bad sound system. 'Don't worry, I'm not staying.'

She started to move past him, into the house.

He caught her arm. 'Wait.' There was something desperate about the way he was looking at her. He licked his lips. 'Wait – you don't – I have to explain.'

'Forget about it,' Heather said.

'No. I can't – you have to trust me—' Bishop pushed a hand through his hair, so it stood up straight. Heather felt like she could cry. His clown-hair; his faded Rangers T-shirt and sweatpants spotted with paint; his smell. She had thought it was hers – she'd thought he was hers – but all this time he'd been growing up and hooking up and having secret crushes and becoming someone she didn't know.

And she knew, looking at him holding a stupid bag of trash,

that she was in love with him and always had been. Probably since the kiss freshman year. Maybe even before that.

'You don't have to explain,' she said, and pushed past him into the house. It had been bright outside, and she was temporarily disoriented by the dark, and she took two unsteady steps toward the living room, where she could hear the fan going, as Bishop flung open the door behind her.

'Heather,' he said.

Before she could respond, another voice called out. A girl's voice. 'Bishop?'

Time stopped. Heather froze, and Bishop froze, and nothing moved except the black spots across Heather's eyes as her vision slowly adjusted; as she saw a girl float up out of the shadow, emerging from the darkness of the living room. Weirdly, although they'd gone to school together forever, Heather didn't immediately recognize Vivian Trager. Maybe it was the shock of seeing her there, in Bishop's house, barefooted, holding a mug from Bishop's kitchen. As though she belonged.

'Hey, Heather,' Vivian said, taking a sip from her mug. Over the rim, her eyes connected with Bishop's, and Heather saw a warning there.

Heather turned to Bishop. All she saw was guilt: guilt all over him, like a physical force, like something sticky.

'What are you doing here?' Vivian asked, still casual.

'Leaving,' Heather said. She threw herself forward, down the hall and into the kitchen. She was fighting the feeling that she was going to be sick, fighting the memories threatening to drown her: the times she'd drunk cocoa from that mug, her lips where Vivian's now were, her lips on Bishop's – Vivian's Bishop.

Her phone was still plugged into an outlet near the

microwave. Her fingers felt swollen and useless. It took her several tries before she could unplug it.

She couldn't face passing Bishop and Vivian again, so she just hurtled out the back door, across the porch, and down into the yard. Idiot. She was such an idiot. She tasted tears before she knew she was crying.

Why would Bishop go for her, Heather? He was smart. He was leaving for college. Heather was a nobody. Nill. As in zero. That's why Matt had dumped her too.

No one had ever told her this basic fact: not everyone got to be loved. It was like those stupid bell curves they'd had to study in math class. There was the big, swollen, happy middle, a whale hump full of blissful couples and families eating around a big dining room table and laughing. And then, at the tapered ends, there were the abnormal people, the weirdos and freaks and zeros like her.

She wiped away the tears with her forearm and took a few seconds to breathe and calm down before she returned to the car. Lily was picking at a mosquito bite on her big toe. She stared at Heather suspiciously when Heather got in the car.

'Did you see Bishop?' Lily asked.

'No,' Heather said, and put the car in drive.

WEDNESDAY, AUGUST 3

dodge

DODGE HAD LOST THE RECEIPT FOR NATALIE'S NECKLACE, AND instead had to pawn it for half of what he had paid. He needed the money. It was August 3; he was running out of time. He needed a car for the Joust. A junker would do – he was even thinking of buying one off Bishop. So long as it drove.

He had just finished a shift at Home Depot when he got a text. He hoped for a wild second it was Natalie; instead it was from his mom.

Meet us @ Columbia Memorial ASAP!!

Dayna. Something bad had happened to Dayna. He tried calling his mom's cell phone, and then Dayna's, and got no response.

He barely registered the twenty-minute bus ride to Hudson. He couldn't sit still. His legs were full of itching, and his heart was lodged underneath his tongue. His phone buzzed in his pocket. Another text.

This time, it was from an unknown number.

Time to go solo. Tomorrow night we'll see what you're really made of.

He shut his phone, shoved it in his pocket.

When he reached Columbia Memorial, he practically sprinted from the bus.

'Dodge! *Dodge!*'

Dayna and his mom were standing outside, by the handi-capped ramp. Dayna was waving frantically, sitting up as tall as she could in her chair.

And she was grinning. They both were – smiling so big, he could see all their teeth, even from a distance.

Still, his heart wouldn't stop going as he jogged across the parking lot. 'What?' He was breathless by the time he reached them. 'What is it? What happened?'

'You tell him, Day,' Dodge's mom said, still smiling. Her mascara was smudgy. She'd obviously been crying.

Dayna sucked in a deep breath. Her eyes were shining; he hadn't seen her look so happy since before the accident. 'I *moved*, Dodge. I moved my toes.'

He stared at Dayna, then his mom, then Dayna again. 'Jesus Christ,' he finally burst out. 'I thought something *happened*. I thought you were dead or something.'

Dayna shook her head. She looked hurt. 'Something *did* happen.'

Dodge took off his hat and ran a hand through his hair. He was sweating. He jammed on the hat again. Dayna was watching him expectantly. He knew he was being a dick.

He exhaled. 'That's amazing, Day,' he said. He tried to sound like he meant it. He *was* happy; he was just still wound up from the trip over, from being so afraid. 'I'm proud of you.' He leaned down and gave her a hug. And he felt the tiniest convulsion in her body, like she was holding in a sob. Dodge's mom insisted they go out to eat to celebrate, even though they couldn't really afford it, especially now with all the bills.

They ended up at an Applebee's outside Carp. Dodge's mom ordered a margarita with extra salt and nachos for the table to start. Nachos were Dodge's favorite, but he couldn't bring himself to eat. His mom kept prattling on about Bill Kelly: how Bill Kelly was so nice, so thoughtful, even though he was grieving; how Bill Kelly had set them up with the appointment and made a phone call on their behalf and blah, blah, blah.

Her cell phone rang in the middle of dinner. Dodge's mom stood up. 'Speak of the devil,' she said. 'It's Bill. He might have news . . .'

'What kind of news?' Dodge asked when she had stepped outside. He could see her pacing the parking lot. Under the glare of the lights, she looked old. Tired, kind of saggy. More momlike than usual.

Dayna shrugged.

'Are they screwing or something?' Dodge pressed.

Dayna sighed and wiped her fingers carefully on her napkin. She'd been picking apart her burger, layer by layer. This was something she'd always done: deconstruct her food, put it back together in a way that pleased her. With burgers it was lettuce and tomato on the bottom, then ketchup, then burger, then bun. 'They're friends, Dodge,' she said, and he felt a flicker of irritation. She was speaking to him in her grown-up voice, a voice that had always grated on him. 'Why do you care, anyway?'

'Mom doesn't have friends,' he said, even though he knew it was kind of mean.

Dayna set down her napkin – hard, in her fist, so that the water cups jumped. 'What is up with you?'

Dodge stared at her. 'What's up with *me*?'

'Why do you have to give Mom such a hard time? That doctor isn't cheap. She's trying.' Dayna shook her head. 'Ricky had to leave, like, his whole family to come here—'

'Please don't bring Ricky into this.'

'I'm just saying, we should feel lucky.'

'*Lucky*?' Dodge barked a laugh. 'Since when did you become such a guru?'

'Since when did you become such a brat?' Dayna fired back.

Dodge suddenly felt lost. He didn't know where the feeling came from, and he struggled to get out from underneath it. 'Mom's clueless. That's all I'm saying.' He stabbed at his mac 'n' cheese to avoid meeting Dayna's eyes. 'Besides, I just don't want you to get your hopes up . . .'

Now it was Dayna's turn to stare. 'You're unbelievable.' She spoke in a low voice, and somehow that was worse than if she'd been screaming. 'All this time you've been telling me to keep trying, keep believing. And then I actually make progress—'

'And what about what *I've* been doing?' Dodge knew he was being a brat, but he couldn't help it. Dayna had been on his side – she was the only one on his side – and now, suddenly, she wasn't.

'You mean the game?' Dayna shook her head. 'Look, Dodge. I've been thinking. I don't want you to play anymore.'

'You what?' Dodge exploded; several people at a neighboring table turned to stare.

'Keep your voice down.' Dayna was looking at him the way she used to when he was a little kid and didn't understand the rules of a game she wanted to play: disappointed, a little impatient. 'After what happened to Bill Kelly . . . it's not worth it. It's not right.'

Dodge took a sip of his water and found he could barely work it down his throat. 'You wanted me to play,' he said. 'You asked me to.'

'I changed my mind,' she said.

'Well, that's not how the game works,' he said. His voice was rising again. He couldn't help it. 'Or did you forget?'

Her mouth got thin: a straight pink scar in the face. 'Listen to me, Dodge. This is for you – for your own good.'

'I played for you.' Dodge no longer cared about being overheard. The anger, the sense of loss, ate away the rest of the world, made him careless. Who did he have? He had no friends. He'd never stayed in a place long enough to make them or trust them. With Heather he'd thought he'd gotten close; with Natalie, too. He'd been wrong; and now even Dayna was turning on him. 'Did you forget that, too? This is all for you. So that things can go back.'

He hadn't intended to say the last part – hadn't even thought the words until they were out of his mouth. For a second there was silence. Dayna was staring at him, openmouthed, and the words sat between them like something detonated: everything had been blown wide open.

'Dodge,' she said. He was horrified to see that she looked like she felt sorry for him. 'Things can never go back. You know that, right? That's not how it works. Nothing you do will change what happened.'

Dodge pushed his plate away. He stood up from the table. 'I'm going home,' he said. He couldn't even think. Dayna's words were making a storm inside his head. *Things can never go back.*

What the hell had he been playing for, all this time?

'Come on, Dodge,' Dayna said. 'Sit down.'

'I'm not hungry,' he said. He couldn't bring himself to look at her: those patient eyes, the thin, dissatisfied set of her mouth. Like he was a little kid. A dumb kid. 'Tell Mom I said good-bye.'

'We're miles from home,' Dayna said.

'I could use the walk,' Dodge said. He shoved a cigarette in his mouth, even though he didn't feel like smoking, and hoped it wouldn't rain.

heather

HEATHER DIDN'T RETURN TO METH ROW. IT WAS CONVENIENT, in some ways, but there was no privacy in it, now that Dodge knew where she was. She didn't want him to be spying on her, seeing how she was living, maybe running his mouth about it.

Heather had been careful, thus far, to move the car only in the middle of the night, from parking lot to empty road to parking lot, when there was less danger of being spotted. She'd developed a routine: on work days, she set her alarm for four a.m., and, while Lily was still sleeping, headed through the ink-black to Anne's house. She had found a break in the trees just off the driveway where she could park. Sometimes she slept again. Sometimes she waited, watching the black begin to blur and change, turning first to smudgy dark, then sharpening and splitting, peeling off into vivid purple shadows and triangles of light.

She tried very hard not to think about the past, or what was going to happen in the future, or anything at all. Later, when it was almost nine, she'd walk up to the house, telling Anne that Bishop had dropped her off. Sometimes Lily came with her. Sometimes she stayed in the car, or played in the woods.

Twice, Heather had arrived early and chosen to bathe, sneaking through the woods to the outdoor shower. Then she'd stripped, shivering in the cool air, and stepped gratefully under the stream of hot water, letting it run in her mouth and eyes and over her body. Otherwise, she'd been making do with a hose.

Heather had to stop herself from fantasizing about running water, microwaves, air conditioners and refrigerators and toilets. Definitely toilets. It had been two weeks since she'd left her mom's, and she'd gotten two mosquito bites on her butt while peeing at six a.m. and eaten more cold canned ravioli than she could stomach.

What she wanted to do was make it to Malden Plaza, where they'd crossed the highway – to that vast, impersonal parking lot with only a few streetlamps. Truckers came on and off the highway all the time, and cars stayed in the lot overnight. There was a McDonald's, and public restrooms, with showers for the truckers who passed through.

First they needed gas. It wasn't yet dark, and she didn't want to stop in Carp. But she'd been running on fumes for almost twenty-four hours, and she didn't want to break down, either. So she pulled into the Citgo on Main Street, which was the least popular of the three gas stations in town because it was the most expensive and didn't sell beer.

'Stay in the car,' she told Lily.

'Yeah, yeah,' Lily mumbled.

'I'm serious, Billy.' Heather wasn't sure how long she could take this: the sniping, the back-and-forth. She was losing it. Cracking up. Grief had its hands around her neck; she was being choked. She kept seeing Vivian sipping from Bishop's mug, her black hair hanging in wisps around a pretty, moon-white face. 'And don't talk to anybody, okay?'

She scanned the parking lot: no police cars, no cars she recognized. That was a good sign.

Inside, she put down twenty dollars for gas and took the opportunity to stock up on whatever she could: packages of ramen soup, which they would eat dissolved in cold water; chips and salsa; beef jerky; and two fresh-ish sandwiches. The man behind the counter, with a dark, flat face and thinning hair slicked to one side, like weeds strapped to his forehead, made her wait for change. While he counted singles into the register, she went to the bathroom. She didn't like standing under the bright lights of the store, and she didn't like the way the man was looking at her either – like he could see through to all her secrets.

While she was washing her hands, she dimly registered the jangle of the bell above the door, the low murmur of conversation. Another customer. When she left the bathroom, he was blocked from view by a big display of cheap sunglasses, and she was almost at the counter before she noticed his uniform, the gun strapped to his hip.

A cop.

'How's that Kelly business going?' the man behind the counter was saying.

The cop – with a big belly pushing out over his belt – shrugged. 'Autopsy came in. Turns out Little Kelly didn't die in that fire.'

Heather felt like something had hit her in the chest. She

tugged her hood up and pretended to be looking for chips. She picked up a package of pretzels, squinted at it hard.

'That right?'

'Sad story. Looks like OD. He'd been taking pills since he came back from the war. Probably just went to that Graybill house for a nice warm place to get high.'

Heather exhaled. She felt an insane, immediate sense of relief. She hadn't realized, until now, that she had held herself accountable, at least a little bit, for his murder.

But it wasn't murder. It hadn't been.

'Still, someone started that fire,' the cop said, and Heather realized she'd been staring at the same package of pretzels for several seconds too long, and now the cop was staring at her. She shoved the pretzels back on their rack, ducked her head, and headed for the door.

'Hey! Hey, miss!'

She froze.

'You forgot your groceries. I got change for you too.'

If she bolted, it would look suspicious. Then the cop might wonder why she'd freaked. She turned slowly back to the counter, keeping her eyes trained on the ground. She could feel both men staring at her as she collected the bag of food. Her cheeks were hot, and her mouth felt dry as sand.

She was almost at the door again, almost in the clear, when the cop called out to her.

'Hey.' He was watching her closely. 'Look at me.'

She forced her eyes up to his. He had a pudgy, doughlike face. But his eyes were big and round, like a small kid's, or an animal's.

'What's your name?' he said.

She said the first name that came to her: 'Vivian.'

He moved gum around in his mouth. 'How old are you, Vivian? You in high school?'

'Graduated,' she said. Her palms were itching. She wanted to turn and run. His eyes were traveling her face quickly, like he was memorizing it.

The cop took a step closer to her. 'You ever heard of a game called Panic, Vivian?'

She looked away. 'No,' she said in a whisper. It was a stupid lie, and immediately she wished she'd said yes.

'I thought everybody played Panic,' the cop said.

'Not everyone,' she said, turning back to him. She saw a spark of triumph in his eyes, as though she'd admitted to something. God. She was messing this up. The back of her neck was sweating.

The cop stared at her for a few more beats. 'Go on, get out of here,' was all he said.

Outside, she took a few deep breaths. The air was thick with moisture. A storm was coming – a bad one too, judging from the sky. It was practically green, like the whole world was about to get sick. She shoved her hood back, letting the sweat cool off her forehead.

She jogged across the parking lot to the pump.

And stopped.

Lily was gone.

There was a resonant *boom*, a sound so loud she jumped. The sky opened up, and rain hissed angrily against the pavement. She reached the car just as the first fork of lightning tore across the sky. She jiggled the door handle. Locked. Where the hell was Lily?

'Heather!' Lily's voice rang out over the rain.

Heather turned. A cop was standing next to a blue-and-white patrol car. He had his hand around her sister's arm.

'Lily!' Heather ran over, forgetting to be worried about cops or being careful. 'Let go of her,' she said.

'Calm down, calm down.' The cop was tall and skinny, with a face like a mule. 'Everyone be calm, okay?'

'Let go of her,' Heather repeated. The cop obeyed, and Lily barreled over to Heather, wrapping her arms around Heather's waist, like she was a little kid.

'Hold on now,' the cop said. Lightning flashed again. His teeth were lit up, gray and crooked. 'I just wanted to make sure the little lady was okay.'

'She's fine,' Heather said. 'We're fine.' She started to turn away, but the cop reached out and stopped her.

'Not so fast,' he said. 'We still got a little problem.'

'We didn't *do* anything,' Lily piped up.

The cop squinted at Lily. 'I believe you,' he said, his voice a little softer. 'But that right there' – and he pointed to the beat-up Taurus – 'is a stolen car.'

The rain was coming down so hard, Heather couldn't think. Lily looked sad and extra skinny with her T-shirt sticking to her ribs.

The cop opened the back door of the squad car. 'Go on and get in,' he said to Lily. 'Dry off.' Heather didn't like it – she didn't want Lily anywhere near the police car. That's how they got you: they were nice, and they lured you into thinking you were safe, and then they flipped the tables without warning. She thought of Bishop and felt her throat squeeze. That was how everyone got you.

But Lily had scooted inside before Heather could say, *Don't*.

'How about we go somewhere and talk?' the cop said. At least he didn't sound mad.

Heather crossed her arms. 'I'm fine,' she said, hoping he wouldn't see her shiver. 'And I didn't steal that car,' she said. 'It's my mom's car.'

He shook his head. 'Your mom said you stole it.' She could barely hear him over the rain. 'You got quite the setup in the backseat. Food. Blankets. Clothes.' A bead of rain rolled off the tip of his nose, and Heather thought he looked almost as pathetic as Lily had.

She looked away. She felt the need to tell, to spill, to explain, swelling like a balloon inside her chest, pressing painfully against her ribs. But she just said, 'I'm not going home. You can't make me.'

'Sure I can.'

'I'm eighteen,' she said.

'With no job, no money, no home,' he said.

'I have a job.' She knew she was being stupid, stubborn, but she didn't care. She'd promised Lily they wouldn't go back, and they wouldn't. Probably if she told on her mom, told about the partying and the drugs, she wouldn't have to go back. But maybe they'd stick her mom in jail and put Lily in some home with strangers who didn't care about her. 'I have a good job.'

And suddenly it occurred to her: Anne.

She looked at the cop. 'Don't I get one phone call or something?'

For the first time, he smiled. But his eyes were still sad. 'You're not under arrest.'

'I know,' she said. She was suddenly so nervous, she felt like she would puke. What if Anne didn't care? Or worse, sided with the police? 'But I want my phone call, just the same.'

dodge

DODGE HAD ONLY MADE IT HALFWAY HOME WHEN THE SKY split open and it began to pour. Just his fucking luck. Within a few minutes, he was totally soaked. A car passed, blaring its horn, sending a fierce spray of water across his jeans. He was still two miles from home.

He was hoping the storm would let up, but it got worse. Lightning ripped across the sky, quick flashes that gripped the world in a weird green glow. Water accumulated fast in the ditches, driving leaves and paper cups onto his shoes. He was practically blind; he couldn't see the oncoming traffic until it was nearly on top of him.

He realized, suddenly, that he was only a few minutes away from Bishop's. He turned off the road and started jogging. With any luck, Bishop would be home, and he could wait it out or bum a ride.

But when he came up the driveway, he saw the whole house was dark. Still, he went up to the porch and knocked on the front door, praying that Bishop would answer. Nothing.

He remembered the back porch was screened in, and circled the house through the slog of mud. He banged his shin against an old lawn mower and went stumbling forward, nearly face-planting, cursing.

The screen door was, of course, locked. He was wet and so miserable he briefly considered punching a hole through it – but then lightning bit through the sky again, and in that half-second of unnatural brightness, he saw a kind of gardening shed, a little ways back and half-obscured by the trees.

The door to the shed was protected by a padlock, but Dodge had his first bit of luck: the lock wasn't actually in place. He pushed into the shed and stood shivering in the sudden dryness and coolness, inhaling the smell of wet blankets and old wood, waiting for his eyes to adjust. He couldn't see shit. Just outlines, dark objects, probably more junk.

He pulled out his cell phone for light and saw the battery was almost out. He couldn't even call Bishop and ask where he was and when he would be home. Great. But at least in the glow of the screen he could make a better scan of the shed, and he was surprised to see that it was actually wired: a plain bulb was screwed into the ceiling, and there was a switch on the wall, too.

The bulb was dim, but it was better than nothing. Immediately he saw that the shed was better organized than he'd thought. Certainly cleaner than the junkyard. There was a stool and a desk and a bunch of shelves. A bunch of betting slips, water-warped and weighted down with a metal turtle, were piled on the desk.

Next to the betting slips was a pile of old AV and recording equipment, and one of those cheap pay-per-use cell phones, the kind that required no subscription.

His second piece of luck: the cell phone powered on and didn't require a password.

He looked in his contacts for Bishop's cell phone number and managed to retrieve it just before his cell went dead.

He thumbed it into the keypad of the cell phone he'd found and listened to it ring. Five times, then Bishop's voice mail. He hung up without leaving a message. Instead he flipped over to the texts, planning to shoot off a 911 to Bishop. He had to come home sometime. Where could he be in this weather, anyway?

And then: he froze. The driving of the rain on the roof, even the weight of the cell phone – all of it receded, and he saw only the words of the last outgoing text.

Time to go solo. Tomorrow night we'll see what you're really made of.

He read it again, and a third time.

The feeling returned in a rush.

He scrolled down. More texts: instructions for the game. Messages to other players. And at the very bottom, a text to Heather's number.

Quit now, before you get hurt.

Dodge replaced the phone carefully, exactly where it had been. Now everything looked different: recording equipment. Cameras. Spray paint stacked in the corner, and plywood leaning against the shed walls. All the stuff Bishop had needed for the challenges.

A half-dozen mason jars were lined up on one shelf; he bent down to examine them and then cried out, stumbling away, nearly upsetting a stack of plywood.

Spiders. The jars were full of them – crawling up the glass, dark brown bodies blurring together. Meant for him, probably.

'What are you doing here?'

Dodge spun around. His heart was still beating hard; he was imagining the feel of a hundred spiders on his skin.

Bishop was standing in the doorway, totally immobile. The storm was still raging behind him, sending down sheets of water. He was wearing a hooded rain poncho, and his face was in shadow. For a second, Dodge was truly afraid of him; he looked like a serial killer in some bad horror movie.

Dodge had a sudden flash of clarity: this was what the game was really about. This was what true fear was – that you could never know other people, not completely. That you were always just guessing blind.

Then Bishop took another step into the shed, shoving off his hood, and the impression passed. It was just Bishop. Some of Dodge's fear eased too, although his skin was still prickling, and he was uncomfortably aware of the spiders in their thin glass jars, only a few feet away.

'What the hell, Dodge?' Bishop burst out. His fists were balled up.

'I was looking for you,' Dodge said, raising both hands, just in case Bishop was thinking of swinging at him. 'I just wanted to get out of the rain.'

'You're not supposed to be in here,' Bishop insisted.

'It's all right,' Dodge said. 'I know, okay? I already know.'

There was a minute of electric silence. Bishop stared at him. 'Know what?' he said at last.

'Come on, man. Don't bullshit,' Dodge said quietly. 'Just tell me one thing: why? I thought you hated Panic.'

Dodge thought Bishop might not answer, might still try to deny the whole thing. Then his body seemed to collapse, like someone had pulled the drain in his center. He tugged the door closed behind him, then sagged into the chair. For a moment, he sat with his head in his hands. Finally he looked up.

'Why did you play?' he asked.

Revenge, Dodge thought, and *Because I have nothing else.* But out loud he said, 'Money. Why else?'

Bishop gestured wide with his hands. 'Same.'

'Really?' Dodge watched him closely. There was a look on Bishop's face he couldn't identify. Bishop nodded, but Dodge could tell he was lying. It was more than that. He chose to let it go.

Everyone needed secrets.

'So what now?' Bishop asked. He sounded exhausted. He looked exhausted too. Dodge realized how much it must have weighed on him this summer – all the planning, all the lies.

'You tell me,' Dodge said. He leaned back against the desk. He was feeling slightly more relaxed, and grateful that Bishop was positioned so that he could no longer see the spiders.

'You can't tell Heather,' Bishop said, sitting forward, suddenly wild. 'She *can't* know.'

'Calm down,' Dodge said. His mind was ticking forward, already adjusting to the new information, thinking of how he could use it. 'I'm not going to tell Heather. But I'm not going to do the solo challenge either. You're just going to say I did.'

Bishop stared at him. 'That's not fair.'

Dodge shrugged. 'Maybe not. But that's how it's going to go.' He wiped his palms on his jeans. 'What were you planning to do with those spiders?'

'What do you think?' Bishop sounded annoyed. 'All right. Fine. You'll go straight to Joust. Okay?'

Dodge nodded. Abruptly, Bishop stood up, kicking the chair so it scootched forward a few inches. 'Jesus. Do you know, I'm actually kind of glad you found out? I was almost hoping you would. It's been awful. Fucking awful.'

Dodge didn't say anything stupid, like that Bishop could have said no when he was approached about being a judge.

So he just said, 'It'll be over soon.'

Bishop was pacing. Now he whirled around to face Dodge. Suddenly he seemed to fill the whole space. 'I killed him, Dodge,' he said, choking a little. 'I'm responsible.'

A muscle flexed in Bishop's jaw; it occurred to Dodge that he was trying not to cry. 'It was part of the game.' He shook his head. 'I never meant to hurt anyone. It was a stupid trick. I lit some papers in a trash can. But the fire got out of control so quick. It just . . . exploded. I didn't know what to do.'

Dodge felt a brief moment of guilt. Earlier tonight, when he'd gone off on Dayna about Bill Kelly, he hadn't been thinking of Little Kelly at all. And about how awful his father must feel. 'It was an accident,' he said softly.

'Does it matter?' Bishop asked. His voice was strangled. 'I should go to jail. I probably will.'

'You won't. Nobody knows.' It occurred to Dodge, though, that Bishop must have a partner. There were always at least two judges. He knew that Bishop wouldn't tell him if he asked, though. 'And I won't say anything. You can trust me.'

Bishop nodded. 'Thanks,' he whispered. Again, the energy seemed to leave him at once. He sat down again and put his head in his hands. They stayed like that for a long time, while the rain drummed on the roof, like fists beating to get in. They stayed until Dodge's leg started to get numb where he was leaning on it, and the noise of the rain receded slightly, and became the light scratching of nails.

'I have a favor to ask you,' Bishop said, looking up.

Dodge nodded.

Bishop's eyes flashed: an expression gone too quickly to interpret. 'It's about Heather,' he said.

SATURDAY, AUGUST 6

heather

ANNE HAD DECIDED THAT HEATHER WAS READY TO FEED THE tigers. She had shown Heather how to unlock the pen and where to place the bucket of meat. Anne took her time doing it – sometimes, she even wound up and threw a steak, like a player hurling a Frisbee, and occasionally one of the tigers would snap it up in midair.

Heather always waited until the tigers were on the other side of the pen or lying underneath the trees, where they liked to spend the sunniest afternoons. She worked as quickly as possible, never taking her eyes off them. The whole time she could practically feel the heat of their breath, the sharp rip of their teeth in her neck.

'Do you think they miss home?'

Heather turned around. Lily. Earlier that morning, Lily had helped Anne wrestle Muppet into a bath, and her legs were spotted with muddy water. But she looked cleaner, healthier, than she had in weeks. From the other side of the barn, they could hear Anne humming as she pulled daffodils from the garden.

'I think they're pretty happy,' Heather said, although she'd never really thought about it one way or another. She triple-checked that she'd locked the pen, then turned once again to Lily. Lily's face was puckered, like she was trying to swallow something too big.

'What about you, Bill?' she asked, resting a hand briefly on Lily's head. 'Do you miss home?'

Lily shook her head so hard her braid whipped her in the face. 'I want to stay here forever,' she said, and Heather knew that the words had been the too-big thing that was choking her.

Heather had to bend down awkwardly to give Lily a hug. Still, Lily was growing; she was nearly at Heather's chest. It was just one more thing that had changed while Heather wasn't paying attention. Like Bishop. Like her friendship with Nat.

'No matter what, we'll be together. Okay? We'll be fine.' Heather put her thumb on Lily's nose, and Lily swatted at her. 'Do you believe me?'

Lily nodded, but Heather could tell that she didn't, not entirely.

It had been three days since Heather had been picked up by the cops, and for now Anne had agreed to let Heather and Lily stay with her. They were sleeping in the 'blue room': wallpaper patterned with blue posies, blue coverlets, ruffled blue curtains. Heather thought it was the most beautiful room she'd ever seen. Earlier that morning, she'd woken up and Lily's bed had been empty. For a moment, she was seized with panic, until she heard the sound of laughter from outside. When she went to the window, she saw Lily was helping Anne feed the chickens and laughing hysterically as one of them chased her, pecking up feed.

The day before, Krista had arrived in the Taurus, which the cops had returned to her. She refused even to acknowledge Anne, but made a big show of embracing Lily, who stood rigidly, her face squashed against Krista's sun-freckled chest. Heather had expected her to be angry about the car, and maybe she was, but she was sober, at least, and trying to put on a good show. She reeked of perfume, and she was wearing her work pants and a blue blouse that puckered under her boobs.

She told Heather she was sorry, and she wasn't partying anymore, and she was going to do a better job of paying attention to Lily. But she recited the words stiffly, like an actress reading lines that bored her.

'So? You gonna come home?' she said.

Heather shook her head. And then she'd seen it: Krista's face had, for just a minute, transformed.

'You can't stay here forever,' Krista said in a low voice, so Anne couldn't hear. 'She'll get sick of you.'

Heather felt something open up deep in her stomach. 'Good-bye, Krista,' she said.

'And I won't let you take my baby, either. Don't think you're taking Lily from me.' Krista had reached out and grabbed Heather's elbow, but seeing Anne move toward them, had quickly released it.

'I'll be back soon,' Krista said loudly with her plastic smile. The words were like a threat. And Heather had walked around for the rest of the day with that empty, raw feeling, even after Anne had approached, unexpectedly, unasked, and given Heather a big hug.

Don't worry, she'd said. *I'm here for you.*

Heather wished she could truly believe it.

The tigers had moved across the pen now, toward the meat

– lazily at first, as though uninterested. They sprang on it in one quick, fluid motion, jaws opening, teeth gleaming momentarily in the sun. Heather watched them tear into it and felt a little queasy. What had Anne said on her first day of work? She liked taking in broken and damaged things. But Heather couldn't imagine the tigers needing the help.

Her phone buzzed in her back pocket. Natalie. They hadn't spoken since her birthday.

'Heather?' Natalie's voice sounded distant, as though she were speaking from underwater. 'Did you see the newest?'

'Newest what?' Heather asked. Cradling the phone between her ear and shoulder, she shoved open the door to the toolshed and replaced the keys to the tiger pen.

'The betting slips,' Natalie said. 'Dodge beat his solo challenge. Spiders.' She paused. 'One of us is next.'

Heather's stomach gave another twist. 'Or Ray. Or Harold Lee,' she pointed out.

'But it'll be our turn soon,' Nat said. She paused. 'Have you . . . have you spoken to him?'

Heather knew right away that Nat was talking about Dodge. 'Not really,' she said. She hadn't told Natalie about what Dodge had said: that their deal was off. She suspected that Nat knew as much.

Nat sighed. 'Let me know, okay?'

'Yeah, sure,' Heather said. There was an awkward pause. She remembered how hysterical Nat had been in the bathroom the other night, with her hands scraped nearly raw from scrubbing. She felt a sudden wave of emotion – love for Natalie, grief for all the things that were never said.

'And Heather?' Nat said.

'What's up?'

Nat's voice was quiet. 'I couldn't have done this without you. I would never have gotten this far. You know that, right?'

'The game's almost done,' Heather said, trying to keep her voice light. 'Don't turn melty on me now.'

As soon as she hung up, she saw she'd missed a text. She clicked over to her messages and felt her breath stick in her mouth.

Tomorrow it's your turn, the message read.

SUNDAY, AUGUST 7

heather

'I'd be better if you'd stop jerking the wheel,' Heather said. Then, immediately: 'I'm sorry.'

'It's all right,' Nat said. Her knuckles were tiny half-moons on the wheel.

As soon as Heather saw the sign for Fresh Pines Mobile Park, she felt like her stomach might drop out her butt. They were headed to Lot 62, only a few rows down from Krista's house. Even though no one had lived there for ages, it was wired and fitted with a fridge, a table, and a bed.

Heather knew that people used Lot 62, which had been empty for as long as she could remember, for partying and probably for other stuff she didn't want to think about. Once, when she was eight or nine, she and Bishop had gone on a rampage there, emptying out all the beers in the fridge, shaking the cigarette packs and bags of weed they found in the cupboards into the trash cans – like that would stop anyone.

Heather wondered what Bishop was doing right now, and

whether he'd heard it was her turn for a challenge. Probably not. Then she found that thinking of him was too painful, so she forced herself to concentrate on Natalie's awful driving.

'At least you're getting it over with,' Nat said. Heather knew she was trying to be helpful. 'I almost wish it was my turn.'

'No, you don't,' Heather said. Already, they were at Lot 62. The shades were pulled, but she could see light glowing in the windows, and people turned to silhouettes inside. Great. So she'd have an audience, too.

Natalie cut the engine. 'You're going to be great,' she said. She started to get out of the car.

'Hey.' Heather stopped her. Her mouth was dry. 'You know what you said earlier? Well, I could never have gotten this far without you, either.'

Nat smiled. She looked sad. 'May the best girl win,' she said softly.

Inside, the air was hazy with cigarette smoke. Diggin was back, his face still swollen and shiny, patterned all over with bruises. He was showing off his injuries like they were badges of honor. Heather was annoyed to see that Ray had come – probably to watch her fail.

There were a few cheap bottles of liquor and some plastic cups on the counter. A group of people was sitting around the table; as Heather and Nat entered, they turned around as one. Heather's heart stopped. Vivian Trager had come.

And so had Matt Hepley.

'What are you doing here?' She directed the question to Matt. She didn't move from the doorway. She kept thinking that this was part of the test – like a setup. *Panic challenge: see how long Heather can last without crying in a small trailer with her ex-boyfriend and Bishop's new girl. Bonus points for not puking.*

Matt stood up from the table so quickly, he nearly overturned his chair. 'Heather. Hey.' He waved awkwardly, like they were standing at a distance instead of five feet from each other. Heather could feel Vivian watching her, looking slightly amused. Bitch. And Heather had never been anything but nice to her. 'Diggin asked me to come. For help with . . .' He trailed off.

'With what?' Heather felt cold. She couldn't feel her mouth, even as it made words.

Matt turned a deep red. Heather used to like that about him – how he was an easy blusher.

Now she thought he just looked stupid. 'With the gun,' he said finally.

For the first time, Heather became aware of the object on the table, around which everyone had gathered. Her breath froze in her throat, became a hard block. She couldn't swallow.

Not a pack of cards: a gun.

The gun – the one Heather had stolen from Trigger-Happy Jack's place.

But no, that was impossible. She was losing it. Bishop had taken the gun and locked it away in his glove box. Heather wasn't sure she could tell the difference between guns, anyway. They all looked the same: like horrible metal fingers, pointing the way to something evil.

She remembered, suddenly, listening as a small child while Krista was drinking with the neighbors in the kitchen. 'Now Heather's father . . . *he* was a mess. Offed himself right after the baby came along. Came home and found his brain splattered on the wall.' Pause. 'Can't say I blame him, sometimes.'

'Please? Just for a minute?' Matt had come even closer. He was staring at Heather with his big cow eyes, pleading; she belatedly registered that he had asked her whether they could talk. He lowered his voice. 'Outside?'

'No.' Everything Heather thought was taking a long time to turn into words, into action.

'What?' Matt looked momentarily confused. He probably wasn't used to having Heather stand up for herself. Probably Delaney always said yes to him too.

'If you want to talk, you can talk to me here.' Heather was aware that Nat was doing her best to pretend she wasn't listening. Vivian, on the other hand, was still staring at her.

Matt coughed. He blushed again. 'Look, I just wanted to tell you . . . I'm sorry. For the way everything happened between us. The Delaney thing . . .' He looked away. He was doing his best to seem apologetic, but Heather knew that he was gloating, just a little bit, to be in the position of *having* to apologize. He was in control. He shrugged. 'You have to believe, it just kind of . . . *happened*.'

She felt a rush of hatred for him. How had she ever believed she was in love with him? He was a dolt, just like Nat said. At the same time, an image of Bishop rose up in her mind: Bishop in his stupid sweatpants and flip-flops, grinning at her; sharing an iced coffee, sharing the same straw, mindless of backwash and the fact that Heather always chewed her straws to bits; lying side by side on the hood of his car, surrounded by crushed cans, which Bishop said would make the aliens more likely to abduct them. Saying, *Please, please, take me away from here, alien friends!* And laughing.

'Why are you telling me this now?' Heather said.

Matt looked startled, as though he'd expected her to thank him. 'I'm telling you now because you don't have to do this.

You don't have to go through with it. Look, I *know* you, Heather. And this isn't you.'

She felt like she'd been socked in the stomach. 'You think this is about you? About what happened?'

Matt sighed. She could tell he thought she was being difficult. 'I'm just saying you don't have to prove anything.'

A vibration went through Heather – tiny electrical pulses of anger. 'Fuck off, Matt,' she said. By now, the people in the room were no longer pretending not to be listening. But she didn't care.

'Heather—' He reached for her arm as she started to move past him.

She shook him off. 'This was never about you.' That wasn't, she realized, 100 percent true. She had entered – at least, she *thought* she had – out of a sense of desperation, a sense that her life was over when he dumped her. But she was playing for herself now, for herself and Lily; she was playing because she had made it this far; she was playing because if she won, it would be the first and only time she had ever won something in her life. 'And you *don't* know me. You never did.'

She was hoping he would leave, now that he had come to say what he had to say, but he didn't. He crossed his arms and leaned against the bathroom door, or the sheet of graffiti-printed plywood where the bathroom door *should* have been – the plumbing lines hadn't been connected. Just for a second, she saw Matt Hepley and Ray Hanrahan exchange a glance. Almost imperceptibly, Matt gestured to him. Like, *I did what I could.*

She felt a twin surge of disgust and triumph. So now Ray was enlisting Matt's help to get Heather to drop out. It was probably Ray who'd sent her that text in June telling her to quit Panic. He obviously thought she was a real threat.

And that made her feel powerful.

'What is this?' she said, gesturing with her chin to the gun. Her voice was overloud, and she was aware that everyone was watching her – Matt, Ray, Nat, Vivian, and all the rest of them. It was like a painting; and at the center, framed in light, was the gun.

'Russian roulette.' Diggin sounded almost apologetic. He added quickly, 'You only have to pull the trigger once. Harold had to do it too.'

'But Harold *didn't* do it.' Vivian spoke up. Her voice was deep and slow, and reminded Heather of warmer places. Places where it never rained.

She forced herself to meet Vivian's eyes. 'So Harold is out?'

Vivian shrugged. 'Guess so.' She had one foot on the chair, knee up to her chest, and she fiddled unconcernedly with the necklace she was wearing. Heather could see her collarbones protruding from her tank top. Like baby bird bones. She had an image of Bishop kissing that spot and looked away.

So Harold was out. That left just four players.

'All right,' she said. She could hardly swallow. 'All right,' she repeated. She knew she should get it over with, but her hands wouldn't move from her sides. Nat was staring at her, horrified, as though Heather was already dead.

'Is it loaded?' someone asked.

'It's loaded.' It was Ray who answered. 'I checked.' But even he looked kind of queasy, and he wouldn't meet Heather's eyes.

Don't be afraid, she told herself. But it had the opposite effect. She was rooted, paralyzed with fear. How many chambers were in a gun? What were her chances? She'd always been crap at things like that – probabilities.

She kept hearing her mom's voice: *Came home and found his brain splattered on the wall . . .*

She had no choice unless she wanted the game to end here, now. Then what would Lily do?

But what would happen to Lily if Heather blew her brains out?

She saw her hand leave her side and reach for the gun. Her hand looked pale and foreign, like some weird creature you'd find living in the ocean. Behind her, Nat gasped.

Suddenly the door flew open behind them, with such force that it banged hard against the wall. Everyone turned simultaneously, as though they were all puppets on the same string.

Dodge.

Heather felt immediately disappointed; she knew that deep down, she'd been hoping for Bishop.

'Hey,' she said. But Dodge didn't answer. He just crossed the small space toward her, practically shoving Matt out of the way.

'It was you,' he said. His voice was low and full of spite.

Heather blinked. 'What?'

'You told someone about the spiders,' he said. He glared at Natalie next. 'Or you did.'

Ray snickered. Dodge ignored him.

'What are you talking about?' It had not occurred to Heather to wonder how the judges had known about Dodge's fear of spiders. But now she did. How did they know about any of them?

'Neither of us said anything, Dodge, I promise.' That was Natalie.

Dodge stared at each of them in turn. Then, unexpectedly, he reached out and seized the gun. Several people gasped and Diggin actually ducked, like he expected Dodge to start firing.

'What are you doing?' Vivian said.

Dodge did something with the gun – opened the chamber, Heather thought, although his fingers moved so quickly, she couldn't be sure. Then he replaced it on the table.

'I wanted to be sure it was loaded,' he announced. 'Fair's fair.' Now he wouldn't look at Heather at all. He just crossed his arms and waited.

'Poor Dodge,' Ray said. He didn't bother to stifle a laugh. 'Afraid of itsy-bitsy spiders.'

'Your turn's coming, Hanrahan,' Dodge said calmly. This made Ray stop laughing.

The room got quiet. Heather knew there would be no more interruptions. No more distractions. She felt as though someone had turned the lights up. It was too hot, too bright.

She took the gun. Heather heard Nat say, *'Please.'* Heather knew that everyone was still watching her, but she could make out no individual faces: everyone had been transformed into vague blobs, suggestions of color and angles. Even the table began to blur.

The only real thing was the gun: heavy and cold.

She fumbled a little to get her finger on the trigger. She couldn't feel her body anymore from the waist down. Maybe this was what it was like to die: a slow numbing.

She placed the gun to her temple, felt the cool bite of metal on her skin, like a hollow mouth. *This was what my father must have felt like,* she thought.

She closed her eyes.

Nat screamed, 'Don't do it!' At the same time, a chair clattered to the floor and several voices called out at once.

She squeezed the trigger.

Click.

Nothing. Heather opened her eyes. Instantly, the room was a roar of sound. People were on their feet, cheering. Heather was so weak with joy and relief she found she couldn't hold on to the gun and let it fall to the floor. Then Natalie had rocketed into Heather's arms. 'Oh, Heather, oh, Heather,' she kept saying. 'I'm so sorry.'

Heather was saying, 'It's okay, it's okay,' but she didn't feel the words leave her mouth. Her lips were numb, her tongue was numb, her body was quivering like it was preparing to disintegrate. When Nat released her, Heather thudded into a chair.

It was over.

She was alive.

Someone pressed a drink into her hand, and she sipped gratefully before noticing it was warm beer. Then Diggin was in front of her, saying, 'I didn't think you'd do it. Wow. Holy shit.' She didn't know whether Matt congratulated her; if he did, she didn't register it. Vivian smiled at her but said nothing.

Even Dodge came over. 'Look, Heather,' he said, kneeling so they were at eye level. For a second, his eyes searched hers, and she was sure he was going to tell her something important. Instead he just said, 'Keep this safe, okay?' and pressed something into her hand. She slipped it mindlessly into her pocket.

Suddenly Heather wanted to get out of there more than anything. Away from the too-close smells of beer and old cigarettes and other people's breath; far away from Fresh Pines, where she had never intended to return in the first place. She wanted to be back at Anne's house, in the blue room, listening to the wind sing through the trees, listening to Lily's sleep murmurs.

It took her two attempts to get to her feet. She felt like her body had been sewn together backward.

'Let's go, okay?' Nat said. Her breath smelled a little like beer, and normally Heather would have been annoyed that she was drinking right before they were going to drive. But she didn't have the strength to argue, or even to care.

'That was *epic*,' Nat said, as soon as they were in the car. 'Seriously, Heather. Everyone will be talking about it – probably for years. I do think it's kind of unfair, though. I mean, your challenge was, like, a billion times harder than Dodge's. You could have *died*.'

'Can we not talk about this?' Heather said. She unrolled her window a little, inhaling the smell of pine and climber moss. Alive.

'Sure, yeah.' Nat looked over at her. 'Are you okay?'

'I'm okay,' Heather said. She was thinking her way into the deepness of the woods, the soft spaces of growth and shadow. She shifted to lean her head against the window and felt something in her pocket. She remembered what Dodge had given her. She wondered whether he felt guilty about his earlier outburst.

She reached into her pocket. Just then they passed under a streetlamp, and as Heather uncurled her fingers, time seemed to stop for a second. Everything was perfectly still: Nat with both hands on the wheel, mouth open to speak; the trees outside, frozen in anticipation; Heather's fingers half-uncurled.

And the bullet, resting in the fleshy middle of her palm.

SUNDAY, AUGUST 14

heather

IT WAS ALREADY THE SECOND WEEK OF AUGUST. THE GAME was drawing to a close. Four players remained: Dodge, Heather, Nat, and Ray.

For the first time since the game began, people began to place bets that Heather would win, although Ray and Dodge were still evenly split for the favorite.

Heather heard that Ray passed his solo challenge: he'd broken into the county morgue in East Chatham and stayed locked up next to the corpses all night. Creepy, but not likely to kill him; Heather was still angry that her challenge had been the worst.

But then, of course, there was the fact that Dodge had ensured her challenge would be harmless too. Dodge, who had palmed a bullet while making a show of checking the gun for ammo.

Dodge, who now refused to pick up her phone calls. It was such a joke. Bishop called Heather incessantly. She called Dodge. Krista called Heather. No one picked up for anyone else. Like some mixed-up game of telephone.

Nat stayed out of it. She had still not been given her solo challenge. Every day, Nat grew paler and skinnier. For once, she wasn't chattering endlessly about all the guys she was dating. She'd even announced, solemnly, that she thought she might try and stay away from guys for a while. Heather didn't know if it was the game or whatever had happened on the night of Nat's birthday, but Nat reminded Heather of a painting she'd once seen reproduced in a history textbook, of a noble-woman awaiting the guillotine.

A week after Heather's challenge, the blade fell.

Heather and Nat had taken Lily to the mall to see a movie, mostly to get out of the heat – it had been a record ninety-five degrees for three straight days, and Heather felt as if she was moving through soup. The trees were motionless in the shimmering heat.

Afterward, they returned in Nat's car to Anne's house. Nat knew, at last, that Heather wasn't living at home, and had offered to come sleep at Anne's with her, even though she disliked the dogs and wouldn't even get close to the tigers' pen. But Anne had left town for the weekend to visit her sister-in-law in Boston, and Heather hated being in the big, old house without her. That was one good thing about the trailer: you always knew what was what, where the walls were, who was home. Anne's house was different: full of wood that creaked and groaned, ghost sounds, mysterious thumps and scratching noises.

'Get it,' Nat said when her phone dinged between her legs.

'Ew. I'm not reaching for it,' Heather said.

Nat giggled and tossed the phone at her, taking her hand off the wheel only briefly. She swerved, and Lily yelped from the backseat.

'Sorry, Bill,' Nat said.

'*Don't* call me that,' Lily said primly. Nat laughed. But Heather was sitting with the phone in her lap, ice running through her wrists, into her hands.

'What's the matter?' Nat asked. Then her face got serious. 'Is it—?' She cut herself off and glanced in the rearview at Lily, who was listening attentively.

Heather read the text again. Impossible. 'Did you tell anyone you were sleeping over at Anne's tonight?' she asked, in a low voice.

Nat shrugged. 'My parents. And Bishop. I think I mentioned it to Joey, too.'

Heather slid Nat's phone shut and chucked it into the glove compartment. Suddenly she wanted it as far from her as possible.

'What?' Nat asked.

'Someone knows that Anne's gone,' Heather said. She turned the radio up so Lily couldn't eavesdrop. 'The judges know.' Who had Heather told? Dodge – she'd mentioned it to him in a text. Said he should come over so they could talk, so she could thank him. And of course, Anne had told some people, probably; it was Carp, and people talked because they had nothing else to do.

The implication of what Heather had just read – what Nat would have to do – sank in. She unrolled her window, but the blast of hot air gave her no relief. She shouldn't have drunk so much soda at the movie theater. She was nauseous.

'What is it?' Nat said. She looked afraid. Unconsciously, she'd begun tapping out a rhythm on the steering wheel. 'What do I have to do?'

Heather looked at her. Her mouth tasted like ash, and she

found she could not even speak a complete sentence. 'The tigers,' she said.

dodge

THE CHALLENGES WERE ALWAYS POPULAR, BUT THIS YEAR, many spectators had been staying away. It was too risky. The police had threatened to haul in anyone associated with Panic, and everyone was worried about taking the rap for the fire at the Graybill house. Rumor was Sadowski wanted someone – anyone – to take the fall. The roads, usually so empty, were infested with police cars, some from other counties.

But the word – *tigers* – was too much to resist. It had its own lift and momentum: it flitted through the woods, stole its way into houses barred up against the heat, spun into the rhythm of fans that cycled in bedrooms across Carp. By afternoon, all the players and ex-players and spectators and bettors and welshers and squealers – everyone who cared even remotely about the game and its outcome – had heard about the tigers of Mansfield Road.

Dodge was lying naked on his bed with two fans going at once when the text came in from Heather. For a second he wasn't sure whether he was sleeping or awake. His room was dark and as hot as a mouth. He didn't want to open the door, though. Ricky was over again and he'd brought food for Dayna, stuff he'd cooked himself at the diner, rice and beans and shrimp that smelled like burned garlic. They were watching a movie, and occasionally, despite the noise of the ancient fans and the closed door, he could hear the muffled sound of laughter.

The effort of sitting up made Dodge begin to sweat. He punched in Bishop's number.

'What the hell?' he said, when Bishop picked up. No preamble. No bullshit. 'How could you do it? How could you make *her* do it?'

Bishop sighed. 'Rules of the game, Dodge. I'm not the only one in control of this shit.' He sounded exhausted. 'If I don't make it hard enough, I'll get replaced. And then I won't be able to help at all.'

Dodge ignored him. 'She'll never go through with it. She shouldn't.'

'She doesn't have to.'

Dodge felt like throwing his phone against the wall, even though he knew what Bishop said was true. In order for Dodge's plan to succeed, Nat would have to drop out anyway, and soon. Still, it felt unfair. Too hard, too dangerous, like Heather's challenge. But at least there, Bishop – and Dodge – had made sure she wouldn't be in any real danger.

'Heather will find a way to help her,' Bishop said, as though he could read Dodge's thoughts.

'You don't know that,' Dodge said, and hung up. He didn't know why he was so angry. He'd known the rules of Panic from the start. But somehow everything had gotten out of control. He wondered whether Bishop would show tonight, whether he could face it.

Poor Natalie. He thought about calling her and trying to convince her to drop out, to leave it, but then he thought about how she'd returned the necklace to him, and what he'd said to her that night – about opening her legs. It made him hot with shame. She had a right not to speak to him. She had a right to hate him, even.

But he would go tonight. And even if she did hate him, even if she ignored him completely, he wanted her to know that he was there. That he was sorry, too, for what he had said.

Time, for him, was running out.

heather

ONE OF HEATHER'S PROBLEMS – OUT OF ABOUT A HUNDRED big problems – was what to do about Lily. Anne had left them food for the weekend – mac 'n' cheese, not from a box, but made with real cheese and milk and little spiral pasta, and tomato soup. Just heating it up made Heather feel like a criminal: Anne had invited them into her home, was taking care of them, and Heather was plotting behind her back.

Heather watched Lily polish off three portions. She didn't know how Lily could eat in this heat. All the fans were going, all the windows were open, but it was still sweltering. She couldn't have taken even a bite. She was sick with guilt and nerves. It wouldn't be long before sundown, and game time. Heather wondered what Natalie was doing. She'd been locked in upstairs for the past three hours. Heather had heard the shuddering of pipes, the gush of water in the shower, three times.

After Lily ate, Heather brought her into the den: a big, dark room that still bore the mark of Anne's late husband – beat-up leather couches and mohair blankets and carpet that smelled a little like wet dog. Here it was a little cooler, although the leather stuck uncomfortably to Heather's thighs when she sat down.

'I need you to promise me that you won't come outside,' Heather said. 'There will be people. And you might hear noises. But you have to stay right here, where it's safe. Promise me.'

Lily frowned. 'Does Anne know?' she asked.

That guilty feeling rode a wave up into Heather's throat. She shook her head. 'And she won't,' she said.

Lily picked at a bit of stuffing that had begun to poke out of the couch. She was silent for a second. Heather wished, suddenly, she could take Lily into her arms and squeeze her, tell her everything – how scared she was, how she didn't know what would happen to either of them.

'This is about Panic, isn't it?' Lily said. She looked up. Her face was expressionless, her eyes flat. They reminded Heather of the tigers' eyes: ancient, all-seeing.

Heather knew there was no point in lying. So she said, 'It's almost over.'

Lily didn't move when Heather kissed her head, which smelled like grass and sweat. The leather released Heather's skin with a sharp sucking sound. She put on a DVD about a zoo, which Lily had requested – another gift from Anne.

Anne, Heather knew, was a good person. The best person Heather had ever met. So what did that make Heather?

She was at the door when Lily spoke up. 'Are you going to win?'

Heather turned around to her. She'd left the lights off, so it would stay cool, and Lily's face was in shadow.

Heather tried to smile. 'I'm already winning,' she lied, and closed the door behind her.

The haze of the sky, milk white and scorched, at last turned to dark; and the trees impaled the sun, and all the light broke apart. Then they came: quietly, tires moving almost soundlessly on the dirt, headlights bouncing like overgrown fireflies through the woods.

There was no thudding music, no shouting. Everyone was on alert for cops.

Heather stood outside, waiting. The dogs were going crazy; she kept feeding them treats, trying to get them to shut up. She knew there were no neighbors around for miles, but she couldn't shake the feeling that someone would hear – that Anne would know, somehow, be summoned back to the house by the barking.

Nat had still not come down.

Heather had fed the tigers more than double their normal amount. Now, as the last light drained from the sky, and the stars began to pulse through the liquid haze of heat, they were lying on their sides, seemingly asleep and indifferent to all the cars. Heather prayed they would stay that way – that Nat could do whatever she needed to do, and get out.

Car after car: Diggin, Ray Hanrahan, even some of the players who'd been eliminated, like Cory Walsh and Ellie Hayes; Mindy Kramer and a bunch of her dance team friends, still dressed in bikinis and cutoffs and bare feet, like they'd just come from the beach; Zev Keller, eyes red-rimmed and liquid, obviously drunk, with two friends Heather didn't recognize; people she hadn't seen since the challenge at the water tower. Matt Hepley, too, and Delaney. He walked right by Heather, pretending she didn't exist. She found she didn't care.

They drifted across the yard and gathered around the tigers' pen, silent, disbelieving. Flashlights clicked on as it got darker; the floodlights on the barn, motion-detected, came on too, illuminating the tigers, sleeping almost side by side, so still they might have been statues, held in a flat palm of earth.

'I don't believe it,' someone whispered.

'No fucking way.'

But there they were: no matter how many times you blinked or looked away. Tigers. A bit of a miracle, a circus-wonder, right there on the grass under the Carp trees and the Carp sky.

Heather was relieved to see Dodge arrive on his bicycle. She still hadn't had a chance to thank him in person for what he'd done.

Almost immediately, he asked, 'Is Bishop here?'

She shook her head. He made a face.

'Dodge,' she said. 'I wanted to say—'

'Don't.' He put a hand on her arm, and squeezed gently. 'Not yet.'

She didn't know exactly what he meant. She wondered, for the first time, what Dodge was planning to do this fall, and whether he would remain in Carp, or whether he had plans for a job somewhere – or even college. She'd never paid any attention to how he did in school.

Suddenly the thought of Dodge leaving made her sad. They were friends, or something like it that was close enough.

It struck her how sad it was that all of them – the kids standing here, her classmates and friends and even the people she'd hated – had grown up on top of one another like small animals in a too-small cage, and now would simply scatter.

And that would be the end of that. Everything that had happened – those stupid school dances and basement after-parties, football games, days of rain that lulled them all to sleep in math class, summers swimming at the creek and stealing sodas from the coolers at the back of the 7-Eleven, even now, this, Panic – would be sucked away into memory and vapor, as though it hadn't even happened at all.

'Where's Natalie?' That was Diggin. He was speaking softly, as if afraid to wake the tigers. Hardly anyone made a sound. They were all still transfixed by the sight of those dreamlike creatures, stretched long on the ground like shadows.

'I'll get her,' Heather said. She was grateful to have an excuse to go into the house, even for a moment. What she was doing, what she was helping Nat do, was too horrible. She thought of Anne's face, her smile pulling her eyes into a squint. She'd never felt so much like a criminal, not even when she'd taken her mom's car and run away.

Another car was arriving, and she knew from the spitting and hissing of its engine that it was Bishop. She was right. Just as she reached the front door, he climbed out of his car and spotted her.

'Heather!' Even though he wasn't shouting, his voice seemed to her like a slap in the silence.

She ignored him. She stepped into the kitchen and found Natalie sitting at the table, eyes red. There was a shot glass in front of her, and a bottle of whiskey.

'Where'd you get that?' Heather asked.

'In the pantry.' Nat didn't even look up. 'I'm sorry. I only had a sip, though.' She made a face. 'It's awful.'

'It's time,' Heather said.

Nat nodded and stood up. She was wearing denim shorts

and no shoes; her hair was still wet from the shower. Heather knew that if Nat weren't so afraid, she would have insisted on putting on makeup, on doing her hair. Heather thought Nat had never looked so beautiful. Her fierce and fearful friend – who loved country music and cherry Pop-Tarts and singing in public and the color pink, who was terrified of germs and dogs and ladders.

'I love you, Nat,' Heather said on impulse.

Nat looked startled, as though she'd already forgotten Heather was there. 'You, too, Heathbar,' she said. She managed a small smile. 'I'm ready.'

Bishop was standing a little ways from the house, pacing, bringing his fingers up to his lips and down again as though he were smoking an invisible cigarette. As Nat moved into the crowd, he caught up with Heather.

'Please.' His voice was hoarse. 'We need to talk.'

'This is kind of a bad time.' Her voice came out harsher, more sarcastic, than she'd intended. It occurred to her that she hadn't seen Vivian, and she wondered whether Bishop had begged her not to come. *Please, babe. Just until I can patch things up with Heather. She's jealous, you know . . . she always had a thing for me.* The thought made her throat knot up, and a part of her just wanted to tell Bishop to fuck off.

Then there was the part of her that wanted to put her arms around his neck and feel his laughter humming through his chest, feel the wild tangle of his hair on her face. Instead she crossed her arms, as if she could press the feeling down.

'I need to tell you something.' Bishop licked his lips. He looked awful. His face was sickly, different shades of yellow and green, and he was too skinny. 'It's important.'

'Later, okay?' Before he could protest, she moved past him.

Natalie had reached the fence, closer to the tigers than she had ever allowed herself to go. Unconsciously, the crowd had backed off a little, so she was surrounded by a halo of negative space – like she was contaminated with something contagious.

Heather jogged over to her. Now the dogs started up again, shattering the stillness, and Heather hushed them sharply as she passed the kennel. She pushed easily through the crowd and stepped into Nat's open circle, feeling as if she were trespassing.

'It's okay,' she whispered. 'I'm here.' But Nat didn't seem to hear her.

'The rules are simple,' Diggin said. Even though he was speaking at a normal volume, to Heather it sounded like he was shouting. She began praying the tigers wouldn't wake up. They still hadn't even lifted their heads. She noticed a bit of the steak she'd given them earlier was still untouched, buzzing with flies, and couldn't decide if that was a good thing or not. 'You go into the pen, you stand with the tigers for ten seconds, you get out.' He emphasized this last part just slightly.

'How close?' Nat said.

'What?'

'How close do I have to get?' she asked, turning to him.

Diggin shrugged. 'Just inside, I guess.'

Nat pushed out a small breath. Heather smiled at her encouragingly, even though she felt like her skin was made of clay about to crack. But if the tigers slept, Nat would have no problem. They were a full forty feet away from the gate. Nat wouldn't even have to go near them.

'I'll time you,' Diggin said. Then: 'Who has the key to the gate?'

'I do.' Heather stepped forward. She heard a slight rustle,

as everyone turned to stare at her; she felt the heat of all those eyes on her skin. The air was leaden, totally still.

Heather fumbled in her pocket for the key to the padlock. Nat's breathing was rapid and shallow, like an injured animal's. For a second, Heather couldn't feel the key and didn't know whether to be relieved; then her fingers closed around metal.

In the silence and the stillness, the click of the padlock seemed as loud as a rifle report. She unlooped the heavy chain carefully and laid it on the ground, then slid the metal latches back, one by one, desperately trying to stall, trying to give Nat a few more seconds.

As the final latch clanged open, both tigers lifted their heads in unison, as though sensing that something was coming.

The whole group inhaled as one. Nat let out a whimper.

'It's okay,' Heather told her, gripping Nat by the shoulders. She could feel Nat trembling under her hands. 'Ten seconds. You just have to step inside the gate. It'll be done before you know it.'

People had started buzzing, giggling nervously, shifting. Now the stillness was replaced with an electric energy. And as Nat took one halting step toward the gate, and then another, the tigers, too, stood up – twisting onto their feet, stretching, yawning their enormous jaws so their teeth glistened in the floodlights – as though they had decided to perform.

Nat paused with a hand on the gate. Then her other hand. Then both hands. Her mouth was moving, and Heather wondered if she was counting or praying, whether for Nat they were the same thing. Dwarfed by the gate, silhouetted against the sharp, unnatural light, she looked unreal, one-dimensional, like a cardboard cutout.

'You don't have to do it.' Dodge's voice was loud, and so

unexpected that everyone turned to stare. Nat turned too, and Heather saw her frown.

Then she pulled open the gate and stepped inside.

'Start the timer,' Heather cried out. She saw Diggin fumbling for his phone. *'Now.'*

'Okay, okay,' Diggin said. 'Time!'

It was too late. The tigers had started to move. Slowly, their massive heads swinging between their shoulder blades like some awful clock pendulum . . . *tick, tick, tick.* But still they were too close, already too close; three strides and they covered five yards, mouths open, grinning.

'Three seconds!' Diggin announced.

Impossible. Surely Nat had been in the pen for ten minutes, for half an hour, forever. Heather's heart was bursting out of her throat. No one spoke. No one moved. Everything was a black sea, dim and featureless: everything but the bright circle of white light, and the cardboard-cutout Nat, and the long shadow of the tigers. Nat was shaking now, and whimpering, too. Heather feared for a second that she would collapse.

Then what? Would the tigers pounce? Would she, Heather, be brave enough to try to stop them?

She knew she wouldn't. Her legs were water, and she could hardly breathe.

'Seven seconds!' Diggin's voice was shrill, like an alarm.

The tigers were less than eight feet from Nat. They would be on top of her in two more paces. Heather could hear them breathing, see their whiskers twitching, tasting the air. Nat had started to cry. But she still held herself there, rigid. Maybe she was too scared to move. Maybe their eyes, like deep black pools, had transfixed her.

'Eight seconds!'

Then one of the tigers twitched; a muscle flexed, and Heather knew it was getting ready to pounce, *felt* it, knew it would jump on Natalie and tear her apart and they would all stand, watching, helpless. And just as she was trying to scream *Run* but couldn't, because her throat was too thick with terror, Nat *did* run. Maybe someone else screamed it. There was noise suddenly – people shouting – and Nat was out of the gate and slamming it shut, leaning back, crying.

Just as the tiger, the one Heather had been sure was moving to spring, lay down again.

'Nine seconds,' Diggin said above the sudden roar of sound. Heather registered a small burst of triumph – Nat was out of the game – and then a stronger pull of shame. She pushed over to Nat and drew her into a hug.

'You were amazing,' she said into the top of Nat's hair.

'I didn't make it,' Nat said. Her voice was muffled and her face sticky against Heather's chest.

'You were still amazing,' Heather said.

Nat was the only one who wasn't celebrating. She returned almost immediately to the house. But everyone else seemed to forget about the threat of cops, forget about what had happened at the Graybill house and about the body of Little Kelly, found charred and blackened in the basement – for a short while, it felt almost as it had at the beginning of the summer, when the players had first made the Jump.

It took more than an hour for Heather to get everyone out, into their cars and off the property, and the whole time the dogs were going crazy and the tigers were still again, as though deliberately making a point. By the time the yard was almost empty of cars, exhaustion numbed Heather's fingers and toes.

But it was over, thank God. It was all over, and Anne would never have to know.

There were only three players left. And Heather was one of them.

'Heather,' Bishop tried again when almost everyone had gone. 'We need to talk.'

'Not tonight, Bishop.'

There were a few people lingering, leaning up against their cars, hands down each other's pants, probably. Strange how just a few months ago she had been one of them, hanging out at parties with Matt, her capital-B Boyfriend, flaunting it however she could. Wearing his sweatshirts, his baseball hats, like a badge of something – that she was lovable, that she was fine and normal and just like everybody else. Already the old Heather seemed like someone she barely knew.

'You can't avoid me forever,' Bishop said, deliberately moving in front of her as she stooped to collect a cigarette pack, half-trampled into the grass.

She straightened up. His hair was poking out from every side of his hat, like something alive trying to get out. She resisted the urge to reach up and try and wrestle it into shape. The worst was that when she looked at him now, she still saw their kiss: the heat that had roared through her and the soft-ness of his lips and the brief electric moment when his tongue had found hers.

'I'm not avoiding you,' she said, looking away so she wouldn't have to remember. 'I'm just tired.'

'When, then?' He looked lost. 'It's important, okay? I need you. I need you to listen.'

She was tempted to ask him why Vivian couldn't listen, but she didn't. He looked awful, and miserable, and she loved him even if he didn't love her. The thought that he was upset, in pain, was a worse feeling than her own pain.

'Tomorrow,' she said. Impulsively, she reached out and squeezed his hand. He looked startled, and she dropped it quickly, as though it might burn her. 'I promise, tomorrow.'

MONDAY, AUGUST 15

heather

IN THE MORNING, HEATHER WAS WOKEN UP BY SHOUTING.
Lily was calling her name, pounding up the stairs; then the
door flew open, so hard it struck the wall.

Lily said, 'The tigers are gone.' She was breathing hard,
her face red and damp with sweat. She smelled a little like
manure – she must have been out feeding the animals.

'*What?*' Instantly Heather was awake and sitting up.

'The gate is open and they're gone,' Lily said.

'Impossible.' Heather was already pulling on clothes, shoving
her legs into shorts, wrestling on a T-shirt. She didn't even
bother with a bra. 'Impossible,' she repeated, but even as she
said it, a dull thud of terror began, bringing back images from
last night, disjointed memories – hugging Nat, latching the
gates . . . Had she replaced the padlock? She couldn't remember.
Mindy Kramer had been talking to her about her job at Anne's,
and then she'd had to yell at Zev Keller for trying to get into
the pigpen.

She must have replaced the padlock. Maybe the tigers weren't really missing. Maybe they were just hiding out in the trees somewhere, where Lily hadn't spotted them.

Downstairs, Heather saw that it was already eleven a.m., that she'd overslept, that Anne would be home soon. Lily followed her outside. It was another day of thick heat, but this time the sky was overcast, and there was moisture shimmering in the air like a curtain. It would rain.

She was halfway across the yard when she saw it: the padlock, coiled in the grass like a metal snake, exactly where she had placed it last night when she unlocked the gate for Natalie.

And the gate, now swinging open.

There was no need to search the whole enclosure. They were gone. She could *feel* it. Why hadn't the dogs barked? But maybe they had and she hadn't heard. Or maybe they'd been frightened, bewitched like the crowd last night.

Heather closed her eyes. For a second she thought she might faint. The tigers were gone, it was her fault, and now Anne would despise her and throw her out. She'd have every right to.

She opened her eyes, fueled by a wild panic: she had to find them, now, quickly, before Anne came home.

'Stay here,' she told Lily, but she didn't have the strength to argue when Lily followed her back into the house. She hardly knew what she was doing. She found a bucket under the sink, dumped out a bunch of shriveled sponges and cleaning supplies, and filled it with some half-thawed steaks. Then she was out of the house again and plunging into the woods. Maybe they hadn't gone far, and she could lure them back.

'Where are we going?' Lily asked.

'Shhh,' Heather said sharply. She felt the bite of tears in her eyes. How could she be such an idiot, such an absolute moron? The bucket was heavy and she had to pull it with both hands, scanning from left to right, looking for a flash of color, those luminous black eyes. *Come on, come on, come on.*

Behind Heather, there was a rustling in the undergrowth, a shift in the air – a presence, animal, watchful. All of a sudden it struck Heather that what she was doing was idiotic: charging off into the woods with Lily, searching for the tigers like they were lost kittens, hoping to lure them home. If she did find the tigers, they'd probably tear her head off for a snack. A hard zip of fear went up her spine. She was overconscious of every rustle, every snapping twig, the diamond patterns of light and shadow that could easily conceal a pair of eyes, a swath of tawny fur.

'Take my hand, Lily,' she said, trying to keep the fear out of her voice. 'Let's go back inside.'

'What about the tigers?' Lily asked. She thought it was some kind of adventure, obviously.

'We'll have to call Anne,' Heather said, and instantly knew it was true. She still had the unmistakable sense of something Other watching her, watching them. 'She'll know what to do.'

A raccoon poked its head suddenly from between the fat leaves of a spirea bush, and Heather felt a flood of relief that nearly made her pee. She abandoned the bucket in the woods. It was too heavy, and she wanted to move quickly.

As they were emerging from the woods just next to the outdoor shower, Heather could hear tires spitting on the driveway and thought that Anne must be home. She didn't know whether to feel grateful or afraid. She was both.

But then she saw the rusted hood of Bishop's Le Sabre and remembered she'd promised him they could talk today.

'Bishop!' Lily was running to him before he had even fully extricated himself from the car. 'The tigers are gone! The tigers are gone!'

'What?' He looked even worse than he had the night before, as though he hadn't slept at all. He turned to Heather. 'Is it true?'

'It's true,' she said. 'I forgot to padlock the gates.' All of a sudden the truth hit her like a hard punch to the stomach, and she was crying. She'd get kicked out of Anne's house; they'd have to move back to Fresh Pines or go on the run. And Anne would be devastated. Anne, who was practically the only person who gave a shit about Heather.

'Hey, hey.' Bishop was next to her. She didn't resist when he hugged her. 'It's not your fault. It's gonna be okay.'

'It *is* my fault.' She buried her face in the hollow of his shoulder and cried until she coughed, while he rubbed her back and her hair, touched her lightly on her cheek, murmured into the top of her head. Only Bishop could make her feel small. Only Bishop could make her feel protected.

She didn't even hear the approach of Anne's car, until a door was slamming and Anne's voice, frantic, called, 'What's the matter? What's wrong?'

Heather stepped away from Bishop and immediately, Anne seized her by the shoulders. 'Are you okay? Are you hurt?'

'It's not me.' Heather swiped an arm across her nose. Her mouth was thick with the taste of phlegm, and she couldn't look Anne in the eye. 'I'm fine.' She tried to say it. *The tigers are gone. The tigers are gone.*

Lily was quiet, her mouth moving soundlessly.

It was Bishop who spoke. 'The tigers got out,' he said.

Anne's face turned colors, as though Heather was watching her on a screen and someone had just adjusted the contrast. 'You're . . . you're joking.'

Heather managed to shake her head.

'How?' Anne said.

Before Heather could speak, Bishop cut in, 'It was my fault.'

At last Heather found her voice. 'No. Bishop had nothing to do with it. It was me. It was . . . the game.'

'The game?' Anne squinted at Heather like she'd never seen her before. 'The game?'

'Panic,' Heather said. Her voice was hoarse. 'I opened the gates . . . I must have forgotten to lock them again.'

For a second, Anne was silent. Her face was awful to see: white and ghastly. Horrified.

'But I was the one who told her to do it,' Bishop said suddenly. 'It's my fault.'

'No.' Heather was embarrassed that Bishop felt he had to stand up for her, even as she was grateful to him. 'He had nothing to do with it.'

'I did.' Bishop's voice got louder. He was sweating. 'I told her to do it. I told all of them to do it. I started the fire at the Graybill place. I'm the one . . .' His voice broke. He turned to Heather. His eyes were pleading, desperate. 'I'm a judge. That's what I wanted to tell you. That's what I wanted to explain. What you saw the other day, with Vivian . . .'

He didn't finish. Heather couldn't speak either. She felt like time had stopped; they were all transformed to statues. Bishop's words were sifting through her like a snow, freezing her insides, her ability to speak.

Impossible. Not Bishop. He hadn't even wanted her to play . . .

'I don't believe it.' She heard the words, and only then realized she was speaking.

'It's true.' Now he turned back to Anne. 'It wasn't Heather's fault. You have to believe me.'

Anne brought her hand briefly to her forehead, as though pressing back pain. She closed her eyes. Lily was still standing several feet away, shifting her weight, anxious and silent. Anne opened her eyes again. 'We need to call the police,' she said quietly. 'They'll need to put out the alert.'

Bishop nodded. But for a second no one moved. Heather wished Anne would yell – it would be so much easier.

And Bishop's words kept swirling through her: *I told her to do it. I told all of them to do it.*

'Come on, Lily,' Anne said. 'Come inside with me.'

Heather started to follow them into the house, but Anne stopped her. 'You wait out here,' she said sharply. 'We'll talk in a bit.'

Her words brought little knife-aches of pain to Heather's stomach. It was all over. Anne would hate her now.

Lily shot Heather a worried glance and then hurried after Anne. Bishop and Heather were left standing alone in the yard, as the sun pushed through the clouds and the day transformed into a microscope, focusing its heat.

'I'm sorry, Heather,' Bishop said. 'I couldn't tell you. I wanted to – you have to know that. But the rules—'

'The *rules*?' she repeated. The anger was bubbling up from a crack opening inside her. 'You lied to me. About everything. You told me not to play, and all this time—'

'I was trying to keep you safe,' he said. 'And when I knew you wouldn't back down, I tried to *help* you. Whenever I could, I tried.' Bishop had moved closer and his arms were out – he was reaching for her. She took a step backward.

'You almost got me killed,' she said. 'The gun – if it wasn't for Dodge—'

'I told Dodge to do it,' Bishop cut in. 'I made sure of it.'

Click-click-click. Memories slotted together: Bishop insisting on taking the shortcut that led past Trigger-Happy Jack's house. The fireworks at the Graybill house on the Fourth of July, which Bishop made sure she would see. A clue: fire.

'You have to believe me, Heather. I never meant to lie to you.'

'So why *did* you do it, Bishop?' Heather crossed her arms. She didn't want to listen to him. She wanted to be angry. She wanted to give in to the black tide, let it suck away all her other thoughts – about the tigers, about how badly she had disappointed Anne, about how she would be homeless again. 'What did you need to prove so badly, huh?' More parts of her were flaking off. *Crack.* 'That you're better than us? Smarter than us? We get it, okay? You're *leaving*.' *Crack.* 'You're getting out of here. That makes you smarter than the whole fucking rest of us put together.'

Bishop's mouth was as thin as a line. 'You know what your problem is?' he said quietly. 'You *want* everything to be shitty. You have a sister who loves you. Friends who love you. I love you, Heather.' He said it fast, in a mumble, and she could not even be happy, because he kept going. 'You've outlasted almost everyone in Panic. But all you see is the crap. So you don't have to believe in anything. So you'll have an excuse to fail.'

Crack. Heather turned around, so if she started crying again, he wouldn't see. But she realized she had nowhere to go. There was the house, the high bowl of the sky, the sun like a laser. And she, Heather, had no place in any of it. The last bits of her broke apart, opened like a wound: she was all hurt and anger. 'You know what I wish? I wish you were gone already.'

She thought he might start yelling. She was almost hoping he would. But instead he just sighed and rubbed his forehead. 'Look, Heather. I don't want to fight with you. I want you to understand—'

'Didn't you hear me? Just go. Leave. Get out of here.' She swiped at her eyes with the palm of her hand. His voice was screaming through her head. *You want everything to be shitty . . . so you'll have an excuse to fail.*

'Heather.' Bishop put a hand on her shoulder, and she shook him off.

'I don't know how many other ways I can say it.'

Bishop hesitated. She felt him close to her, felt the warmth of his body, like a comforting force, like a blanket. For one wild second, she thought he would refuse, he would turn around and hug her and tell her he was never ever leaving. For one wild second, it was what she wanted more than anything.

Instead she felt his fingers just graze her elbow. 'I did it for you,' he said in a low voice. 'I was planning to give you the money.' His voice cracked a little. 'Everything I've ever done is for you, Heather.'

Then he was gone. He turned around, and by the time she couldn't stand it anymore and her legs were about to give out and the anger had turned to eight different tides pulling her to pieces, and she thought to turn around and call out for him – by then he was in the car, and couldn't hear her.

*

It was an upside-down day for Carp. Bishop Marks turned himself in to the police for the murder of Little Kelly – even though, as it turned out, Little Kelly hadn't been killed in the fire at the Graybill house. Still, no one could believe it: Bishop Marks, that nice kid from down the way, whose dad had a frame shop over in Hudson. Shy kid. One of the good ones.

At the police station, Bishop denied the fire had anything to do with Panic. A prank, he said.

Upside down and inside out. Sign of the messed-up times we're living in.

That night, Kirk Finnegan came outside when his dogs began to go crazy. He was carrying a rifle, suspecting drunk kids or maybe his piece-of-shit neighbor, who'd recently started parking on Kirk's property and couldn't be convinced that it wasn't his right.

Instead he saw a tiger.

A fucking tiger, right there in his yard, with its enormous mouth around one of Kirk's cocker spaniels.

He thought he was dreaming, hallucinating, drunk. He was so scared he peed in his boxer shorts and didn't notice until later. He acted without thinking, swung the rifle up, fired four shots straight into the tiger's flank, kept firing, even after it collapsed, even after by some grace-of-God miracle its jaws went slack and his spaniel got to his feet and started barking again – kept firing, because those eyes kept staring at him, dark as an accusation or a lie.

TUESDAY, AUGUST 16

heather

HEATHER HAD SUCCESSFULLY MANAGED TO AVOID TALKING TO Anne for a whole day. After her fight with Bishop, she had walked two miles to the gully and spent the afternoon cursing and throwing rocks at random things (street signs, when there were any; fences; and abandoned cars).

His words played on endless repeat in her head. *You want everything to be shitty . . . so you'll have an excuse to fail.*

Unfair, she wanted to scream.

But a second, smaller voice in her head said, *True.* Those two words – *unfair* and *true* – pinged back and forth in her head, like her mind was a giant Ping-Pong table.

By the time she returned from the gully it was evening, and both Anne and Lily were gone. She was seized with a sudden and irrational fear that Anne had taken Lily back to Fresh Pines. Then she saw a note on the kitchen table.

Grocery store, it said simply.

It was only seven thirty, but Heather curled up in bed, under the covers, despite the stifling heat, and waited for sleep to put a stop to the Ping-Pong game in her mind.

But when she woke up – early, when the sun was still making its first, tentative entry into the room, poking like an exploratory animal through the blinds – she knew there was no avoiding it anymore. Overnight, the Ping-Pong game had been resolved. And the word *true* had emerged victorious.

What Bishop had said was true.

Already, she could hear Anne noises from downstairs: the *clink-clink-clink* of dishes coming out of the dishwasher, the squeak of the old wooden floorboards. When waking up in Fresh Pines to the usual explosion of sounds – cars backfiring, people yelling, doors banging and dogs barking and loud music – she had dreamed of just this kind of home, where mornings were quiet and mothers did dishes and got up early and then yelled at you to get up.

Funny how in such a short time, Anne's house had become more like home than Fresh Pines had ever been.

And she had ruined it. Another truth.

By the time she came downstairs, Anne was on the porch. She called Heather out to her immediately, and Heather knew: this was it.

Heather was shocked to see a squad car parked a little ways down the drive, half pulled off into the underbrush. The cop was outside, leaning his butt against the hood of the car, drinking a coffee and smoking.

'What's he doing here?' Heather said, forgetting for a moment to be scared.

Anne was sitting on the porch swing without swinging. Her knuckles around her mug of tea were very white. 'They think the other one might come back.' She looked down. 'The ASPCA would at least use a stun gun . . .'

'The other one?' Heather said.

'You didn't hear?' Anne said. And she told her: about Kirk Finnegan and his dog and the gunshots, twelve in total. By the time she was done, Heather's mouth was as dry as sand. She wanted to hug Anne, but she was paralyzed, unable to move.

Anne shook her head. She kept her eyes on the mug of tea; she hadn't yet taken a sip. 'I know it was irresponsible, keeping them here.' When she finally looked up, Heather saw she was trying not to cry. 'I just wanted to help. It was Larry's dream, you know. Those poor cats. Did you know there are only thirty-two hundred tigers left in the wild? And I don't even know which one was killed.'

'Anne.' Heather finally found her voice. Even though she was standing, she felt like she was shrinking from the inside out until she was little-kid-sized. 'I'm so, so, so sorry.'

Anne shook her head. 'You shouldn't be playing Panic,' she said, and her voice momentarily held an edge. 'I've heard too much about that game. People have died. But I don't blame you,' she added. Her voice softened again. 'You're not very happy, are you?'

Heather shook her head. She wanted to tell Anne everything: about how she'd been dumped by Matt just when she was ready to say *I love you*; about how she realized now she hadn't really loved him at all, because she had always been in love with Bishop; about her fears that she would never get out of Carp and it would eat her up, swallow her as it had her mom, turn her into one of those brittle, bitter women who is old and drug-eaten and done at twenty-nine. But she couldn't speak. There was a thick knot in her throat.

'Come here.' Anne patted the swing next to her. And then, when Heather sat down, she was shocked: Anne put her arms around her. And all of a sudden Heather was crying into her shoulder, saying, 'I'm sorry, I'm sorry, I'm so sorry.'

'Heather.' Anne pulled away but kept one hand on Heather's shoulder. With her other hand, she brushed the hair back from Heather's face, where it was sticking to her skin. Heather was too upset to be embarrassed. 'Listen to me. I'm not sure what this means for you and Lily. What I did – keeping the tigers here – was illegal. If your mom wants to make a big deal out of it, if the county wants to – the police might force you to go home. I'll do everything I can to keep you here for as long as you and Lily want to stay, but—'

Heather nearly choked. 'You – you're not kicking me out?'

Anne stared at her. 'Of course not.'

'But . . .' Heather couldn't believe it. She must have misheard. 'I was the one who let the tigers out. It's all my fault.'

Anne rubbed her eyes and sighed. Heather never thought of Anne as old, but in that moment, she truly looked it. Her fingers were brittle and sun-spotted, her hair a dull and uniform gray. Someday she would die. Heather's throat was still thick from crying, and she swallowed against the feeling.

'You know, Heather, I was with my husband for thirty years. Since we were kids, really. When we first got together, we had nothing. We spent our honeymoon hitchhiking in California, camping out. We couldn't afford anything else. And some years were very hard. He could be moody . . .' She made a restless motion with her hands. 'My point is, when you love someone, when you care for someone, you have to do it through the good and the bad. Not just when you're happy and it's easy. Do you understand?'

Heather nodded. She felt as though there was a glass ball in her chest – something delicate and beautiful that might shatter if she said the wrong word, if she disturbed the balance in any way.

'So . . . you're not mad at me?' she asked.

Anne half-laughed. 'Of course I'm mad at you,' she said. 'But that doesn't mean I don't want you to stay. That doesn't mean I've stopped caring.'

Heather looked down at her hands. Once again, she was too overwhelmed to speak. She felt as though, just for a second, she had understood something vastly important, had had a glimpse of it: love, pure and simple and undemanding.

'What's going to happen?' she said, after a minute.

'I don't know.' Anne reached over and took one of Heather's hands. She squeezed. 'It's okay to be scared, Heather,' she said, in a low voice, like she was telling her a secret.

Heather thought of Bishop, and the fight she'd had with Nat. She thought about everything that had happened over the summer, all of the changes and tension and weird shifts, as though the air was blowing from somewhere totally unfamiliar. 'I'm scared all the time,' she whispered.

'You'd be an idiot if you weren't,' Anne said. 'And you wouldn't be brave, either.' She stood up. 'Come on. I'm going to put the kettle on. This tea is ice-cold.'

Bishop had, for the most part, come clean to the police. He'd been questioned for the better part of three hours and had at last been released back home to his father, pending official charges.

But he'd lied about one thing. The game wasn't over. There were still three players left.

It was time for the final challenge.

It was time for Joust.

THURSDAY, AUGUST 18

dodge

DODGE KNEW IT WAS JUST A MATTER OF TIME BEFORE BISHOP came to see him. He didn't wait long. Just three days after Bishop had turned himself in to the police for the Graybill fire, Dodge came home from work and spotted Bishop's car. He wasn't outside, though; Dodge was surprised to see that Dayna had let him in. Bishop was sitting on the couch, hands on his knees, knees practically to his chin, he was so tall and the couch was so low. And Dayna was reading in the corner, like it was normal, like they were friends.

'Hey,' Dodge said. Bishop stood up, looking relieved. 'Let's go outside, okay?'

Dayna looked at Dodge suspiciously. He could tell she was waiting for a sign, an indication that everything was okay. But he refused to give it to her. She had betrayed him – by changing, by suddenly flipping the script. Panic had been *their* game, a plan they had made together, a shared desire for revenge.

He knew, obviously, that nothing could bring his sister back, and that hurting Ray, or even killing him, wouldn't restore

Dayna's legs. But that was the whole point: Ray and Luke Hanrahan had stolen something Dodge could never get back. So Dodge was going to steal something from them.

Now that Dayna was shifting, turning into someone he didn't know or recognize – telling him he was immature, criticizing him for playing, spending all her time with Ricky – he felt it even more strongly. It wasn't fair. It was all their fault.

Someone had to pay.

Outside, he gestured for Bishop to follow him into Meth Row. For once, there were signs of life here. Several people were sitting out on their sagging porches, smoking, drinking beers. One woman had snaked a TV out into the front yard with her. Everyone was hoping to catch a glimpse of the tiger; in just a few days, it had become an obsession.

'I'm out, you know,' Bishop said abruptly. 'I won't get my cut or anything. It was all pointless.' His voice was bitter. Dodge felt almost bad for him. He wondered why Bishop had ever agreed to judge, to go along with it. Or why anyone else agreed to it, for that matter. Maybe all of them – the players, the judges, Diggin, even – had their own secrets. Maybe the money was only part of it, and the stakes were much higher for each of them.

Dodge said, 'We're almost at the end. Why back out now?'

'I don't have a choice. I broke the rules. I talked.' Bishop took off his hat, ran a hand through his hair, then smashed his hat back on. 'Besides, I *hate* it. I always have. Fucking Panic. It drives people crazy. It *is* crazy. I only did it because . . .' He looked down at his hands. 'I wanted to give Heather my cut,' he said quietly. 'When she started playing, I had to keep going. To help her. And keep her safe.'

Dodge said nothing. In a screwed-up way, they were both

acting out of love. Dodge felt sad that he hadn't gotten to know Bishop better. There was so much he regretted. Not spending more time with Heather, for example. They could have been real friends.

And Nat, of course. He'd royally screwed things up with her.

He wondered if all of life would be like this: regret piled on regret.

'Did you ever do something bad for a good reason?' Bishop blurted out suddenly.

Dodge almost laughed. Instead he simply answered, 'Yes.'

'So what does that make us?' Bishop said. 'Good, or bad?'

Dodge shrugged. 'Both, I guess,' he said. 'Like everybody else.' He felt a sudden pang of guilt. What he was doing – what he wanted to do to Ray – was really bad. Worse than anything he'd ever done.

But there was that old saying: an eye for an eye, a tooth for a tooth. That's all he was doing. Getting even.

After all, he wasn't the one who had started this.

Bishop turned to him and stopped walking. 'I need to know what you're going to do,' he said.

Bishop looked so lost, standing there with his big arms and legs as if he didn't know how to work them.

'I'm going to keep playing,' Dodge said quietly. 'We're almost done. But not quite. Not yet.'

Bishop exhaled loudly, as though Dodge had just punched him in the stomach, even though he must have been expecting it. And Dodge suddenly knew how he could make Bishop feel better, how he could do something good for a change, and how he could make sure that Ray lost.

'I can keep Heather safe,' Dodge said. Bishop stared at him.

'I can make sure she doesn't go up against Ray. I'll make sure she doesn't get hurt. Deal?'

Bishop watched him for several long minutes. Dodge could tell he was struggling with something; he probably didn't trust Dodge completely. Dodge couldn't blame him.

'What do I have to do?' Bishop said.

Dodge felt a weight lift from his chest. One step closer. Everything was slotting into place.

'A car,' he said. 'I need to borrow a car.'

Dodge had been worried Heather wouldn't listen to him. After all, he was the one who'd told her all deals were off, no splits. But when he asked her to meet him at Dot's, she agreed. It was ten p.m. – the only time the diner was ever empty, in between the dinner rush and the late-night crowd, when couples blasted from the bar next door came in for pancakes and coffee to sober them up.

He explained what he needed her to do. She'd ordered a coffee, made it light with cream. Now she stared at him mid-sip. She set her cup back down.

'You're asking me to lose?' she said.

'Keep your voice down,' Dodge said. His mom had worked the early shift and was probably out with Bill Kelly – they were practically goddamn inseparable at this point – but he knew everyone else in Dot's. Including Ricky, who he could see every time the kitchen door opened and closed, grinning and waving at him like an idiot. Dodge had to admit the kid was pretty nice. He'd already sent out a free grilled cheese and some mozzarella sticks.

'Look, you don't want to go up against Ray, do you? The kid's a beast.' Dodge felt a tightening in his throat. He thought about why he was doing this – thought about Dayna wheeled home for the first time, Dayna falling out of bed in the night and crying for help, unable to climb back into bed. Dayna wheeling around, hopped up on pain meds, practically comatose. And even though she'd seemed better and happier lately – hopeful, even – he, Dodge, would never forget. 'He'll knock you off the road, Heather. You'll end up losing anyway.'

She made a face but said nothing. He could tell she was thinking about it.

'If we play it my way, you still win,' he said, leaning over the table, tacky from years of accumulated grease. 'We split the money. And nobody gets hurt.' *Except for Ray.*

She was quiet for a minute. Her hair was swept back into a ponytail, and she was flushed from a summer outside. All her freckles had kind of merged into a tan. She looked pretty. He wished he could tell her that he thought she was great. That he was sorry they had never been closer.

That he had fallen for her best friend, and had messed it up.

But none of that mattered now.

'Why?' she asked finally, turning back to him. Her eyes were clear, gray-green, like an ocean reflecting the sky. 'Why do you want it so bad? It's not even the money, is it? It's about the win. It's about beating Ray.'

'Don't worry about it,' Dodge said a little roughly. The kitchen doors swung open again and there was Ricky, his cook's whites streaked with marinara sauce and grease, grinning and giving him the thumbs-up. Jesus. Did Ricky think he was on a date? He turned his attention back to Heather. 'Listen. I promised Bishop I would—'

'What's Bishop got to do with it?' she asked sharply, cutting him off.

'Everything,' Dodge said. He drained his Coke glass of ice, enjoying the burn on his tongue. 'He wants you to be safe.'

Heather looked away again. 'How do I know I can trust you?' she said finally.

'That's the thing about trust.' He crunched an ice cube between his teeth. 'You don't know.'

She stared at him for a long second. 'All right,' she said finally. 'I'll do it.'

Outside, at the edge of the parking lot, the trees were dancing in the wind. Some of the leaves had already begun to turn. Gold ate up their edges. Others were splotched with red, as though diseased. Less than three weeks until Labor Day and the official end of summer. And only a week until the final showdown. After saying good-bye to Heather, Dodge didn't go home straightaway, but spent some time walking the streets.

He smoked two cigarettes, not because he wanted them, but because he was enjoying the dark and the quiet and the cool wind, the smells of autumn coming: a clean smell, a wood smell, like a house newly swept and sprayed down. He wondered whether the tiger was still loose. It must be; he hadn't heard anything about its capture. He half-hoped he would see it, and half-feared he would.

All in all, the conversation with Heather had gone easier than he'd expected. He was so close.

Rigging the explosion, he knew, would be the hard part.

MONDAY, AUGUST 22

heather

IN THE DAYS FOLLOWING THE TIGERS' ESCAPE, HEATHER WAS so anxious she couldn't sleep. She kept expecting Krista to show up with some court order, demanding that Lily return home. Or, even worse, for the cops or the ASPCA to show up and haul Anne off to jail. What would she do then?

But as more days passed, she relaxed. Maybe Krista realized she was happier with her daughters out of the house. That she wasn't meant to be a mother. All the things Heather had heard her say a million times. And although the cops floated in and out, still trying to locate the second tiger, still patrolling Anne's property, and the ASPCA showed up to verify the conditions of the other animals and make sure they were all legal, Anne wasn't clapped in handcuffs and dragged away, as Heather had feared.

Heather knew, deep down, that her situation at Anne's was temporary. She couldn't stay here forever. In the fall, Lily had to go back to school. Anne was floating them, paying for them, but how long would that last? Heather had to get a job, pay

Anne back, do something. She kept clinging to the hope that Panic would fix it: that with the money she earned, even if she had to split it with Dodge, she could rent a room from Anne or get her own space with Lily.

The longer she stayed away from Fresh Pines, the more certain she became: she would never, ever go back there. She belonged here, or somewhere like it – somewhere with space, where no neighbors were crawling up your butt all the time and there was no shouting, no sounds of bottles breaking and people blasting music all night. Somewhere with animals and big trees and that fresh smell of hay and poop that somehow wasn't unpleasant. It was amazing how much she loved making the rounds, cleaning out the chicken coop and brushing the horses down and even sweeping the stalls.

It was amazing, too, how good it felt to be wanted some-where. Because Heather believed, now, what Anne had said to her. Anne cared. Maybe even loved her, a little bit.

Which changed everything.

Three days until the final challenge. Now that Heather knew how it would go down – that she would only be called on to lose in the first round of Joust, to Dodge – she felt incredibly relieved. First thing she was going to do with the money was buy Lily a new bike, which she'd been eyeing when they took a trip to Target the other day.

No. First she would give Anne some money, and *then* she would buy a bike.

And then maybe a nice sundress for herself, and strappy leather sandals. Something pretty to wear when she finally worked up the courage to talk to Bishop – *if* she did.

She fell asleep and dreamed of him. He was standing with her on the edge of the water tower, telling her to jump, jump.

Beneath her – far beneath her – was a swollen rush of water, interspersed with bright white lights, like unblinking eyes pasted in the middle of all that black water. He kept telling her not to be afraid, and she didn't want to tell him she was terrified, so weak she couldn't move.

Then Dodge was there. 'How are you going to win if you're scared of the Jump?' he was saying.

Suddenly Bishop was gone, and the ledge under her feet wasn't metal, but a kind of wood, half-rotten, unstable. Boom. Dodge was swinging at it with a baseball bat, whittling away the wood, sending showers of splinters down toward the water. *Boom*. 'Jump, Heather.' *Boom*. 'Heather.'

'Heather.'

Heather woke up to doubleness – Lily whispering her name urgently, standing in the space between their beds; and also, like an echo, a voice from outside.

'Heather Lynn!' the voice cried. *Boom*. The sound of a fist on the front door. 'Get down here! Get down here so I can talk to you.'

'Mom,' Lily said, just as Heather placed the voice. Lily's eyes were wide.

'Get in bed, Lily,' Heather said. She was awake in an instant. She checked her phone: 1:13 a.m. In the hall, a small fissure of light was showing underneath Anne's bedroom door. Heather heard sheets rustling. So she'd been woken too.

The banging was still going, and the muffled cries of 'Heather! I know you're in there. You gonna ignore your own mother?' Even before reaching the door, Heather knew her mom was drunk.

The porch light was on. When she opened the door, her mom was standing with one hand to her eyes, like she was shielding them from the sun. She was a mess. Hair frizzy; shirt so low Heather could see all the wrinkles of her cleavage and the white half-moons where her bikini had prevented a tan; jeans with stains; enormous wedge heels. She was having trouble standing in one place and kept taking miniature steps for balance.

'What the hell are you doing here?'

'What am I doing here?' she slurred. 'What are you doing here?'

'Leave.' Heather took a step onto the porch, hugging herself. 'You have no right to be here. You have no right to come barging—'

'Right? Right? I got every right.' Her mom took an unsteady step forward, trying to move past her. Heather blocked her, grateful, for once, that she was so big. Krista started shouting, 'Lily! Lily Anne! Where are you, baby?'

'Stop it.' Heather tried to grab Krista by the shoulders, but her mom reeled away from her, swatting her hand.

'What's going on?' Anne had appeared behind them, blinking, wearing an old bathrobe. 'Heather? Is everything okay?'

'You.' Krista took two steps forward before Heather could stop her. 'You stole my babies.' She was weaving, swaying on her shoes. 'You goddamn bitch, I should—'

'Mom, stop!' Heather hugged herself tight, trying to keep her insides together, trying to keep everything from spilling out.

And Anne was saying, 'Okay, let's calm down, let's everyone calm down.' Hands up, like she was trying to keep Krista at bay.

'I don't need to calm down—'

'Mom, stop it!'

'Get out of my way—'

'Hold on, just hold on.'

And then a voice from the darkness beyond the porch: 'What's the trouble?' A flashlight clicked on, just as the porch light went off. It swept over all of them in turn, like a pointed finger. Someone emerged from the dark, came heavily up the stairs, as the porch light, in response to his movement, clicked on again. The rest of them were momentarily frozen. Heather had forgotten there was a patrol car parked in the woods. The cop was blinking rapidly, like he'd been sleeping.

'The problem,' Krista said, 'is that this woman has my babies. She stole them.'

The cop's jaw was moving rhythmically, like he was chewing gum. His eyes moved from Krista, to Heather, to Anne, then back again. His jaw hinged left, right. Heather held her breath.

'That your car, ma'am?' he said finally, jerking his head over his shoulder, to where Krista's car was parked.

Krista looked at it. Looked back at him. Something flickered in her eyes. 'Yeah, so?'

He kept chewing, watching her. 'Legal limit's .08.'

'I'm not drunk.' Krista's voice was rising. 'I'm as sober as you are.'

'You mind stepping over here for a minute?'

Heather found herself ready to throw her arms around his neck and say thank you. She wanted to explain, but her breath was lodged in her throat.

'I *do* mind.' Krista sidestepped the cop as he took a step toward her. She nearly stumbled over one of the flowerpots. He reached out and grabbed her elbow. She tried to shake him off.

'Ma'am, please. If you could just walk this way . . .'

'Let *go* of me.'

Heather watched it in slow motion. There was a swell of noise. Shouting. And Krista was swinging her arm, bringing her fist to the officer's face. The punch seemed amplified by a thousand: a ringing, hollow noise.

And then time sped forward again and the cop was twisting Krista's arms behind her as she bucked and writhed like an animal. 'You are under arrest for assaulting a police officer—'

'Let go.'

'You have the right to remain silent. Anything you say can and will be used against you in a court of law.'

She was handcuffed. Heather didn't know whether to feel relieved or terrified. Maybe both. Krista was still shouting as the cop led her off the porch, toward the squad car – calling up to Lily, screaming about her rights. Then she was in the car and the door closed and there was silence, except for the engine gunning on, the spit of gravel as the cop turned a circle. A sweep of headlights. Then darkness. The porch light had gone off again.

Heather was shaking. When she could finally speak, the only thing she could say was: 'I hate her.' Then again: 'I hate her.'

'Come on, sweetie.' Anne put her arm around Heather's shoulders. 'Let's go inside.'

Heather exhaled. She let the anger go with it. They stepped into the house together, into the coolness of the hall, the patterns of shadow and moonlight that already looked familiar. She thought of Krista, raging away in the back of a cop car. Her stomach started to unknot. Now everyone would know the truth: how Krista was, and what Heather and Lily were escaping.

Anne gave Heather a squeeze. 'It's going to be okay,' she said. '*You're* going to be okay.'

Heather looked at her. She managed a smile. 'I know,' she said.

The end of August was the saddest time of the year in Carp. Maybe the saddest time everywhere.

Every year, no matter what the weather, the public pools were suddenly clogged with people, the parks carpeted in picnic blankets and beach towels, the road packed bumper-to-bumper with weekenders descending on Copake Lake. A shimmering veil of exhaust hung over the trees, intermingling with the smell of charcoal and smoke from hundreds of barbecues. It was the final, explosive demonstration of summer, the line in the sand, a desperate attempt to hold fall forever at bay.

But autumn nibbled the blue sky with its teeth, tore off chunks of the sun, smudged out that heavy veil of meat-smelling smoke. It was coming. It would not be held off much longer.

It would bring rain, and cold, and change.

But before that: the final challenge. The deadliest challenge.

Joust.

THURSDAY, AUGUST 25

dodge

THE DAY OF JOUST WAS WET AND COLD. DODGE DRESSED IN his favorite jeans and a worn T-shirt, emerged sockless into the den, ate cereal from a mixing bowl, and watched a few reality TV shows with Dayna, making some jokes about the douche bags who would let their whole lives get filmed. She seemed relieved that he was acting normal.

But the whole time, his mind was several miles away, on a dark straightaway, on engines gunning and tires screeching and the smell of smoke.

He was worried. Worried the fire would start too early, when Dodge was driving the car. And worried that Ray wouldn't go for the switch.

He was *counting* on that, had rehearsed a speech in his head. 'I want to change cars,' he'd say, after Heather let him win the first round. 'So I know it's fair. So I know he didn't go turbo on his engine, or screw with my brakes.'

How could Ray say no? If Dodge drove carefully, no more than forty miles per hour, the engine shouldn't heat up too much, and the explosion wouldn't get triggered. Heather had to let him win even if he was going at a crawl. Ray would never suspect.

And then Ray would get in the car, floor it, and the engine would start smoking and sparking and then . . .

Revenge.

If everything went according to plan. If, if, if. He hated that stupid word.

At three p.m. Bill Kelly came by to take Dayna to physical therapy. Dodge didn't understand how Kelly had just wormed his way into their lives. Dayna was practically up his ass. Like they were suddenly all one big happy family unit, and Dodge was the only one who could remember: they weren't family, would never be. It had always been Dodge and Dayna and no one else.

And now, he'd even lost her.

'You gonna be okay?' she asked. She was getting good with her chair, spinning herself around furniture, bumping up the place where the floor was slightly uneven. He hated that she'd had to get good at being crippled.

'Yeah, sure.' He deliberately didn't look at her. 'Just gonna watch some TV and stuff.'

'We'll be back in a couple of hours,' she said. And then: 'I think it's really working, Dodge.'

'I'm happy for you,' he said. He was surprised to feel his throat getting tight. She was halfway out the door when he called her back. 'Dayna,' he said. *All for you.*

She turned. 'What?'

He managed to smile. 'Love ya.'

'Don't be a dick,' she said, and smiled back. Then she wheeled out of the house and closed the door behind her.

heather

WITH EVERY PASSING MINUTE, SHE WAS CLOSER TO THE END.

Heather should have felt a sense of relief, but instead she was gripped, all day, with dread. She told herself that all she had to do was lose. She'd have to trust that Dodge would keep his promise about the money.

He wasn't playing for the money. She had always known that on some level. But she wished she'd really pushed him about what motivated him. Maybe that was making her jumpy: now, even at the very end of the game, she didn't understand his end goal. It made her feel as though there were other games going on, secret rules and pacts and alliances, and she was just a pawn.

Around five o'clock, the storm passed, and the clouds started to shred apart. The air was thick with moisture and mosquitoes. The roads would be slick. But she reminded herself it wouldn't matter. She could pretend to chicken out, or really chicken out, at the last second. Then Dodge and Ray could face off and she'd be done.

Still, the sick feeling – a weight in her stomach, an itch under her skin – wouldn't leave her.

Joust had been moved. There had been no formal messages about it, no texts or emails. Bishop was lying low, just in case anyone was angry about the way the game had shaken out. Heather didn't blame him. And presumably Vivian, too, was keeping her head down. For the first time in the history of the game, the final challenge would proceed with or without the judges.

But word had come back to Heather, as it always did in a town so small, with so little but talk to feed it. The cops were posted all around the runway where Joust traditionally occurred. So: a change in location. A spot not far from the gully and the old train tracks.

Heather wondered, with another pang, whether Nat would show up.

It was six o'clock when she left. Her hands were already shaking, and she worried that in another hour or so, she'd be too nervous to drive or she'd chicken out entirely. Anne had agreed to let Heather use the car for the night, and Heather hated herself for lying about why she needed it. But she told herself that this was it, the end – no more lies from here on out. And she would be extra careful, and pull the car off the road well before Dodge came anywhere close to her.

She didn't say good-bye to Lily. She didn't want to make a big deal of it. It wasn't a big deal.

She'd be home in a few hours, tops.

She had just turned out of the driveway when she felt her phone buzz. She ignored it, but the calls started up again right away. And then a third time. She pulled over and fished her phone from her pocket.

Nat. As soon as she picked up, she knew something was very, very wrong.

'Heather, please,' Nat was saying, even before Heather said hello. 'Something bad is going to happen. We have to stop it.'

'Hold on, hold on.' Heather could hear Nat sniffling. 'Calm down. Start at the beginning.'

'It's going to happen tonight,' Nat said. 'We have to do something. He'll end up dead. Or he'll kill Ray.'

Heather could barely follow the thread of the conversation. 'Who?'

'Dodge,' Nat wailed. 'Please, Heather. You have to help us.'

Heather sucked in a deep breath. The sun chose that moment to break through the clouds completely. The sky was streaked with fingers of red, the exact color of new blood.

'Who's us?'

'Just come,' Nat said. 'Please. I'll explain everything when you get here.'

dodge

DODGE DROVE PAST THE GULLY JUST AFTER SIX O'CLOCK. THE car Bishop had lent him – a Le Sabre that Dodge knew could never be returned – was old and temperamental, and drifted to the left whenever he didn't correct it. It didn't matter. Dodge didn't need it for very long.

He parked on the side of the road on one side of the straightaway that had been selected for the challenge. The road was pretty dead – maybe people were discouraged by the bad weather. Dodge was glad. He couldn't risk being spotted.

It didn't take long. It was surprisingly easy – kid stuff, which was ironic, especially considering that Dodge had failed chemistry twice and wasn't exactly a science guy. Funny how easily you could look this shit up online. Explosives, bombs, Molotov cocktails, IEDs . . . anything you wanted. Learning how to blow someone up was easier than buying a frigging beer.

Earlier, he'd dissolved a bit of an old Styrofoam cooler in some gasoline and poured the whole mixture into a mason jar. Homemade napalm – easy as making salad dressing. Now he carefully duct-taped a firecracker to the outside of the jar and nestled the whole thing down into the engine bay. Not *too* close to the exhaust manifold – he needed to get through the challenge with Heather first. And he would drive carefully, make sure the engine didn't get too hot.

Then the car would go to Ray. Ray would gun it, and the firecracker would ignite, and the jar would shatter, discharging the explosives.

Kaboom.

All he had to do now was wait.

But almost immediately, he got a text from Heather. *Need to pick u up. Emergency. We have to talk.*

And then: *Now.*

Dodge cursed out loud. Then he had a sudden fear: she was going to back out. That would ruin everything. He wrote her back quickly. *Corner of Wolf Hill and Pheasant. Pick me up.*

Coming, she wrote back.

He walked circles while he waited for her, smoking cigarettes. He had been calm before, but now he was filled with anxiety, a crawling, itching sensation, as though spiders were scurrying under his skin.

He thought of Dayna in the hospital bed as he'd first seen her after the accident – wide-eyed, a little blood and snot crusted above her mouth, saying, 'I can't feel my legs. What happened to my legs?' Getting hysterical in the hospital room, trying to stand, and landing instead in Dodge's lap.

He thought of Luke Hanrahan, driving off with fifty grand; and the night Dodge had stood outside the Hanrahans' house with a baseball bat and been too afraid to act.

And by the time Heather pulled up, he felt a little better.

*

Heather wouldn't tell him anything in the car. 'What's this about?' he asked her.

But she just kept repeating, 'Just hold on. Okay? She'll want to tell you herself.'

'She?' His stomach flipped.

'Nat,' she said.

'Is she okay?' he asked. But Heather just shook her head, indicating she would say no more. He was getting annoyed now. This was a bad time; he needed to focus. His stomach was tight with nerves. But at the same time he was flattered that Heather needed him – flattered, too, that Nat might have asked to see him. And they still had two hours before full dark. More than enough time.

There were two cars in Nat's driveway, one of them a battered Chevy truck he didn't recognize. He wondered if this was some kind of intervention for her and got that crawling feeling under his skin again.

'What's going on?' he asked again.

'I told you,' Heather said. 'She'll want to explain it herself.'

The door was unlocked. Weirdly, although the light was rapidly fading outside, there were no lamps on in the house. The air was dull and gray, lying like a textured blanket over everything, smudging out details. Walking into Nat's house, Dodge had the feeling he used to get in church: like he was trespassing on sacred ground. There was wood everywhere, lots of nice-looking furniture, things that screamed money to him. But not a sound.

'Is she even here?' he asked. His voice sounded overloud.

'Downstairs.' Heather moved ahead of him. She opened a door just to the right of the living room. A set of unfinished stairs led down into what was obviously a basement. Dodge thought he heard movement, maybe a whisper, but then it stopped.

'Go ahead,' Heather said. He was going to tell her to go first, but he didn't want her to think he was afraid. Which he was, for whatever reason. Something about this place – the silence, maybe – was freaking him out. As if sensing his hesitation, Heather said, 'Look, we'll be able to talk down there. She'll tell you everything.' Heather paused. 'Nat?' she called out.

'Down here!' Nat's voice came from the basement.

Reassured, he headed down the stairs, into the musty, humid, underground air. The basement was large and filled with discarded furniture. He had just reached the bottom of the stairs and turned around to look for Nat when the lights went off. He froze, confused.

'What the—' he started to say, but then he felt himself roughly seized, heard an explosion of voices. He thought for one second this must be part of the game, a challenge he hadn't anticipated.

'Over here, over here!' Nat was saying. Dodge struck out, struggling, but whoever was holding him was big, fleshy, and strong. A guy. Dodge could tell by his size, and by the smell, too – menthol, beer, aftershave. Dodge kicked out; the guy cursed, and something toppled over. There was the sound of breaking glass. Natalie said, 'Shit. Here. Here.'

Dodge was forced into a chair. His hands were twisted behind him, tied up with something. Duct tape. His legs, too.

'What the fuck?' He was yelling now. 'Get the fuck off me.'

'Shhh. Dodge. It's okay.'

Even now, here, Dodge was paralyzed by the sound of Natalie's voice. He couldn't even struggle. 'What the hell is this?' he said. 'What are you doing?' His eyes were slowly adjusting to the dark. He could just make her out, the wide contours of her eyes, two sad, dark holes.

'It's for you,' she said. 'For your own good.'

'What are you talking about?' He thought, suddenly, of the car parked on Pheasant Lane, the mason jar of gasoline and Styrofoam, nestled in the engine like a secret heart. He strained against the duct tape binding him. 'Let me go.'

'Dodge, listen to me.' Nat's voice broke, and he realized she'd been crying. 'I know – I know you blame Luke for what happened to your sister. For the accident, right?'

Dodge felt something ice-cold move through him. He couldn't speak.

'I don't know exactly what you're planning, but I won't let you go through with it,' Nat said. 'This has to stop.'

'Let me go.' His voice was rising. He was fighting a panicked feeling, a sense of dull dread in his whole body, the same feeling he'd had two years earlier, standing on the lawn in front of the Hanrahans' house, trying to get his feet to move.

'Dodge, listen to me.' Her hands were on his shoulders. He wanted to push her off, but he couldn't. And another part of him wanted her and hated her at the same time. 'This is for you. This is because I care.'

'You don't know anything,' he said. He could smell her skin, a combination of vanilla and bubblegum, and it made him ache. 'Let me go, Natalie. This is insane.'

'No. I'm sorry, but no.' Her fingers grazed his cheek. 'I won't let you do anything stupid. I don't want you to get hurt.'

She leaned even closer, until her lips were nearly touching his. He thought she might be leaning in to kiss him, and he was unable to turn away, unable to resist. Then he felt her hands moving along his thighs, groping.

'What are you—?' he started to say. But just then she found his pocket and extracted his keys and phone.

'I'm sorry,' she said, straightening up. And she did truly sound sorry. 'But believe me, it's for the best.'

A wave of helplessness overtook him. He made a final, futile attempt to free himself. The chair jumped forward a few inches on the concrete floor. 'Please,' he said. 'Natalie.'

'I'm sorry, Dodge,' Nat said. 'I'll be back as soon as the challenge is over. I swear.'

She was fumbling with his phone, and the screen lit up temporarily, casting her face in brightness, showing the deep, mournful hollows of her eyes, her expression of pity and regret. And lighting up, too, the guy behind her. The one who'd wrestled Dodge into the chair.

He'd gained weight – at least thirty pounds – and he'd let his hair get long. Fifty grand wasn't sitting too well on him. But there was no mistaking his eyes, the hard set of his jaw, and the scar, like a small white worm, cutting straight through his left eyebrow.

Dodge felt a fist of shock plunge straight through him. He could no longer speak, or even breathe.

Luke Hanrahan.

heather

HEATHER WAITED IN THE CAR WHILE NATALIE AND LUKE DID whatever they had to do. She was trying to breathe normally, but her lungs weren't obeying and kept fluttering weirdly in her chest. She would have to go up against Ray Hanrahan now. There was no giving in or weaseling out.

She wondered what Dodge had had planned for tonight. Luke hadn't exactly known either, although he'd shown Nat and Heather some of the threatening messages that had come from Dodge. It was surreal, sitting in Nat's kitchen with Luke Hanrahan, football star Luke Hanrahan, the homecoming king who'd gotten kicked out of homecoming for smoking weed in the locker room during the announcement of the court. Winner of Panic. Who'd once assaulted a cashier at the 7-Eleven in Hudson when the guy wouldn't sell him cigarettes.

He looked like shit. Two years away from Carp hadn't done him any good, which was shocking to Heather. She thought all you needed to do – all any of them needed – was to get out. But maybe you carried your demons with you everywhere, the way you carried your shadow.

He'd found Nat, he said, because of a betting slip that had reached him all the way in Buffalo. And because of that stupid video – the one filmed at the water towers, which showed Dodge with his arm slung around Nat. Nat had been the easiest of the remaining players to locate, and he was hoping he could talk her into helping him convince Dodge to bow out.

Nat emerged from the house at last. Heather watched her talking with Luke on the front porch; he was nearly double her size. Crazy how several years ago, Nat would have freaked at the idea that Luke might ever look in her direction or know who she was. It was so strange, the way that life moved forward: the twists and the dead ends, the sudden opportunities.

The promise was always in the possibility.

'Is Dodge okay?' Heather asked when Nat slid into the car.

'He's mad,' Nat said.

'You did kidnap him,' Heather pointed out.

'For his own good,' Nat said, and for a minute she looked angry. But then she smiled. 'I've never kidnapped someone before.'

'Don't make a habit of it.' They both seemed to have resolved not to mention their fight, and Heather was glad. She nodded at Luke, who was getting into his truck. 'Is he coming to watch?'

Nat shook her head. 'I don't think so.' She paused, and said in a low voice, 'It's awful, what he did to Dayna. I think he must hate himself.'

'He seems like he does,' Heather said. But she didn't want to think about Luke, or Dodge's sister, or legs buried beneath a ton of metal, rendered useless. She was already sick with nerves.

'Are you okay?' Nat said.

'No,' Heather said bluntly.

'You're so close, Heather. You're almost at the end. You're *winning*.'

'I'm not winning yet,' Heather said. But she put the car into gear. There was no more delaying it. There was hardly any light left in the sky – as though the horizon were a black hole, sucking all the color away. Something else occurred to her. 'Jesus. This is *Anne's* car. I'm barely allowed to be driving it. I can't go up against Ray in this.'

'You don't have to.' Nat reached into her purse and extracted a set of keys, jiggling them dramatically.

Heather looked at her. 'Where'd you get those?'

'Dodge,' Nat said. She flipped the keys into her palm and returned them to her bag. 'You can use his car. Better to be safe than sorry, right?'

As the last of the sun vanished, and the moon, like a giant scythe, cut through the clouds, they gathered. Quietly they materialized from the woods; they came down the gully, scattering gravel, sliding on the hill; or they came packed together in cars, driving slowly, headlights off, like submarines in the dark.

And by the time stars surfaced from the darkness, they were all there: all the kids of Carp, come to witness the final challenge.

It was time. There was no need for Diggin to repeat the rules; everyone knew the rules of Joust. Each car aimed for the other, going fast in a single lane. The first person to swerve would lose.

And the winner would take the pot.

Heather was so nervous, it took her three tries to get the key in the ignition. She'd found the Le Sabre pulled over on the side of the road, practically buried in the bushes. It was Bishop's car – Dodge must have borrowed it.

She was unreasonably annoyed that Bishop had helped Dodge in this way. She wondered if Bishop had risked coming tonight – somewhere in the crowd, the dark masses of people, faces indistinguishable in the weak moonlight. She was too proud to text him and see. Ashamed, too. He'd tried to talk to her, to explain, and she had acted awful.

She wondered whether he would forgive her.

'How are you feeling?' Nat asked her. She'd offered to stay with Heather until the last possible second.

'I'm okay,' Heather said, which was a lie. Her lips were numb. Her tongue felt thick. How would she drive when she could barely feel her hands? As she pulled the car up to her starting position, the headlights lit up clusters of faces, ghost-white, standing quietly in the shadow of the trees. The engine was whining, like there was something wrong with it.

'You're going to be fine,' Nat said. She twisted in her seat. Her eyes were suddenly wide, urgent. 'You're going to be *fine*, okay?' She said it like she was trying to convince herself.

Diggin was gesturing to Heather, indicating she should turn the car around. The engine was making a weird grinding noise. She thought she smelled something weird too, but then thought she must be imagining it. It would all be over soon, anyway. Thirty, forty seconds, tops. When she managed to get her car pointed in the right direction, Diggin rapped on her windshield with his fingers, gave her a short nod.

At the other end of the road – a thousand feet away from her, a thousand miles – she saw the twin circles of Ray's headlights. They went on and off again. On and off. Like some kind of warning.

'You should go,' Heather said. Her throat was tight. 'We're about to start.'

'I love you, Heather.' Nat leaned over and put her arms around Heather's neck. She smelled familiar and Nat-like, and it made Heather want to cry, as though they were saying goodbye for the last time. Then Nat pulled away. 'Look, if Ray doesn't swerve – I mean, if you're close and it doesn't look like he's going to turn . . . You have to promise me you will. You can't risk a collision, okay? Promise me.'

'I promise,' Heather said.

'Good luck.' Then Nat was gone. Heather saw her jog to the side of the road.

And Heather was alone in the car, in the dark, facing a long, narrow stretch of road, pointing like a finger toward the glow of distant headlights.

She thought of Lily.

She thought of Anne.

She thought of Bishop.

She thought of the tigers, and of everything she'd ever screwed up in her life.

She swore to herself that she wouldn't be the first to swerve.

While in a dark basement, with the smell of mothballs and old furniture in his nose, Dodge realized, too late, why Nat had taken his keys – and, crying out, fought against his

restraints, thinking of a little time-bomb heart, ticking slowly
away . . .

Something in the engine was smoking. Heather saw little trails
of smoke unfurling from the hood of the car, like narrow black
snakes. But just then Diggin stepped into the center of the
road, shirtless, waving his T-shirt above his head like a flag.

Then it was already too late. She heard the high-pitched
squeal of tires on asphalt. Ray had started to move. She slammed
her foot onto the accelerator and the car jumped forward,
skidding a little. The smoke redoubled almost instantly; for a
second her vision was completely obscured.

Panic.

Then it broke apart and she could see. Headlights growing
bigger. The slick sheen of the moon. And smoke, pouring like
liquid from the hood. Everything was fast, too fast – she was
hurtling down the road, there was nothing but two moons,
growing larger . . . closer . . .

The stink of burning rubber and the scream of tires . . .

Closer, closer . . . She was hurtling forward. The speedometer
ticked up to sixty miles per hour. It was too late to swerve
now, and he wasn't swerving either. It was too late to do
anything but crash.

Flames leaped suddenly out of the engine, a huge roar of
fire. Heather screamed. She couldn't see anything. The wheel
jerked in her hand, and she struggled to keep her car on the
road. The air stank like burning plastic, and her lungs were
tight with smoke.

She slammed on the brakes, suddenly overwhelmed with
certainty: she would die. She saw movement from somewhere
on her left – someone running into the road? – and realized,

a second later, that Ray had swerved to avoid it, had jerked his wheel to the left and was plunging straight into the woods.

There was a shuddering crash as she sailed past him, flames licking her windshield. She was screaming. She knew she had to get out of the car now, before she hit anything.

Skidding, shuddering, spinning in circles; the car was slowing, it was drifting toward the woods. Heather fought to open the door. The handle caught and she thought she would be trapped there as the fire consumed her. Then she shoved with her shoulder and the door popped open and she jumped, rolled, felt the bite of pavement on her arm and shoulder, tasted dirt and grit, heard a distant roar of sound as if people were yelling her name. Sparks showered from the wheels of the car as it flipped off the road and into the woods.

There was an explosion so loud, she felt it through her whole body. She covered her head. Now she could hear that people *were* calling her name – and Ray's, too. A siren wailed in the distance. For a second, she thought she must be dead. But she could taste blood in her mouth. If she were dead, she wouldn't be able to taste any blood.

She looked up. The car was in ruins; a column of flame was eating it, turning it to rubber and metal. Amazingly, she managed to sit up, and then to stand. She felt no pain, as if she were watching a movie about her own life. And now she couldn't hear anything. Not the voices calling to her, urging her out of the road, away from the car – not the sirens, either. She was in a watery, deep place of silence.

She turned and saw Ray struggling to get out of his car. There was blood trickling down his face; three people were trying to pull him from the wreck. When he'd swerved, he'd gone straight into a tree; the hood was crumpled, compressed nearly in half.

And now she saw why.

Standing in the middle of the road, perfectly still, not twenty feet away, was the tiger.

It was watching Heather with those deep black eyes, eyes that were old and sorrowful, eyes that had watched centuries go to dust. And in that moment, she felt a jolt go through her, and she knew that the tiger was afraid – of the noise and the fire and the people shouting, crowding the road on both sides.

But she, Heather, wasn't afraid anymore.

She was compelled forward by a force she couldn't explain. She felt nothing but pity and understanding. She was alone with the tiger on the road.

And in the final moment of the game, as smoke billowed in swollen plumes into the air and fire licked the sky, Heather Nill walked without hesitation to the tiger, and placed her hand gently on its head, and won.

SATURDAY, OCTOBER 8

heather

IN EARLY OCTOBER, CARP ENJOYED A WEEK OF FALSE SUMMER. It was warm and bright and, if it weren't for the trees that had already changed – deep reds and oranges interspersed with the deep green of the pines – it might have been the beginning of summer.

One day, Heather woke up with the sudden, strong impulse to return to where the game had begun. A mist rose slowly over Carp, shimmering, dispersing finally in the mounting sun; the air smelled like moist ground and freshly cut grass.

'How'd you like to go swimming, Bill?' she asked Lily when Lily rolled over, blinking, hair scattered across the pillow. Heather could see the light pattern of freckles on Lily's nose, individual lashes highlighted by the sun, and thought her sister had never looked so pretty.

'With Bishop, too?' Lily asked.

Heather couldn't stop herself from smiling. 'With Bishop, too.' He had been driving home every weekend from college, to fulfill his community service duties. And to see Heather.

In the end, she decided to invite Nat and Dodge, too. It seemed right, somehow. When the small yellow envelope containing a single gold key – the key to a strongbox at a local bank – had arrived mysteriously in the mail, she had collected and divided the money among the three of them. She knew Dodge had given most of his portion to Bill Kelly; they were building a small memorial for Little Kelly at the site of the Graybill house, which had been demolished. Nat was taking some acting classes in Albany, and she'd gotten a job modeling clothes on weekends at the Hudson Valley Mall.

And starting in January, Heather would enroll in the Jefferson Community College's program in veterinary services.

Heather packed the trunk with a blanket, beach towels, mosquito repellent, and sunscreen; a stack of old, waterlogged magazines from Anne's living room; a cooler full of iced tea; several bags of chips; and creaky beach chairs with faded, striped seats. She could sense that tomorrow the weather would turn again, and the air would be edged with cold. Soon Krista would get out of her thirty-day program, and then Heather and Lily might have to return to Fresh Pines, at least temporarily. And soon the months of rain would come.

But today was perfect.

They arrived at the estuary just before lunch. Nobody had spoken much in the car. Lily had squeezed in between Dodge and Nat in the backseat. Nat braided a portion of Lily's hair and whispered quietly to her about which movie stars she thought were the cutest; Dodge had leaned his head back against the window, and it was only from the occasional way his mouth twitched into a smile that Heather knew he wasn't asleep. Bishop kept one hand on Heather's knee as she drove. It still seemed miraculous to see it there, to know that he was hers – as he always had been, in some way. But everything was different now.

Different and better.

Once out of the car, all their restraint lifted. Lily went whooping into the woods, holding her towel over her head so it flapped behind her like a banner. Nat chased after her, swatting away the branches in her path. Dodge and Bishop helped Heather clear out the trunk, and together they all went pushing through the woods, loaded down with towels and beach chairs and the cooler clinking ice.

The beach looked cleaner than usual. Two trash cans had been installed at the far end of the shore, and the sand-and-gravel strip of beach was free of the usual cigarette butts and beer cans. Sunlight filtering through the trees patterned the water in crazy colors – purples and greens and vivid blues. Even the steep face of the rock wall across the water, from which all the players had jumped, now looked beautiful instead of frightening: there were flowers growing out of fissures in the rock, Heather noticed, tangled vines sweeping down toward the water. The trees at the top of the jumping point were fire-red already, burning in the sun.

Lily trotted back to Heather as she was shaking out the blanket. There was a light breeze, and Heather had to tamp down the corners with different belongings: her flip-flops, Bishop's sunglasses, the beach bag.

'Is that it, Heather?' Lily pointed. 'Is that where you jumped?'

'Nat jumped too,' Heather said. 'We all did. Well, except Bishop.'

'What can I say?' He was already unlacing his Converses. He winked at Lily. 'I'm chicken.'

Briefly, his eyes met Heather's. After all this time, she still couldn't quite believe that he had planned Panic, or forgive him for not having told her. She would never have guessed in a million years: her Bishop, her best friend, the boy who used to dare her to eat her scabs and then almost throw up when she did.

But that was the point. He was the same, and different. And that made her hopeful in a way. If people changed, it meant that she was allowed to change too. She could be different.

She could be happier.

Heather *would* be happier – was happier already.

'It isn't *that* high,' Lily said. She squinted. 'How'd you get all the way up there?'

'Climbed,' Heather said. Lily opened her mouth soundlessly.

'Come on, Lily!' Nat was standing by the water, shimmying out of her shorts. Dodge stood a short distance away, smiling out over the river, watching her. 'Race you into the water!'

'No fair!' Lily ran, kicking up sand, struggling out of her T-shirt at the same time.

Heather and Bishop lay down on the blanket together, on their backs. She rested her head on his chest. Every so often, he ran his fingers lightly through her hair. For a while they didn't speak. They didn't need to. Heather knew that no matter what, he would always be hers, and they would always have this: a perfect day, a temporary reprieve from the cold.

Heather had started to drift off to sleep when Bishop stirred. 'I love you, Heather.'

She opened her eyes. She was warm and lazy. 'I love you, too,' she said. The words came with no trouble at all.

He had just kissed her – once, lightly, on the top of her

head; and then, when she tilted her face to his, harder, on the lips – when Lily began to shout.

'Heather! Heather! Look at me! Heather!'

Lily was standing at the very top of the rocks. Heather hadn't seen her climbing; she must have been quick. Heather felt a pulse of fear.

'Get down!' she called.

'She's fine,' Dodge said.

He was now standing in the water with Nat – Heather couldn't believe Nat had managed to convince him to swim, or that he even owned a bathing suit. One arm was wrapped around Nat's waist. They looked amazing together, like statues carved from different-colored rocks.

'Watch me!' Lily crowed. 'I'm going to jump!'

She did; without hesitating, Lily threw herself into the air. For a second she seemed to be suspended there, legs and arms splayed, mouth open and laughing. Then she was hitting the water and surfacing, spitting out a mouthful of water, calling, 'Did you see? I wasn't scared. Not at all.'

A feeling of joy flooded Heather, made her feel light and dizzy. She was on her feet and plunging into the water before Lily could reach the shore, splashing past Nat, who shrieked, tackling her sister as she tried to stand up and dragging her back into the water.

'You weren't scared, huh?' Heather attacked Lily's bare stomach as Lily wriggled away from her, squealing with laughter, calling for Bishop's help. 'Are you scared of being tickled, huh? Are you?'

'Bishop, help me!' Lily screamed, as Heather wrapped her in a bear hug.

'I'm coming, Lily!' Then Bishop was sloshing in after them,

pulling Heather backward so they collapsed together into the
water. She came up spluttering, laughing, pushing him off.

'You can't get rid of me *that* easily,' Bishop said. He kept his
arms around her waist. His eyes were the same blue-green as
the water. Her Bishop. Her best friend.

'Children, children, don't fight,' Nat said, teasing.

The wind lifted goosebumps on Heather's skin, but the sun
was warm. She knew that this day, this feeling, couldn't last
forever. Everything passed; that was partly why it was so
beautiful. Things would get difficult again. But that was okay
too.

The bravery was in moving forward, no matter what.
Someday, she might be called on to jump again. And she would
do it. She knew, now, that there was always light – beyond the
dark, and the fear, out of the depths; there was sun to reach
for, and air and space and freedom.

There was always a way up, and out, and no need to be
afraid.

vanishing girls

Dara and Nick used to be inseparable, but that was *before* – before Dara kissed Parker, before Nick lost him as her best friend, before the accident that left Dara's beautiful face scarred. Now the two sisters, who used to be so close, aren't speaking. In an instant, Nick lost everything and is determined to use the summer to get it all back.

But Dara has other plans. When she vanishes on her birthday, Nick thinks Dara is just playing around. But another girl has vanished, too – nine-year-old Elizabeth Snow – and as Nick pursues her sister, she becomes increasingly convinced that the two disappearances may be linked.

Coming in March 2015

BEFORE

THE FUNNY THING ABOUT ALMOST-DYING IS THAT AFTERWARD everyone expects you to jump on the happy train and take time to chase butterflies through grassy fields or see rainbows in puddles of oil-slick on the highway. *It's a miracle*, they'll say, with an expectant look, as if you've been given a big old gift and you better not disappoint Grandma by pulling a face when you unwrap the box and find a lumpy, misshapen sweater.

That's what life is, pretty much: full of holes and tangles and ways to get stuck. Uncomfortable and itchy. A present you never asked for, never wanted, never *chose*. A present you're supposed to be excited to wear, day after day, even when you'd rather stay in bed and do nothing.

The truth is this: it doesn't take any skill to almost-die, or to almost-live, either.

March 27

NICK

These are the three words I've heard most often in my life. *Want to play?* As four-year-old Dara bursts through the screen door, arms extended, flying into the green of our front yard without waiting for me to answer. *Want to play?* As six-year-old Dara slips into my bed in the middle of the night, her eyes wide and touched with moonlight, her damp hair smelling like strawberry shampoo. *Want to play?* Eight-year-old Dara chiming the bell on her bike; ten-year-old Dara fanning cards across the damp pool deck; twelve-year-old Dara spinning an empty soda bottle by the neck.

Fifteen-year-old Dara doesn't wait for me to answer, either. 'Scoot over,' she says, bumping her best friend Ariana's thigh with her knee. 'My sister wants to play.'

'There's no room,' Ariana says, squealing when Dara leans into her. 'Sorry, Nick.' They're crammed with a half dozen people into an unused stall in Ariana's parents' barn, which smells like sawdust and, faintly, manure. There's a bottle of vodka, half-empty, on the hard-packed ground, as well as a few six-packs of beer and a small pile of miscellaneous items of clothing: a scarf, two mismatched mittens, a puffy jacket, and Dara's tight pink sweatshirt with *Queen B*tch* emblazoned across the back in rhinestones. It all looks like some bizarre ritual sacrifice laid out to the gods of strip poker.

'Don't worry,' I say quickly. 'I don't need to play. I just came to say hi, anyway.'

Dara makes a face. 'You just got here.'

Ariana smacks her cards facedown on the ground. 'Three of a kind, kings.' She cracks a beer open, and foam bubbles up around her knuckles. 'Matt, take off your shirt.'

Matt is a skinny kid with a slightly-too-big nose look and the filmy expression of someone who is already on his way to being very drunk. Since he's already in his t-shirt – black, belongs to him. 'I'm cold,' he whines.

'It's either your shirt or your pants. You choose.'

Matt sighs and begins wriggling out of his t-shirt, showing off a thin back, faintly constellated with acne.

'Where's Parker?' I ask, trying to sound casual, then hating myself for having to try. But ever since Dara started…*whatever* she's doing with him, it has become impossible to talk about my former best friend without feeling like a Christmas tree ornament has landed in the back of my throat.

Dara freezes in the act of redistributing the cards. But only for a second. She tosses a final card in Ariana's direction and sweeps up a hand. 'No idea.'

'I texted him,' I say. 'He told me he was coming.'

'Yeah, well, maybe he *left*.' Dara's dark eyes flick to mine, and the message is clear. *Let it go.* So. They must be fighting again. Or maybe they're not fighting, and that's the problem. Maybe he refuses to play along.

'Dara's got a *new* boyfriend,' Ariana says in a sing-song, and Dara elbows her. 'Well, you do, don't you? A *secret* boyfriend.'

'Shut up,' Dara says sharply. I can't tell whether she's really mad or only pretending to be.

Ari fake-pouts. 'Do I know him? Just tell me if I *know* him.'

'No way,' Dara says. 'No hints.' She tosses down her cards and stands up, dusting off the back of her jeans. She's wearing fur-trimmed wedge boots and a metallic shirt I've never seen before, which looks like it has been poured over her body and then left to harden. Her hair – recently dyed black, and blown out perfectly straight – looks like oil poured over her shoulders. As usual, I feel like the Scarecrow next to Dorothy. I'm wearing a bulky jacket Mom bought me pulled back in its trademark ponytail.

'I'm getting a drink,' Dara says, even though she's been having beer. 'Anyone want?'

'Bring back some mixers,' Ariana says.

Dara gives no indication that she's heard. She grabs me by the wrist and pulls me out of the horse stall and into the barn, where Ariana – or her mom? – has set up a few folding tables covered with bowls of chips and pretzels, guacamole, packaged cookies. There's a cigarette butt stubbed out in a container of guacamole, and cans of beer floating around in an enormous punch bowl full of half-melted ice, like ships trying to navigate the Arctic.

It seems as if most of Dara's grade has come out tonight, and about half of mine – even if seniors don't usually deign to crash a sophomore party, *second semester* seniors never miss any opportunity to celebrate. Christmas lights are strung between the horse stalls, only three of which contain actual horses: Misty, Luciana, and Mr. Ed. I wonder if any of the horses are bothered by the thudding bass from the music, or by the fact that every five seconds some drunk junior is shoving his hand across the gate, trying to get the horse to nibble Cheetos from his hand.

The other stalls, the ones that aren't piled with old saddles and muck rakes and rusted farm equipment that has somehow landed and then expired here – even though the only thing Ariana's mom farms is money from her three ex-husbands – are filled with kids playing drinking games or grinding on each other, or, in the case of Jake Harris and Aubrey O'Brien, full-on making out. The tack room, I've been informed, has been unofficially claimed by the stoners.

The big sliding barn doors are open to the night, and frigid air blows in from outside. Down the hill, someone is trying to get a bonfire started in the riding rink, but there's a light rain tonight, and the wood won't catch.

At least Aaron isn't here. I'm not sure I could have handled seeing him tonight – not after what happened last weekend. It would have been better if he'd been mad – if he'd freaked could hate him. Then it would make *sense*.

But since the break-up he's been unfailingly, epically polite, like he's the greeter at a Gap. Like he's *really* hoping I'll buy something but doesn't want to seem pushy.

'I still think we're good together,' he'd said out of the blue, even as he was giving me back my sweatshirt (cleaned, of course, and folded) and a variety of miscellaneous crap I'd left in his car: pens and a phone charger and a weird snow globe I'd seen for sale at CVS. School had served marinara for lunch and there was a tiny bit of DayGlo sauce at the corner of his mouth. 'Maybe you'll change your mind.'

'Maybe,' I'd said. And I really hoped, more than anything in the world, that I would.

Dara grabs a bottle of Southern Comfort and splashes three inches into a plastic cup, topping it off with Coca-Cola. I bite the inside of my lip, as if I can chew back the words I really want to say: This must be at *least* her third drink; she's already in the doghouse with Mom and Dad; she's supposed to be staying out of trouble. She landed us both in *therapy*, for God's sake.

Instead, I say, 'So. A new boyfriend, huh?' I try and keep my voice light.

One corner of Dara's mouth crooks into a smile. 'You know Ariana. She exaggerates.' She mixes another drink and presses it into my hand, jamming our plastic cups together. 'Cheers,' she says, and takes a big swig, emptying half her drink.

The drink smells suspiciously like cough syrup. I set it down next to a platter of cold pigs 'n blankets, which look like shriveled thumbs wrapped up in gauze. 'So there's no mystery man?'

Dara lifts a shoulder. 'What can I say?' She's wearing gold eyeshadow tonight, and a dusting of it coats her cheeks; she looks like someone who has accidentally trespassed through fairyland. 'I'm irresistible.'

'What about Parker?' I say. 'More trouble in paradise?'

now, hard. 'Want to say *I told you so* again?'

'Forget it.' I turn away, feeling suddenly exhausted. 'Goodnight, Dara.'

'Wait.' She grabs my wrist. Just like that, the moment of tension is gone, and she smiles again. 'Stay, okay? *Stay*, Ninpin,' she repeats, when I hesitate.

When Dara gets like this, turns sweet and pleading, like her old self, like the sister who used to climb onto my chest and beg me, wide-eyed, to wake up, wake up, she's almost impossible to resist. Almost. 'I have to get up at seven,' I say, even as she's leading me outside, into the fizz and pop of the rain. 'I promised Mom I'd help straighten up before Aunt Jackie gets here.'

For the first month or so after Dad announced he was leaving, Mom acted like absolutely nothing was different. But recently, she's been *forgetting*: to turn on the dishwasher, to set her alarm, to iron her work blouses, to vacuum. It's like every time he removes another item from the house – his favorite chair, the chess set he inherited from his father, the golf clubs he never uses – it takes a portion of her brain with it.

'Why?' Dara rolls her eyes. 'She'll just bring cleansing crystals with her to do the work. Please,' she adds. She has to raise her voice to be heard over the music; someone has just turned up the volume, and the floor seems to vibrate with its rhythm. 'You *never* come out.'

'That's not true,' I say. 'It's just that you're *always* out.' The words sound harsher than I'd intended. But Dara only laughs.

'Let's not fight tonight, okay?' she says, and leans in to give me a kiss on the cheek. Her lips are candy-sticky. 'Let's be happy.'

A group of guys – sophomores, I'm guessing – huddled together in the half-dark of the barn, start hooting and clapping. 'All right!' one of them shouts, raising a beer. 'Lesbian action!'

'Shut up, dick!' Dara says. But she's laughing. 'She's my *sister*.'

'That's definitely my cue,' I say.

But Dara isn't listening. Her face is flushed; her eyes bright with alcohol. 'She's my sister,' she announces again, to no one and also to everyone, since Dara is the kind of person other people watch, want, follow. '*And* my best friend.'

More hooting; a scattering of applause. Another guy yells, 'Get it on!'

Dara throws an arm around my shoulder, leans up to whisper in my ear, her breath sweet-smelling, sharp with booze. 'Best friends for life,' she says, and I'm no longer sure whether she's hugging me or hanging on me. 'Right, Nick? Nothing – *nothing* – can change that.'

http://www.theShorelineBlotter.com/march27_accidentsandreports

At 12:55 a.m., Norwalk police responded to a crash on Route 101, just south of the Shady Palms Motel. The driver, Nicole Warren, 17, was taken to Eastern Memorial with minor injuries. The passenger, Dara Warren, 15, who was not wearing her seatbelt, was rushed by ambulance to the ICU and is, at the time of this posting, still in critical condition. We're all praying for you, Dara.

Sooo sad. Hope she pulls through!
posted by: mamabear27 at 6:04 a.m.

i live right down the road heard the crash from a half mile away!!!
posted by: qTpie27 at 8:04 a.m.

These kids think they're indestructible. Who doesn't wear a seat-belt?? She has no one to blame but herself.
posted by: markhhammond at 8:05 a.m.

Have some compassion, dude! We all do stupid things.
posted by: trickmatrix at 8:07 a.m.

Some people stupider than others.
posted by markhammond at 8:08 a.m.

AFTER

http://www.theShorelineBlotter.com/july15_arrests

It was a busy night for the Main Heights P.D. Between midnight and 1 a.m. on Tuesday, three local teens perpetrated a rash of minor thefts in the area south of Route 23. Police first responded to a call from the 7Eleven on Richmond Place, where Mark Haas, 17, Daniel Ripp, 16, and Jacob Ripp, 19, had threatened and harassed a local clerk before making off with two six-packs of beer, four cartons of eggs, three packages of Twinkies; and three Slim Jims. Police pursued the three teens to Sutter Street, where they had destroyed a half dozen mailboxes and egged the home of Mr. Walter Middleton, a math teacher at the teens' high school (who had, this reporter learned, recently been threatening to fail Haas for suspected cheating). The police at last caught and arrested the teens in Carren Park, but not before the three boys had stolen a backpack, two pairs of jeans, and a pair of sneakers from next to the public pool. The clothes, police reported, belonged to two teenage skinny-dippers, both of whom were brought into the Main Heights police station...hopefully, after recovering their clothing.

Dannnnnnny…ur a legend.
posted by: grandtheftotto @ 12:01 p.m.

> *Get a life.*
> *posted by: momofthree @ 12:35 p.m.*

The irony is that these boys will probably be working in the 7-Eleven before too long. Somehow I don't see these three boys as brain surgeons.
posted by: hal.m.woodward @ 2:56 p.m.

Skinny-dipping? Weren't they freezing?? :P
posted by: prettymaddie @ 7:22 p.m.

How come the article doesn't give us the name of 'two teenage skinny-dippers'? Trespassing is a criminal offense, isn't it?
posted by: vigilantescience01 @ 9:01 p.m.

> *Thanks for posting. It is, but neither teen was charged.*
> *posted by admin @ 9:15 p.m.*

Mr. Middleton sux.
posted by hellicat15 @ 11:01 p.m.

July 15

NICOLE

'SKINNY-DIPPING, NICOLE?'

There are many words in the English language that you never want to hear your father say. *Enema. Orgasm. Disappointed.*

But *skinny-dipping* ranks high on the list, especially when you've just been dragged out of the police station at three in the morning wearing police-issue pants and a sweatshirt that likely belonged to some homeless person or suspected serial killer, because your clothing, bag, ID, and cash were stolen from the side of a public pool.

'It was a joke,' I say, which is stupid; there's nothing funny about getting arrested, almost ass-naked, in the middle of the night when you're supposed to be asleep.

The headlights divide the highway into patches of light and dark. I'm glad, at least, that I can't see my dad's face.

'What were you *thinking*? I would never have expected this. Not from you. And that boy, Mike—'

'Mark.'

'Whatever his name was. How old is he?'

I stay quiet on that. *Twenty* is the answer, but I know better than to say it. Dad's just looking for someone to blame. Let him think that I was forced into it, that some bad-influenceguy made me hop the fence at Carren Park and strip down to my underwear, made me take a big belly-flop into a deep end so cold it shocked the breath right out of my body so I came up laughing, gulping air, thinking of Dara, thinking she should have been with me, that she would understand.

I imagine a huge boulder rising up out of the dark, an accordion-wall of solid stone, and have to shut my eyes and reopen them. Nothing but highway, long and smooth, and the twin funnels of the headlights.

'Listen, Nick,' Dad says – an old nickname for me that stuck – 'Your mom and I are worried about you.'

'I didn't think you and mom were talking,' I say, rolling down the window a few inches, both because the air conditioning is barely sputtering out cold air and because the rush of the wind helps drown out Dad's voice.

He ignores that. 'I'm serious. Ever since the accident—'

'Please,' I say quickly, before he can finish. 'Don't.'

Dad sighs and rubs his eyes under his glasses. He smells a little bit like the menthol strips he puts on his nose at night to keep him from snoring, and he's still wearing the baggy pajama pants he's had forever, the ones with reindeers on them. And just for a second, I feel really, truly terrible.

Then I remember Dad's new girlfriend and Mom's silent, taut look, like a dummy with her strings pulled way too tight.

'You're going to have to talk about it, Nick,' Dad says. This time his voice is quiet, concerned. 'If not with me, then with Dr. Lichme. Or Aunt Jackie. Or *someone*.'

'No,' I say, unrolling the window all the way, so the wind is thunderous, and whips away the sound of my voice. 'I don't.'

to be continued . . . March 2015

Visit Lauren at

www.laurenoliverbooks.com

Find Lauren's books on Facebook at

www.facebook.com/lovedelirium
www.facebook.com/laurenoliverbooks

Follow Lauren on Twitter

@OliverBooks